THE
GIRL
FROM
SHADOW
SPRINGS

THE
GIRL
FROM
SHADOW
SPRINGS

ELLIE CYPHER

SIMON & SCHUSTER BFYR

NEW YORK LONDON TORONTO SYDNEY NEW DELHI

For information about special discounts for bulk purchases, please contact
Simon & Schuster Special Sales at 1-866-506-1949 or business@simonandschuster.com.
The Simon & Schuster Speakers Bureau can bring authors to your live event.
For more information or to book an event, contact the Simon & Schuster Speakers Bureau at
1-866-248-3049 or visit our website at www.simonspeakers.com.
Interior design by Hilary Zarycky
The text for this book was set in Jenson.
Manufactured in the United States of America
First Edition
2 4 6 8 10 9 7 5 3 1
Library of Congress Cataloging-in-Publication Data
Names: Cypher, Ellie, author.
Title: The girl from Shadow Springs / Ellie Cypher.
Description: First edition. | New York : Simon & Schuster Books for Young Readers, [2021] |
Audience: Ages 12+. | Audience: Grades 7-9. | Summary: When seventeen-year-old Jorie picks the
wrong corpse to scavenge from the Ice Flats, she and Cody, a gentle Southern boy, find themselves
at the center of a centuries-old secret.
Identifiers: LCCN 2020027490 (print) | LCCN 2020027491 (eBook) |
ISBN 9781534465695 (hardcover) | ISBN 9781534465718 (eBook)
Subjects: CYAC: Fantasy. | Classification: LCC PZ7.1.C95 Gir 2021 (print)
| LCC PZ7.1.C95 (eBook) | DDC [Fic]—dc23
LC record available at https://lccn.loc.gov/2020027490
LC ebook record available at https://lccn.loc.gov/2020027491

To my family. Always.

CHAPTER 1

Penance and Permafrost

T he answer to what freezes first is the eyes.

That ain't something most people would guess. Most folk would say it was the fingers or toes. Or maybe even the guts, if they were out. Once, I'd even heard a man say it was the tongue that froze first. But I know better.

Lowering the ruddy fur lining of my scarf, I let the blistering cold curl in around me, tilting my head at the ice-covered body by my feet. Guess he knew that now too. I scuffed my boot across the side of the dead man's bear-hide coat, sending small swirls of snow, fine as any dust, out into the raw dawn. And just like everything else round here, the wind whipped past and stole 'em away.

Only idiots tried to cross the Ice Flats. The only thing out this way was the cold. And hunger. And death. Way I figured, anyone desperate or dumb enough to think otherwise had it coming. Ain't like they couldn't see all them grave markers out cross the ice. Little gray stone warnings in the permafrost along the outskirts of town, they made a jagged line of snowy teeth. A boundary between life and death. Between the Flats and the whole rest of the world.

I gazed down. The man's ears and head were more than half buried in the remnants of last night's storm. Heavy flakes of snow, thick as any summer cream, clotted at the corners of his face. Above cracked lips, a fine layer of ice coated his gray flesh like a second skin, slinking upward till it crashed against the ragged fur of his hood. His face was a nightmarish web of cold and loss. A spider's kiss of ice.

In the harsh light that marked the birth of yet another miserable day, I reached my hand down to the body.

"Marjorie!" A girl's cry came from over my shoulder.

With a jolt, I snapped my arm back to the beating warmth of my chest. Stars above, can't she just leave me be for three seconds?

"I'm moving fast as I can," I called back. Ain't like I got any more pressing stuff to do.

The holler came again and I stuck out my tongue—and a finger or two—in the vague direction of home. Too bad no one but me and the dead man could see it. Not that it mattered much. Not out here.

Slow as a bull to market, I pulled out my retrieval cord and wrapped it round the dead man's wrist, securing the leather. Making sure to cinch tight enough to crack his brittle gray skin. Only good thing about the frozen dead, far as I can figure, is they don't bleed.

Hiking my scarf back up against the wind, I slung the thick retrieval cord up and over my shoulders. The quiet morning light, like molten glass, was just tipping over the horizon, igniting the empty vastness of the Flats around me.

It took a few deep grunts to get started, but I managed to get movin. I always did. Under foot, flashes of light, deep reds and blues, hummed up through the thick layers of ice, snagging in my prints. Brightening echoes from the cavernous waters below.

I lumbered the last few yards past the house. Not that the place were much to talk about, scrapped together as it was by a thousand rusty nails. And even rustier prayers.

Under my gloves, the door to the shed squealed open in hopeless protest. I let it slam behind me. My sister shouting like a drowning bear. Or three. And she could keep up her hollering; after sixteen years, I were more than used to it. Like as not Brenna were pissed I was late for breakfast. A fault as like to get me a lecture on mindin how much time I spent out on the Flats, as well as a longer one 'bout listening. To her.

Still, even if we couldn't bury them right and proper till spring, this would be the fifth body I pulled in this week, and more bodies meant more money. More money meant more food. And we sure as stars needed that. Especially after last month. And the one before that.

I hoped he'd have something I could sell. Not all of 'em did. I drug the man into the corner, hefting him right next to the others. Knocking the crusts of snow off the thick soles of my leather boots, I ran my eyes over the lot of 'em.

So many bodies. Even for this time of year it weren't right. A pang of something dangerous close to worry caught in my gut. Cause, irresponsible as they'd been, they'd still been people. People that, if you didn't look right at 'em, if ya let them linger at the edge of your eyes, might've only been sleeping. I blinked down at them for longer than I would've liked.

You, I told myself, *won't never be so stupid, Jorie. Their choices aren't your choices.* Running a hand over my face, I scrubbed at my skin for a warmth I did not feel.

Kneeling at the newest body's side, I rifled through his pockets. Weren't much. An antler-handled knife with a broken blade long as my hand and a hide-bound notebook with near all its pages torn were about the only things of worth in the outer pockets. I set them on the lowest shelf and turned the man over.

He couldn't have been more than mid-thirties. Mainly cause he still had all his teeth. But it were the man's deep red hair and blue eyes that made me suck back a breath. He weren't just a stranger then, but an Inlander. A Southerner in particular. People who, when winter had destroyed our crops, our livelihoods froze and our people starved, when we'd needed help most, had simply refused. Said no. Shakin my head, I flipped open the dead man's coat.

Underneath his dirty bearskins, the man wore naught but a single layer of clothes. *Fine* clothes. A pair of thin fine-spun cotton pants and a high-collared blue silk shirt. That was it. I frowned. Man had no business out here, dressed like that. No wonder the idiot had froze.

Better men died with more.

The Southerner's pockets gave only two more things: a broken-faced compass with glittering silver lettering in a language I didn't recognize, which were only *maybe* worth something, and a half-burned whale-fat candle. Squat and fat and yellow, the candle weren't worth much. Still, I tossed it into my pocket. At least we could use it for a little while. Some were always better than none.

Then there was his coat. I pulled it off and held it up. Little circles of light shined through the mud- and frost-caked furs. I ran a finger round the biggest of 'em. *Huh.* Gunpowder. I tossed the coat onto the floor.

Cause even with the bullet holes, two in the back and another grazing the fur of the collar, the coat might still fetch a fair price at market. If we ever had one again. There weren't much left to kill round here that people ain't shot yet. What with the winter we'd just had—were still having—even the heartiest of animals had run 'way or starved. It weren't natural the way the ice stayed, the way the winters crept longer and longer each year, the snows drowning out the sun. But town weren't called Shadow Springs for nothing. An echo of a place that once were, that's all it was. Caribou and all the rest were mighty smart to avoid it.

I placed the broken-faced compass on the table with the other rummaged items, pocketing the knife. I picked up the leather-bound notebook, running my hand over the cover. Pressed into the hide were a series of bare silver stars. I studied the constellation, trying to place it. Weren't one I knew.

I flicked open the cover. Inside were nothing legible. Not that I read all that well. Words and numbers were everywhere. I turned the page, tilting my head. If they were even words. Flipping through the book, slick paper fluttering soft under my fingers, I tried to tell what it was, if there were a pattern to it. Only if there were, it was beyond me.

At the back, some loose pages slipped down. I turned to them. Thick lines of green ink ran everywhere. Just nonsense, muddled drawings that overflowed into the text so that you couldn't right read it. Here too were more of those same words. The ones as like on the silver compass's face.

Frowning, I flipped to the end. But here it were even worse. Page after page torn or missing. One even burned. And if the spine were anything to go by, near half the book were just clear gone. If you angled it and squinted—I tilted the pages—you could maybe make a sketch of something . . . useless. I tossed it onto the pile in the shed with the rest of the goods.

There had to be something else, some reason the man had been out alone. Perhaps—at my back the door from the breezeway flew open. The sudden change in pressure swelling the cramped space, sending soft tendrils of snow in under the door across from me. Unhurried, I finished putting away my gear, stripping off the last three bulky layers of my clothes, until only a fine-spun wool layer remained against my skin. I changed my boots, worn laces cracking under my fingers, for a pair of soft fur-lined slippers. The warmth of them pricking against my toes. I let out a little hiss at the sensation.

"Jorie, ain't you been hearing me?" Brenna's words smashed into my back with 'bout the same warmth as the wind outside.

"Alright, alright, just give me a second will ya." I could practically feel her glare. She reminded me of Ma. A lot.

"A second? I've been calling you for an hour straight. Something's happened," Brenna said, feet shuffling, worry pricking in her voice. "Something bad."

"What's that?" I asked unfazed. Last time she'd gotten so worked up this early, it were cause she thought we'd run out of beans. Still, to be fair, she did seem a right more agitated than usual. And we had been out of beans.

"Up at the house," she said, glancing over her shoulder.

"The house?" That brought me up short. "Did one of them boys from town come and break another window? Are they bothering you again?" A flicker of unease twisted in my gut. Bren weren't foolin. Not this time.

Bren's mouth pressed thin, hedging.

"Show me."

"Jor, hold on—"

"If they think they can just come here . . . I swear we ain't got the time for this," I sputtered, and without stopping, strode past Brenna and toward the house.

"Jorie!" Brenna stumbled after me, trying and failing to keep pace. "Would you just, for once in your life, listen, you bullheaded, stubborn . . ."

Quirkin my lips at the compliments, I strode quick through the covered passageway. Passing the ice-covered rockery, a thin strip of neglected soil that served as our pitiful garden, I opened the heavy door to the main house.

The candlelit room were surprisingly warm; Bren must've been feedin the fire. It were little darker in the corners than usual, but nothing *seemed* broken.

Along the far side of the dim-lit space, Bren's nest of blankets and furs lay under a high, shuttered window. A mix of half-opened leather books, bindings that'd seen far better days, sticks of charcoal and drawings littered atop. A smaller book caught my eye. All faded gold lettering leaking along the spine—it had been our Ma's. Once. I were pretty sure I'd hidden that one. I let out a deep sigh. Weren't Bren the only one who remembered. Weren't only her who cared.

From behind me, an icy draft of air eddied my long black hair about my neck. With it came Brenna, panting in my wake. Her disapproval, near as palpable as the cold. She let out a little flare of a growl. Sighing, I fixed my sister with a look.

"What is it then, Bren? Out with it," I asked, before rifling through a stack of pullovers. I picked the fraying one. Made of fox, it still smelled of the wild. I inhaled deeply as I slipped it down over my head. I never could get tired of that smell.

When I looked up, Bren were clutching the pendant round her neck, eyes unnatural wide. 'Bout the size of a shark's eye and near as lustrous, the ice-stone were held in place by three talons of tarnished silver. Beautiful as they were, ice-stones weren't usually nothing to get excited about. But this one were different. This one had been our

Ma's. And her Ma's before her. Generations of Harlow women had held it. It were the only thing Ma had ever told us about her past.

Like a drop of midnight, Bren slipped the stone back under her sweater, setting her feet square to facing me. I opened my mouth, but Bren cut me off. As stubborn a line across her lips as ever I'd seen settlin in fast. We weren't sisters and still alive out here for nothing.

"Jor, this ain't good." Brenna's voice dropped to a hushed whisper. I shot her a crooked look; she was clasping and unclasping her hands like a seal, her face still odd blanched from the cold. She'd already said that.

"What is?" I said, sudden more cross than I'd any right to be. Regrettin my tone near at once, I relented and pushed open the door to the kitchen. That spark of worry flared hot in my gut. "Sorry, Bren, it's just that I—"

"Don't go in there, there's—" Brenna's sharp cry cut off.

"A visitor," a deep male voice finished for her.

I spun, nerves as tight as steel. In front of me, the man sat at the kitchen table. His long straight back turned to the low-burning fireplace behind him. With a grunt, he stood up, smoothing his hands against rawhide pants, flames licking at his shadow.

Standin, I saw him better. The stranger looked about as happy as the body I'd just stacked in the shed. And if his too-straight bearing and the shock of white hair weren't enough to name him as a stranger, his red-rimmed goggles, etched with a single wolf's fang across the side, certainly were.

Rovers. Particular pestilence of the North. Men that popped up like rats wherever there were people desperate enough or poor enough for them to swindle and steal from. Last time one of 'em had been in town, one of Della's goats had gone missing. And her husband to boot.

Not that Della were likely to miss the beast much. Or the goat.

I shot Bren a look.

"I tried to tell ya, Jorie, but you never listen to me," Brenna whispered. She turned her face from mine. Long red welts on the side of her neck. My unease roared instant to anger.

But Bren caught my eye, shaking her head gently. She were alright. I rounded on the Rover. We'd certain see what he had to say for himself.

I cracked my knuckles, popping each bone in turn and eyeing the man in front of me. Like all vermin, best be rid of him fast. I took a deep breath, steadying my shaking hands. Ain't no good ever come from showing fear to no man.

"You ain't got business here." I sneered, feeling the familiar sharp tug from the long scar that ran from eye to lip. Out on the Flats, it wasn't always you that won. Sometimes, the beasts did.

The stranger smirked. His gaze snagged in mine. It felt like ice down my back. A trembling began building down deep in my arms, my chest, my legs. *Ain't no good ever come of showing fear.* I repeated the mantra in my head.

"You witless as you are unwanted?" I waved my hand round our poorly furnished room. "Can't ya tell we ain't got nothing for you here?"

The man angled his head. I followed his gaze. Brenna had gone still as ice.

"Think again," I snarled. Heat rose in my cheeks. I took a rushing step toward him but stopped short. His smile widened into a leer. I couldn't take him and he knew it. Certain not one on one. I ground my teeth and fixed the Rover with a feral stare.

"If you even reckon—" I began.

"Shhh, Jorie." Bren pulled urgently at my sleeve. "He ain't all that's here. . . ." She gave the most imperceptible of gestures toward the back hall. Toward the tiny bedroom we shared. A low rumble, like leather over stone, purred down the hallway. My breathing hitched. I stood straighter.

But before I could take a step, let alone a stone's breath worth of air, a shape covered in heavy fur and an even heavier darkness exploded out of the hall, sending us sprawling to our knees.

CHAPTER 2

Reckonings

———•———

E verything about me felt like it were twisting. All muddled up. Dark round the edges.

I tried—and failed—to settle my rolling gut. The muted echoes of breaking glass and heavy footfalls floated, disembodied, around me.

I opened and closed my eyes a few times. But no use. Everything swirled. All the light had gone out of the room, save a few candles too far away to be much more than a low smudge of glowing yellow.

I rubbed my eye sockets with the palms of my hands and tried again. It were like squinting through the first green waters of spring, when all them plants and sea silk in the mouth of the bay flowered bright and bitter. Filtering out the light.

My temples pulsed, radiating sharp lines of hurt. They beat in time with the dull thumping coming from the back room. Rover must be searching. And by the increasing frequency of the cracks and rumbling, he weren't finding what he was after.

I took a deep down inhale, stealing up the air from the bottom of my lungs. The pressure pulling on what promised to be dark bruises in my side. But the pain in my chest weren't what made me go still. There was something else in here too. There weren't no mistaking it. Known it since before I knew my own name. Blood smelled like blood. Always.

Which would've been fine, except it weren't mine.

I pushed down a wave of nausea as I half sat, half sprawled on the ground. I groped round. Biting back a curse. Rover must have moved us, cause the smooth tile of the kitchen had given way to the rough wood flooring of the main room. How long had I been out? How long—my thoughts cut off as a streak of blond hair caught my attention.

Forcing panic down, I pulled myself to my sister's side. Slow, I reached down, feeling for the same up-down rising beat of Brenna's heart, the mirror of the one thundering in my chest.

"Bren?" I whispered, squinting. In the dark her flushed too-cold cheeks nothing but rose-tinged stains. I ran my fingers over her hair. They came back wet. And red. The world lurched.

I flicked her eyes open one at a time. The center of the right one were as wide black as a hooked fish's eye, but the blue-rimmed pupil were moving. So too was the brown of the left. Unconscious, but living. A whimper, soft but merciful real, fluttered from her lips. I shifted into sittin, dragging Brenna up with me. Real careful, like a newborn pup, I cradled her head in my lap. She were so cold. Too cold.

"Bren, wake up. I need you to be alright," I whispered, supporting her head, careful to stay still so as to not shake her none. Bren didn't stir. And like a lead brick, a heavy lump formed in the back of my throat. "You're all I've got, Bren, please—"

A loud clatter came from the hall behind us. I went tight as steel. Holding my breath, fighting down the sudden urge to panic. Which only made my lungs push harder, louder, desperate pulling at my sides till the thinness of my bones ached something fierce.

Exhaling, I uncurled my hands from round my sister and tried to stand. Only my foot caught. Something hard went scattering loud cross the floor. I froze. Listening. Waiting. But no one came to see.

Right. We needed to move. With new urgency, I gave Bren's shoulders a gentle shake. And in merciful reply, her eyes stirred. She took a swallow. Hand flexing, she opened her eyes.

"I told ya so, Jorie." Slow, a smile formed at the edge of her lips, eyes worryingly unfocused.

"Brenna." I exhaled her name and tilted my head down to hers till our foreheads pressed together. She smelled of pine and honeyed sweat and all things good. I let the familiar scent fill my lungs. She smelled of Ma and home. Of the only things worth fightin for in this ice-ravaged world.

It can't be that bad, can it? My smile faltered. *But it can, Jorie, and you know it.*

Unbidden, a flash of Pa, his body too still out on the ice, a crimson halo forming under his head, the dogs barking something fierce, his eyes as cold and unseeing as the stars. *I was too late. I had been too late.* I nuzzled a little into Bren. Sudden heat pooled in at the corners of my eyes, and I forced the tears back. I reached my hand out, letting my fingers fall softly around hers. She were my everything.

Since our parents had died, it was just us. Me and Bren. I sniffed hard against the cold of the room, gritting my jaw tight.

"Bren, how's your head? We need to get you warm, your skin is freezin....," I whispered.

Bren raised her hand to the side of my face and let her fingers trail down my cheek. Tracing my scar. "I'm okay, Jor, promise. Just don't move too much, alright." She let out a little sigh. "I need to rest a little while is all. I'm just so tired."

"Bren, *Bren*." Panic gripped me tighter. "You have to stay awake."

I shifted as Bren took her hand back, the lifting of her fingers from mine a sensation colder than the snowfall outside. "You can't fall asleep right now, you just can't."

But this time Bren didn't open her eyes. Instead, her head drooped and her pale lips went slack.

From somewhere behind me, somewhere in the black of the hallway, came a deep marrow-rattling rumble. Adrenaline sharp and silver, quick as a pike, cracked through my bones. Heart thundering, head aching, I reached for my knife. Only to find the broken one I'd pocketed off the dead man. I ground my teeth. Yet something were better than nothing.

Vibrations curled up the soft flesh of my spine. I held my breath. A half-floated memory flooded up. No. It couldn't be. They were gone, weren't they? I touched my scar as the image of a massive wolf-like creature filled my thoughts—bigger again by half the size of a normal beast, smarter than most people round here, and wicked hard to track, Tracers hadn't been spotted this far south in years.

People said they'd all been run out, that the settling of the snows that wouldn't lift and the loss of their prey had all but forced them away. Killed back to nothing but myths in the night. But that growl coming from the darkness of the hall, that weren't pretend—and neither was the crush of padded feet that followed. My hands shook.

Whatever was making that racket, I'd not want to know it—or its teeth—up close.

I redoubled my grip on the broken knife. I needed to get Bren out of here. Get away before whatever were waiting decided to stop toying with its meal ticket and cash in instead. I rolled Bren onto her side. Half cutting, half ripping off my sleeve, I knotted it rough.

I might not be able to carry her, but I sure as stars could drag her.

As I cinched down the fabric careful, Bren let out a little cry.

Focus, Jorie. But it didn't work so well. Not with that breathing rustling out of the blackness behind me. Fast and hot. Or maybe it was just my own. "You ain't never gettin out of being my little sister this easy, Bren."

Before I could do much else, a rough hand grabbed my shoulder, spinning me round. Wood flooring twistin under my feet.

Callused hands dug into my neck, lifting me. The smell of unwashed pelts and stale smoke filled my nose, my mouth.

I scrambled, clawing against the Rover's thick arm, digging my nails in. But it were no use. He yanked me tighter to him. I near gagged. The warmth of him, so close it were suffocatin. My fingers caught on something wrapped tight around his wrist. A silver chain with a ruby pendant, my struggle shaking the faceted stone.

Growling, I kicked out and were rewarded by a pained grunt. Then a heavy hand clamped tight over my mouth, stifling the air. He lifted me higher. Pulled me closer.

I bit and struck out as he dragged me into him, till my soles brushed useless against Bren, her body sprawled at my feet.

The Rover's breath grew hot against the exposed skin of my neck, sending waves of revulsion through me. I swung my arm, every muscle tight. But he pinned it as quick as if I were nothing but flotsam. The man's hand tightened. My broken knife clattered useless to the floor.

I weren't gonna go out like this. No way. We ain't made it this far only to, only to . . . I cried out against a sudden tightening to his grip. My vision swirled. My throat burned from the effort of pulling air. The man hit me once, hard.

The world spun. Sharp taste of copper filled my mouth. Another mark added to the accounting I wouldn't soon forget to pay back. I spit. Growling, the Rover tossed me aside, my body landing on the floor with a thud.

"Now that I've got your undivided attention," the Rover said, looming above me, "let ol' Reeves tell ya just how this is gonna go."

CHAPTER 3

Missing Chances

First things first," the Rover said, resting a hand on the wicked antler hunting knife at his side. "You show me the Scholar."

I shook my head, dazed. "The who?"

"Don't play dumb with me, girl. The Scholar, that's who," he said, lurching into motion.

"What are you talkin about?" I tried to follow his lumbering shape round the room, but my head hurt, everything hurt. I struggled to focus. Had to focus. Had to get to Bren. I pitched forward, only to have the Rover catch me. And smile. A deep leering thing that crept across his face as he lugged me over to the stone fireplace.

He gripped my shoulders tight. "Where'd you hide the bastard's body?"

"The body?" I asked confused, my gaze darting toward the kitchen. Across from where I leaned against the fireplace, Bren's head splayed to the side, streaks of bloody hair plastered across her cheek. My gut lurched.

"Tell me," he demanded.

"You mean the shed?" He must. "I don't know any of them is that—" But before I could get the words out, the Rover dropped me, grunting.

I tried to rise, to get to my sister, but a foot came down hard on my back, forcing me onto the ground. Before I could bite it back, I cried out in pain. Face pressed to floor, I stared over at my sister. Only she weren't alone.

"Just so you don't get any ideas," he snarled.

I stared. And stared. Next to her curled a lick of nightmare made manifest. Something that shouldn't be. Something un-*real*.

Twice the height of a normal wolf, it were near half as thin, with a thick black coat the relentless dark of which were only broke by little tracks of red that curled round its neck. Set deep in the animal's ragged face, two golden eyes burned bright, sharp as knives as it slunk through the light of the dying candles. The creature moved with an unnerving slickness. It weren't natural, that movement. It weren't.

The beast wound closer to Bren's sprawled body, every stride a menace, every breath hungry. Even from where I lay, the smell of cold and smoke and restlessness rolled off the creature.

"Show me. Or Raz there's gonna get a little chummier with your sister. He ain't eaten a good meal in weeks." A heel ground into my back. But this time I didn't right feel it. I clenched my fingers, digging them into the palms of my hands.

The Rover seized my arm, yanking me to my feet. He drug me toward the back of the room, away from Bren. Everything in me screamed out, but my muscles didn't respond. No air escaped my lips. Every motion were impossible, like trying to pull water through the heart of a glacier.

At the Rover's side, the beast twisted its muzzle, licking at the slender spikes of its long yellow teeth. Smiling. Everything went temporary gray around the edges. I blinked sharp. My ears ringing, my blood rushing. A shake and I were stumbling. Falling. Knees crunching on something hard as I hit the floor. *The knife.*

I scrambled for it, just managing to slip it into my sleeve before the Rover tightened his grip on my arm. I moved one foot in front of the other as the Rover drug me toward the kitchen, pale candlelight sputterin harsh in our wake. I opened my mouth, only to have a hand crash over it, stifling my call.

Outside, the wind whipped past, rattlin the aluminum walls with an intensity that promised a rough night. So too did the creeping wave of gray-green mist just visible over the white of the Flats. A storm were coming.

The Rover shoved open the door to the body shed. I stumbled after. Inside the shed were freezing. The Rover dropped my arm. But not before squeezing tight. Only I didn't feel it. I didn't feel anything at all. Numb, I staggered against the wall, the metal door clattering at my back.

The Rover's eyes lit up as he took in what lay before us. Smiling, he stared at me. A shiver ran down my spine. There weren't many people who'd be right happy to see the dead.

"Stay right there, don't move one muscle. I ain't done with you yet." He hurried to the corpse. Quick as cleaning a fresh kill, the Rover stripped off the man's clothes. And without care, he began pickin his way over the corpse—turning, twisting, searching—his fingers leaving deep indents in the softening skin of the dead man. The man's clothes got the same treatment.

"Where the stars is it?" the Rover grumbled. With a growl of frustration, he tossed the dead man's arm back over the body. Spinning, he turned wild eyes on me. With a few quick strides he closed the distance between us, body looming over mine. I did not flinch. I would not flinch.

"Where is it?"

"Where's what?" I spit back.

The Rover looked me up and down before shooting a glance over his shoulder at the body. "The bleeding bastards! Think they can keep me from what's mine. From what I'm *owed*." There were something off in his voice. Something boiling.

I straightened. "Far as I can see, you're the only bleeding bastard here." The words came out strong. Stronger than I'd expected, and I blinked up at him, my body shaking something fierce.

For the longest breath, the Rover didn't move a muscle, still as snow before a fall. Calculating. A wicked curl formed at the edge of his lips. The kind that sent a smart girl running the other way, and a girl like me straight for my gun.

"You." His voice sudden cold.

I clamped my lips shut. His eyes blazed.

"You took it," he said and shook me. "Give it over."

"Give what?" I said finally, gesturing at the shed, at the body, my anger rising. "There ain't nothing else. This is it." *This is all we've got left.*

"I don't like liars," the Rover growled, jutting a glance at the body behind him.

"Neither do I." Whatever business this were, it weren't mine. "If ya'd just tell me straight what you were after, maybe I could—"

The Rover narrowed his gaze, emotions warring across the muscles of his face. I didn't right like a one of 'em.

Finally he dropped my stare and turned to the body. "He had a coat. Where is it?"

"His coat, why?" I asked. "There ain't nothing special about that dirty bearskin coat, less you count the bullet holes in the back." *I certain didn't.*

"Where is it?"

I blinked at him. *Right. Fine.* If he wanted it, he were more than welcome to it. I raised my hand and pointed to the workbench. "Over there." I gestured to the lowest shelves in the back. "With all the rest of the things I found."

Real quick like, the Rover lurched over to them. Muttering something violent about traitors and liars I couldn't quite hear, he rummaged round the piles.

My head still buzzed about the edges and I swallowed down a sudden sprig of nausea. I flicked my gaze to the door. I took a step toward it. The Rover didn't look up. I took another step, shifting my weight to the balls of my feet. *I had to get back to Bren.*

"Worthless, scuttling liars, all of 'em. I knew he'd double-cross me. Where the stars is it?" He were near frenzied. Distracted. I took another step. Only a few more paces . . .

My flight cut off as the Rover flung a metal container fast and hard across the shed. Right at my head. It hit the metal of the wall with an ear-shattering clang. I froze. The Rover was staring right at me.

"I thought I'd gone and told ya not to move." His voice had gone all smooth. Too smooth.

I swallowed. At my back the wind shook the shed. The Rover twisted to the shelves, searching the rest of the dead man's things.

The Rover turned his attention to the silver-faced compass. My heart gave a little flutter. It were broke, but it weren't exactly scrap either. Maybe he'd think I'd lied. And if I lied about one thing . . . The Rover turned it over in his thick hand, a slick smile spreading over his cold-cracked lips before he opened it. Bits of blackened charcoal and sooty ice came tumbling out. Growling, he kicked the pieces, scattering them across the floor till they came to rest against the stack of bodies.

"As useless and empty as all the rest they try and sell," he said. And with a grunt, tossed the compass back into the pile. Pushing aside some rope, he picked up the dead man's notebook. Squinting and grumbling at the pages. He couldn't right read them neither. He flipped hasty to the back, shaking the notebook. A single piece of paper, torn, fluttered to the frozen ground.

He frowned and bent to pick it up, studying the writing. A moment later he gave a cry of frustration, crumpling the page. Whatever he was after weren't there. He turned his fathoms-deep scowl to me as he slipped the notebook and the wrinkled page into his own coat.

"Where is the rest of it?"

I inched closer to the door rattling at my back, my fingers brushing light against the cold metal. "Rest of it?"

"Don't play a fool with me, girl. That won't end well." He jutted his chin toward the house. My fingers froze on the handle. I couldn't outrun him. Him and whatever beast that was back in the room.

"You pocket them? Think maybe you could use 'em yourself? That no one come looking? I trailed that double-crossing dupe for days, watching him, waiting, only to have him run out into that storm." He began pacing. "Then this morning, guess who were standing out there on them Flats? Not him, no. You."

The words sent every hair on my body straight up.

"Out there, draggin his body in from the ice. I tried to be the first one out searching. I did. But when I found him you were already there. So I said to myself, Harden Reeves, now ain't that something? The man's dead but he ain't alone. Has a friend. And the moment I saw the way you looked at him, I knew it true. Why else would a girl slog a dead man in from the ice, unless he'd something she wanted? And she knew where to look."

Knew where to look? Man was losing it. Not that he had much to begin with.

"But I ain't survived this long cause I trust what I see. Double-checked my odds, I did. And in the nearest house, to my good luck, what did I find? But two girls, all alone."

"We ain't all—"

Rover laughed. "Of course you are. Question is, what to do about it now? Cause either you girls are lying to me because you think I ain't smart enough to know otherwise or you're lying to me cause *you* ain't smart enough to know otherwise." He smiled, tilting his head. "Either way don't matter to me. I'll get what I were promised. And you will give it to me."

"But I don't have nothing. I don't even know who that man is. I swear it. I don't. It's the truth." Real panic fluttered in my chest. Cause I knew it then. Truth or no, Rover had already made up his mind.

"Look, I ain't unreasonable. You just tell me what you did with what you took from him, hand them over right and proper, and good ol' Reeves might just overlook it."

I opened my mouth to reply, but he cut me off.

"And mind your words right, cause if I don't like what I hear, there'll be no second chances." The tip of his tongue flicked to the edge of his mouth.

My stomach rolled. I hesitated. My pocket felt sudden heavy.

"There is one thing." I pulled out the broken blade.

Snaking closed the distance between us, the Rover seized it. The brush of his callused hands across my knuckles sent a throb of revulsion through me. The Rover must have seen it cause his lip curled up tight, a lecherous smile tilted in his eyes. He turned the knife over in his palm.

Eyes locked on mine, he raised the handle to his ear and tapped. Dull. Like solid bone. Frowning, he scrutinized the end, fiddling with it, but no amount of twisting opened it. There weren't nothing to open. Just a broken knife. No secrets. Grunting, the Rover tossed it over his shoulder. It landed flat right on top of the belly of the body behind him.

After that he pulled down everything in the shed. Ropes, wood, metal scraps, it all got looked at, cussed at, and tossed away. Everything I'd ever found and cleaned and stored. One by one. The taste of white, bitter and clean, filled my throat. *Cause there ain't nothing in my life has ever been worth stealing.*

Done, the Rover stared at me for a good long while. The kind of stare an adder gives the mouse. Just before.

I refused to look away. My wits, dazed as they were, were coming back. I forced my shoulders square. With a grunt and a curse, the Rover pushed past me rough and stepped out into the passage. I sprinted after him.

Too slow.

He'd already got Bren over his shoulder by the time I got into the room.

"You put her down. Right now." I screamed it, the last of the concussed stupor gone. My body felt aflame. The Rover only laughed, low and loud.

In the flash of an eye, the beast was at his feet, black body whipping back and forth. The Rover put one hand on the door. Smiling at me, he opened it. Outside a blizzard were howling. The world nothing but freezing swirls of grays and green.

"You give her here. Or I'll kill you." I moved, snapping forward, only to come up short. The beast lunged across my path. The Rover laughed harder, hoisting Brenna higher up onto his shoulder.

"That ain't how this is gonna go, girl. I figured he had a friend out here, way he were carrying on. And a liar is a liar. Can smell it right as bear scat in the wild. I sure as stars didn't make it this far for some little girl to stop me getting what I'm owed."

I clenched my fists. The Rover held up a hand.

"And desperate a case as you're making, girl, it ain't till you give me what I know you have that you get her back. Till then, I reckon she's sweet enough to do just fine. People'll pay good for those mismatched eyes of hers."

"Stop! Where are you taking her?"

"Smart girl like you, I'm sure you'll figure it out." He pulled down his goggles, masking his face. "You know, two will sell better than one." And with that, the man strode out into the storm.

I ran after him, hurtling out into the wide frost-eaten earth that surrounded the house.

But I couldn't see them. Couldn't see the Rover, or the wolf, or Bren. I couldn't see much of anything—except there. Soft red drips of Bren's blood fallen in the snow.

I followed, but after only a few steps the color faded. And then were gone. My breath came in short. *No.* I spun. I couldn't lose her.

Shielding my eyes from the wind, I ran on. But the snowstorm was picking up. The storm whipped wickedly at my unprotected face, eating at the warmth of my exposed skin, licking at the edges of my jumper.

Even without the sun reflecting, the snow could be blinding. Tears froze and cracked against my face. I ripped at them wildly. Ripping flesh and ice away in equal raw measure. But no amount of looking would find something that weren't there.

Forcing my body forward, I ignored the burning ache of cold running through my veins. I scanned the ground. A single set of footprints pressed into the snow. Human ones. Trail leading straight into town. I ran. Faster than I'd ever run.

But the footsteps, they began to fade, buried by the falling show. *No, no, no.* I ran harder, stumbling on legs so numb I couldn't feel nothing from my knees down and still I ran.

Then the footprints were gone. Just gone. I twisted, faltering—a wall of freezing gray was all there were.

"Bren! Brenna!" I called, but the wind stole my voice.

My heart thundered in my chest. A frantic rhythm my failing muscles couldn't use. I collapsed to my hands and knees, scraping skin against the cold of the ice and snow. A hard warmth slipped under my hand. I blinked down, barely able to breathe. Half-hidden under the snow, like a shiver of memory, the stone still held to the heat of her skin. I blinked and blinked at it.

Bren's pendant. The silver-blue stone near to purred with familiarity against my skin. My throat tightened. It weren't something Bren would ever leave behind. Not willingly. I tried to rise. To stand. And failed, slipping.

The last two things I remember were the crunch of snow under my fingernails as I clutched at the pendant, and a large dark shape raging out of the blinding whiteness of the storm. Right at me.

CHAPTER 4
Cold Burns Deep

I woke next to a half-smothered fire, cold floor at my back. My face warm as I blinked against the heavy layers of ash settled in my lashes. I sneezed. And then immediately started coughing. I took a long moment to settle, blinking back tears.

Everything hurt fierce. I could just feel my fingers. I wiggled my feet. And only some of my toes. I ran a hand over my face. At least I weren't *currently* freezing.

I rolled over onto my side and wiped at the spit on my lips. The back of my hand came away gray and black. At my side a soft tug, gentle but insistent, pulled at the hem of my shirt. When I looked down, there weren't nothing there. I frowned. At least the fire was warm.

Then, sharp as a crack of lightning cross the midnight sky, everything came flooding back. The storm. The Rover. Brenna. *I had to go. How long had I been asleep, how long*—heart near to seizing, my fingers fumbled for the pocket of my shirt. Till they curled tight around the lump. Breath shot out of me. Cause it were still there. Bren's pendant. Her stone restin warm against my skin, like a second heart beating next to mine.

"Done yourself a disservice, girl." The voice that cut across my addled thoughts were rough, but it was familiar. "Take days to warm you up. And just what kind of fool idea you had stuck in that freckled little noggin of yours, I've no idea. Wandering into a blizzard like that, no coat. Right rum if you ask me."

"I have to find her." I sprang to my feet. Well, at least tried to. Only just caught myself on a haphazard stack of scrap wood in front of the fireplace, shaking something terrible.

"Jorie, you just sit your rear end back down right this second. You hear me?"

I spun round and, knees wobbling, took a step backward. A high-pitched cry filled the room. I looked down, just in time to see one very pissed-off ferret scurrying across the floor. *Well, least I knew who had been harrying my shirt.*

Della shook her chin. "The way you are right now, your mother would've killed me for just letting you stand up on your own. Right now you ain't fit to so much as clean your leathers, let alone go back out there. And there's no small matter 'bout that storm still raging, either."

I darted a glance at the small window where Cur, Della's white-coated ferret, had taken up offended residence. One eye on his groomin, the other on me. Just in case.

Behind him it were a stark contrast. Through the thick bottle-glass window it were dark as night. The blizzard was right raging outside. A low whistle of air rushed in through small gaps between the wooden planks of the one-room house. The storm's breathing stirring the fire's embers like a lick of demon's breath.

Della eyed me, wary. As if maybe she'd have to tackle me from trying to run. She didn't need to bother. Even if I wanted to run out there, storm like this, I'd be froze before I'd even had time to call Bren's name. I slumped back onto the floor. In the silence, determination coiled with guilt in my gut. If I couldn't leave now, I would leave the first second I could. The very first.

"She must be right angry tonight, sending us a storm like that." Della frowned, fingers darting quick over her heart as she muttered out a few words.

I turned away. I learned long ago there just weren't no point arguing that the Ice-Witch weren't someone to believe in. That there weren't no curse to blame for the ice and snow and death that littered the Flats. Weren't no Witch to fault for when children stopped breathing in the night. Or when animals collapsed under the weight of the water freezing in their veins. Or when your pa weren't never gonna come back in from the snow. No matter how much you needed him to. Or how much your sister cried.

Stifling a pang of memory, I let my hands fall into my lap, tryin and failin to rub a little warmth into the tips. The cold had just plain come to stay. Permanent. And there weren't nothing to do about it but live. But Pa'd always said, *Let people find comfort where they can.* Stars above knew there was little enough of that to go around.

I glanced up at the window. Della were right about one thing. That storm. Bad as I'd seen in a long time. Getting worse every year, they were. Longer, colder. Deadlier. As if with each year the winter crept just ever so much closer, unwilling to let go. Times like this, even *I* reckoned it weren't too hard to believe in all them myths after all.

I'd only the fuzziest memories of a time before the ice, when something akin to spring still came to Shadow Springs. Green and bright and full of sun. But it had to be a dream. Cause true spring? This town ain't seen that for a generation. Pa used to tell us about the time he'd seen one once, when he were young, when he met our ma just after she'd arrived in town. But me and Bren hadn't. Not really. Just the pale imitation, a flicker of warmth.

From his gray perch by the window Cur padded his way over to my lap. He nestled into the crook of my arm. Once his pink nose were buried, he let out a half-muffled little chirp. I smiled raw. He smelled of fresh burning pine and something sweet. I held him close.

"Now that you're finally full awake, ya gonna tell me what you were doing out there, besides tryin to get yourself froze to death?" Della asked, rocking back in her chair, eyebrows raised. Before she'd taken to burying bodies for the town—when she grew too old and too married for her first trade—Della had been like me. Making her living scavenging off the Flats. So she knew. Knew I wouldn't have run out there without reason.

"He took her, Della." The words were all scratchy.

"Who took who?" Della demanded. No one messed with Della. She'd had enough knocks for ten lifetimes. And then some.

I took a deep breath, pushing myself to my knees. "A Rover callin himself Reeves."

Della sucked in her breath, stopped rocking. Her hand went to the stock of her gun, displacing the few paltry winter fox and raccoon hides covering it.

"He came for a body, Della. But he took Bren. He just took her." My whole body ached so fierce even my bones hurt, just saying the words out loud. Cause with 'em, any last hope it weren't real evaporated on my tongue.

"You start right from the beginning, Jorie. And mind you tell me everything," Della said, lips curling to expose more than a few missing and blackened teeth.

A knock against the wall. We both started.

"The wind," Della said. "Shifting the snows, that all."

I put my head in my hands, a deep pinch clenching about my heart.

"Della, there weren't nothing I could do. He were waitin for me, like he had a plan." My words felt heavy. "Why would he be doing that? Why?"

Della pursed her lips, rocking back as Cur darted into her lap. "You aren't the only one round here to be seeing strangers, Jorie."

"I don't even know where to start."

"Start at the beginning, and don't leave no detail out, no matter how small. It may be that you saw more than you know."

I closed my eyes, swallowing down the bile of the memory, and told her. Of the Rover in our kitchen, in our living room, of his leering face as he'd carried Bren out into that storm. And away from me. I opened my eyes. My hands had become fists at my sides. "The Rover had a silver chain in his hand, all twisted up his arm—"

Della sudden stopped her rocking. "With a red stone?"

"I—yes. How did you know that?"

"That settles it." Della gave a twist of her lip, face troubled.

"Settles what?" There was something about her look.

Della glanced to the rifle at her side, clearing her throat. "Last night there was a scuffle outside my door. A right toss-up. Thought strays were into the bin again."

I tilted on the edge of my toes.

"Only when I got there it weren't animals that were fightin. It were men. Two of 'em thrashing in the snow, fighting worrisome like. One I couldn't see real well, but I did notice a flash of bright hair. . . . auburn maybe, and the other one, he were real tall. Both of 'em hollering something fierce."

My breathing felt heavy. As if trying to take in air against a wet cloth. "What were they arguing about?"

"Money. Some big trade gone wrong." Della scrunched her brow. "The big man had told something he shouldn't have. Duped into saying it. A result he weren't too keen on, I can tell you that much." Della shook her head, soft. "There were a scream and then a spark of light as the smaller one ran for it."

"It has to be the same Rover. It just does. Maybe he's still here." Please.

"Maybe. But Jorie," Della said, "ya didn't see them, the way they were fighting. Men like that don't tend to stick around. Not after they get what they want."

"Did you see which way they went at least? After, I mean." What were it to me if the Rover had robbed the other man? I only cared what he'd stole from me.

Della shook her head. "They scuttled off right quick when I took that first shot. But that snowstorm were rising too fast, couldn't see naught else." Della's frown deepened. "But mark my words, any man dead desperate enough to think he can run off into the night, he's done for anyways. That and the gun the tall one pulled as he ran after him would settle his blood quick enough."

"Della, can you think of anything else? What about a dog? Did they one of them have some kinda dog with them?" *Dog* was an understatement, but I didn't know what else to call it. Not without sounding as if I'd less wits than Cur. But if she had seen the beast, maybe it would lead me to the Rover.

"No. Nothing, Jorie. I'm sorry." Della pursed her lips, studying me, eyes bright. Finally, with a grunt, she shuffled over to the hearth. Quiet, she lay kindling on and stoked the embers back into flame.

We stared at them together for a long time. We both knew I wasn't leaving.

Cur on her shoulder, Della walked back over and sat in her chair, settling down. "If there's one Rover sniffin round like a mutt in heat, you can bet there's more. And if he's not alone and one of 'em's already targeted you ..." She fixed me with her stare. "Don't you trust no one, Jorie, you hear me. You got something they want, no matter if you know it or not. And there ain't no one round here that can't be got at."

For the right price. I nodded sharp.

"You and your sister's in more trouble than you know."

CHAPTER 5

Shadow Springs

———— •◦• ————

T he storm didn't let up its thrashing till midday next. And like a winter-starved hare, I was up and out before the sun were fully risen cross the horizon.

All around it were like a fresh-cleaned skin of white. The blizzard had smoothed and smothered everything. Tree boughs hung thick, tucked down against sleet-covered trunks. Not a lick of life to be seen. No tracks. No directions. No way to tell me I weren't the only living thing in the world.

Shoving at the thigh-high deep snow, I tugged Della's jacket tight. At least the wind had merciful settled down. Though the silence, still and cold and sharp as cut glass, were near as uncanny as the storm. Hunkering down, I let the broken wooden mouth of Della's fallow garden gate bang shut behind me, boards rattlin loose, and took my first step toward town.

Shadow Springs was as much a set of half-caved-in boarded-up shacks as it was a town. More so, maybe. Three streets wide, with only one central road, it weren't much to see. Less you liked rotting wood. And didn't mind that nothing sat at right angles to nothing else.

It had been something, once. Something big, Pa had said. When people from towns all over the North would come and stay. Try their luck at prospecting or trapping or hunting out on the ice. But the gold and the furs—just like the hope—had never really panned out. Then winter had come. And the only people who showed up in town weren't after the furs.

Still, taking the turn around the last abandoned building on the edge of town—the pine walls of the old jailhouse stuck up like giant ribs jutting from the snow—I kept my eyes keen. And my ears alert.

The bar, which also served as the only inn in town, was the biggest and squarest building on Main Street. It were also the only place I was likely to find someone.

Frowning, I took the crumbling stairs outside the bar three at a time. I shoved at the door, which were tall and thin, the hinges giving a cough of rusty protest. Kicking the bags of sand blocking the bottom seam of the doorway to the side, I shook off the fine dusting of snow from my coat.

I stamped my feet and gave a snort. Room sure was packed. A whole three people. The same drunks there always were, slumped about the room, more drenched leather and unwashed body than real men. The room smelled of stale smoke and the dank rot of slow blackening wood.

Dev wasn't out in the main room, but he'd like as not be in the back minding his stock, refilling the liquor bottles or attempting to repair something that were near to as hopeless as this whole stars-forsaken town. The various clocks, storm glass and barometers lined up behind the bar ticked slow and steady, the only motion in stillness as I made my way toward the long bar. Halfway there, I froze, my stride pulled short.

A boy, one I didn't right know, slumped against the far side of the bar, his body half hid by shadow in the stale yellow light. Careful eye on him, I strode the rest of the way over.

This close, the smell of whiskey floated off his thin frame. It were dank. I wrinkled my nose and leaned over to grab a bottle from under the counter. A pile of half-washed glasses clanked.

The boy didn't look up.

I hooked my foot and kicked a stool out from the bar, the wood legs gritting over the uneven floor. Dev's scarred face appeared from the back room, cleaning rag tossed over his shoulder. He gave me his familiar grunt of a greeting. A flutter of guilt brushed against my gut. It had been a long time since I'd come to visit him. It weren't nothing against Dev. Opposite, really. He and Pa had been close as brothers once. Then Pa had died, fallen out on the ice. It were an accident. That there must've been a flaw in the pack ice he didn't see. They said that there were nothing anyone could've done. He'd hit his head and bled out. Alone. Cause I weren't there to help him. You lived out here long enough, eventually you died. It weren't like I didn't get that. But even in this stars-forsaken town he didn't have to die alone.

And no matter what no one said, for that I could blame myself. I could have gone out hunting with him that morning. But I didn't. I hadn't. That's what caring for people got you. Pain. And avoiding Dev meant avoiding all of that. Of thinking about that day. Of thinking about Pa. So I stayed away. Till now.

Outside, the wind began to shake. Clattering the loose glass windows in their splintering frames. A racket not unlike the rattling of broken teeth. Behind me, Dev cleared his throat.

I turned to him. "I need information."

Dev raised an eyebrow. "Don't we all."

"You know I wouldn't be asking if it weren't important." I gave Dev what I hoped to be a grin.

Dev took one look at me and, grunting, placed a glass on the bar in front of me. The measure he poured weren't short. He set the flask down on the bar. I took a long, deep swallow of the sweet amber liquid from my cup. Heat flooded my guts. And for something with no liquor it sure did a good job of making a girl feel warm. A syrupy mix of Dev's own imagining, it had been known to keep a man alive out on the ice when little else could.

I set the glass down and took the rest of the flask, sliding it into my pocket. I'd be needing it.

In the yard out back, Dev's pack of snow hounds began barking. A right howling chorus, their calls filled the stillness of the bar. Again a little twist of unease fluttered in my stomach. Time, like the weather, were not on my side.

Without meaning to, I brushed the scar on my face. My hand came down shaky. "I need to know about a man."

"There plenty of them about, Jorie. Don't know that there are any worth knowing here right now," Dev said, running a heavy hand through his long graying beard, rings glinting. The silver one clear broken, the setting empty and gaping wide. Dev tilted his head. We stared at each other. "Why?"

"Because they took something important from me. And I aim to take it back."

My words had the expected effect. Dev froze mid-pour.

"When?" Dev asked, eyes turning hard. Had to give Dev credit. He had always been, if not kind, then well at least helpful. But Della were the only person left I could trust. Much as I liked Dev, he'd always had *enough*.

Enough food. Enough drink. Enough money. When no one round here ever had enough. Not if they were honest.

"Two days past," I kept my voice calm as Dev digested the information. He filled my glass before picking up a dirty one.

"And you think they brought it here?" Dev glanced around the inn, looking confused. "Jorie, no one *brings* things to Shadow Springs. They take 'em."

I know that all too well. "That ain't what I'm sayin, Dev. What I want to know is if there's been any strangers in town. Recent, mind. *Big* strangers. Scary ones. Like, say, Rovers."

Dev's smooth cleaning hitched just for the barest of seconds, so short I didn't right know if I'd actually seen the hesitation before he picked it up again. "Now, why would you be askin after men like that?" He fixed me with what could be considered an uninterested stare. Only I knew it weren't.

"I wouldn't be asking if it weren't important." I wanted to shake him. "And you know it."

Dev let low a whistle. "Strictly speaking, no."

That wasn't an answer. I opened my mouth. But he cut me off with a grunt, holding up a hand.

"I haven't, Jorie, and that's the truth. I would tell you if I had. Though . . ." Dev inclined his head at the slumped boy. "Far as I'm concerned, if you want to ask about trouble, you could do worse than starting right there."

My eyebrows shot up. "I ain't interested in shaking down your customers for tips, Dev. This is important."

Dev gave a snort. "I've always found unassuming packages the most surprising. Though I ain't sure you want to open this one, Jorie. You think real hard on it before you get yourself into more trouble than it's worth."

Great. Cryptic. Thanks, Dev. I turned my gaze between Dev and the boy. Who began to murmur incoherent like. And then belch. Nice. Real classy.

"He ain't no Rover, Dev. What's there to worry about?" I stared. "He's just a boy." Strange, true, but near enough my age I weren't too worried 'bout who'd get the upper hand. He didn't right look like much I couldn't handle.

"Be careful, is all I'm saying," Dev said. "And don't trust no one, you hear me, Jorie? People aren't always who they seem to be." A brief flash of something I could swear were regret filled his eyes before it were gone, his expression hardening. "There's just too much your pa ain't never got a chance to tell you before he died. Before he and your ma—"

Irritation bloomed hot on my cheeks, and I cut him off. I knew exactly where this were going, and I didn't care for it. "I ain't here to talk about my pa, Dev," I said, shiftin on the barstool, pulling my coat tighter round me. "So you can spare me the 'you never know what you don't know' speech. I sure can handle some simple, jelly-legged—"

Before I could say anything else, the boy shot up off his barstool, crashing hard to his knees. Cups scattering everywhere. I blinked real rapid.

"Don't you touch me!" The boy came up swinging. "Don't you *dare* touch me."

Both me and Dev looked at him, surprised. Dev recovered first.

"If he carries on like that, he ain't gonna be a problem for too much longer. Yours or mine," Dev said, seeming oddly relieved by the idea. I frowned. Took a special kind of stupid to be getting drunk out here, especially if you were alone.

The boy lurched to his left, crashing into his barstool, sending it spiraling out into the room. He spun, arms out. But there weren't no one harrying him. I gawked, disbelieving, as with the last of his listless punches he took a few empty bottles down to the dust-coated floor with him.

He was like as to wreck himself carrying on like that. Out of the corner of my eye I saw some of the other men in the bar finally stir, reaching for their sides.

Drunk men. What was it about them and fighting? One whiff of testosterone and they was like hungry bears to the hive.

Behind the bar Dev was already reaching under the counter where he stored his gun. One that ain't never missed its target yet. Human or otherwise.

I stood up and walked over to where the boy had fallen to his knees, curled in on himself. If Dev were right, the boy might be worth a question or two sobered up. *If.* "You'd better be right, Dev."

"I am." Dev slid the key to the boy's rooms along the bar. "Two things I know. First, there ain't such things as coincidence. And two? No one skips out of here without paying." I looked between him and the key before finally nodding.

Dev wouldn't run me on a false trail. If he said there were something, there were something.

"And Jorie." He twisted a warning look at the other guests. The drunkards rumbled themselves to a belligerent stop. "You make sure to ask him about the other one was with him."

CHAPTER 6

Honey Like Lies

———◆———

The other one?" I asked, confused. "Other *who?*"

But before Dev could answer, the boy bent double and heaved. It weren't dry neither. I took a step back to avoid the splatter. The smell of half-eaten fish and rotten apples hit me like a squall. I cupped a hand over my face.

Right. Maybe a day of sleeping it off with Dev's dogs out back was needed. For most of the men round here it were usually the ticket.

As I reached out to take his arm, the boy jolted his face upward. This time his eyes weren't stuck in the corner, but right on mine. Green and bright, they were faultless. An aurora across a midnight sky.

The boy bent forward, eyes still locked on mine, and raised his hand. The soft flesh of his fingers brushing against the exposed cold of my wrist, moving toward my face. His face rose level with mine. The white curl of his breath rushing cool past the red of my flushed cheek.

"I don't . . . your eyes, that scar . . . it's . . ." Light as the press of a summer breeze, his fingers fluttered over my face. He leaned in, but instead of words, he chucked up the rest of his gut. All over my shoes.

Sharp, I snapped away, blinking back the dim light of the inn, staring down at the top of his cap.

Below me, the boy's shoulders tightened as he retched what little were still left. I glanced at Dev. Fingers fiddling with the empty setting on his silver ring, he gave me a deep frown. His mutterings only mostly obscured by his thick beard.

"I'll take care of it," I said. My eyes hard I looked over the boy. "Outside for you it is."

I grabbed the key in one hand and the boy in the other and dragged him out toward the yard. The boy let out a low groan as I pulled him over the threshold and into the cold. Only noise he made. Otherwise he put up no fight. Just let me haul him out back. When I released my grip, he slumped down awkward against the cluttered porch. He listed dangerous to the right. Sighing, I propped him back into sitting.

The boy's lips were a nasty shade of blue, but he weren't shivering. Drink did that to you. Made your body as much a fool as your wits. But if he couldn't walk, there was little chance I'd be able to get him up to his rooms.

I twisted my hair into a knot at the base of my neck and strode across the low-roofed porch. He might not have been a Rover, but he sure weren't from around here. Two Southerners in near as many days. . . . Dev was right, we didn't believe in coincidences. Not round here. So we'd just see what this stranger had to say.

I drug over one of the big wood barrels. Rolling to a stop right at the boy's feet. The guts of the drum sloshed about wet inside.

Though it weren't their food bucket, Dev's dogs picked up their barking. Reckon someone had to be optimistic around here. I gave the dogs a sharp whistle. The barking cut off. Grinning, I wedged up the barrel's lid.

There were two ways to keep your water from freezing up round here: make it salty or make it drink. Excepting, of course, this one trick.

Standing on my tiptoes, I reached into the barrel and pulled out a black glass orb about the size of my fist. The sphere was warm, and though there were ice crystals humming round the edges of the water, it weren't froze like everything else round here. Just cold. They scuttled around the water, some only half submerged and others— the empty ones—clear sunk to the bottom.

That was cause the inside of the orbs was filled with tiny bubbles of gas, and as the hot gas escaped, the orbs sunk. Putting the hot gas into the orb had been my pa's trick. Once. It was the same gas that gurgled up out of ice 'bout a mile into the Flats from our house, where the white of the snow turned yellow. The waters grew thick with the smell of sulfur and the ice became littered with the bones of animals driven mad enough with thirst to try and drink it.

Scrunching up my nose, I gripped the black orb. We'd soon find out what he knew about Bren. With one fast motion, I pulled the stopper open and stuck it right under the boy's nose.

He was on his feet faster than an adder skidding on ice. Did the trick every time. Scurrying back and wicked off-balance, he pressed his spine deep into the pillar behind him, blinking and rubbing violent like at his nose. It didn't hurt. Just smelled. Real bad.

I took a step toward him, closing the space between us.

"Don't know about you, and don't care to," I said, advancing, porch boards creaking under my feet, ice crystals breaking between the grains. The wind picked up.

The boy turned his gaze back to me. When it landed, it was like a blow. Not like I ain't never seen a good-looking boy before, but they was usually looking at Bren. Not me.

I moved closer, blood warm in my veins. I leaned in tight. And going by the wide, puffy black patches under his eyes, I weren't the only one not sleeping.

"Ain't no use trying to run." I placed one finger slow and careful right over his heart. And tapped. "Cause there ain't anyone here but you and me."

CHAPTER 7

Nightmares and Shades

———— ◆ ————

N ame?" I demanded.

The boy swallowed, staring numb up at me. I tossed a hand in the air. Every moment here were a moment longer I weren't with Bren. And I really weren't great at patience. I tried again.

"Come on now, everybody's got a name." I looked him up and down. "Even if it ain't a good one. Here, I'm Jorie." I took a step closer, leaning down. "What's yours?"

He cleared his throat. "Cody. Cody Colburn." His head bobbed. "Excuse me, but do I know you?"

"Do you?" I asked, my eyes narrowing. The boy shifted. After a long moment, he cleared his throat, pulling at the pale green of his high-collared shirt.

"I—no." He blinked slowly as his eyes focused first on the gathering clouds, then on Dev's dogs. "Do you live out here?"

I stared at him with disbelief. "Do you *think* I live here?"

He followed my gaze, the scrap metal, the broken wood. The kennels. The lack of anything remotely like a house. "I—right, sorry. Of course not. That was rude of me."

Oh good. The boy had *manners*. Soft Southern manners. Too bad those wouldn't get him anything out here but dead.

I curled a stray stand of hair out of my face. Spoiled Southerners.

They deserved all the bad luck they got, seeing as how it was their greed that kept the North so poor and the South so rich. It weren't even like we got the good weather—though we had once. A soft white blanket of snow began to fall from the gray sky, flakes swirling up and around the roof caught in a hard wind, too shy yet to land.

In front of me the boy's lips were turning a deeper, more alarming shade of blue; he needed to get warm. It weren't my problem whether a man drank too much and didn't wake up. Never had been. Never would be. Trouble were, I actually wanted something from this one.

"Well, Cody Colburn, I guess it's your lucky day." I spread my arms wide.

"Why is that?" Cody blinked lazy at me, eyes half closed.

"Cause it ain't every day a Southern boy like you gets to be helpful." *Usually you just get yourselves killed.* My mind briefly flashed back to the richly-but-poorly-dressed body in the shed. *Fools, the lot of 'em.* Arrogant, entitled, useless. A perfect trifecta. I placed a hand over my heart. "Lucky you."

It were a sentiment not dislodged when, rather than reply, Cody began to laugh. And not like something were funny. But hard. Like something hurt. Something deep down and buried.

"Help *you?*" His whole body shaking. "You want me to help you?"

My face flushed hot. "You heard me." I could feel the hairs on the back of my neck stand up. "If this is cause I'm a girl, I can assure you I can tear your . . ."

His laughter only got louder. I bit back the rest of my words. Right. I hauled him to his feet, none too gentle. "You seem sober enough to me. Where's your rooms?"

Cody regarded me through long, rose-tinged lashes. Like feathers. I had the oddest urge to run my fingers across them. *Don't be an idiot, Jorie.*

Cody quirked pale lips and raised a finger toward the stairway at the back of the inn. "Top floor," he said. "I think."

"Of course it is." Grinding my jaw, I set his arm over my shoulders, and I half walked, half drug him up the short flight of back stairs. We made it, just.

"My rooms," he said, twisting his arm from my grip, and with a dogged effort fumbled about his pockets. Only I had the key. I held it up. He beamed.

"I really ain't got time for this," I muttered, turning and sliding the key into the lock. A dead bolt with fresh gouge marks all over the wood. Seems I weren't the first interested party to pay a visit. I shoved open the door.

Inside the well-lit room, the smell of a low-burning fire filled the air. As did the thick odor of mold and some other scent I couldn't quite place. Light filtered down cold and gray from the snow-covered skylights.

In the far corner, near the stone fireplace, a large telescope sat blind, its lens covered by thick black cloth. And like scattered constellations, expensive silks and gilded metal and exotic wood boxes littered the floor around it. Facing this were two leather armchairs. One toppled over, the other's fabric split down the back. Books were tossed everywhere, their spines cracked and broken, pages torn out, strewn across the floor.

Whoever had paid a visit before me, they weren't none too gentle.

Cody moved to right the fallen chair, indicating I should sit in the other. I stayed by the door.

"Oh no you don't," I said. "You've got questions to answer for. Starting now."

Cody lowered his way into the leather seat and let out a long sigh, dragging a bearskin blanket over him as he sat.

"I do not feel so well. And you are rude," he said.

I fixed him with a dark look. "The faster you answer me, the sooner I leave."

Cody mumbled something I couldn't hear. I took a step toward him. But he held up a hand. "Just give me a moment is all," he said, taking out an engraved metal dosette box from his pocket. The sharp tang of black cohosh spiked the air as Cody pulled a pinch from the inside and began to chew it. Not that the bitter herb was even gonna touch the headache he was about to have. "I promise to help, but only if you promise not to be mean to me again."

I stared at him. Bren were missing and this drunk were worried that I was rude? I clamped my first reply behind my lips. This were for Bren. I could be nice for Bren. "Fine, but don't take too long about it." I crossed my arms. "I ain't gonna wait nice forever."

Cody yawned, running a hand over his face before giving me a half-hearted smile. I was not moved. I began a careful survey round the room, taking it in. Pa had always told me that if you knew how to look, a girl could learn more about a person by what they kept round them than what they said. I stopped at the desk and picked up a fine blue metal pen, a stone of something that shone like glass, only it weren't, and a series of—old harbor maps? I weren't sure. All of 'em for countries I didn't know.

A broken brass sextant and an overturned inkwell—the pooled black ink long dried—bout made the rest of what covered the desk. But other than rich and careless, I didn't see what this half-ransacked room said about the boy in the chair. Other than . . . I stopped. Cody had taken off his cap. Red hair rustled down over his face. Now that were certain something.

Dev's words filtered back to me. *Ask about the other one. The other one.*

Setting down the sextant, I glanced over. Cody were still too far out of it to be useful, eyes closed and his breathing soft. The gentlest horizon of red just returning to his cheeks. Careful, I snuck down the hall to the back room. Only to find it disappointingly empty. Save for a whole bunch of books.

Tons of 'em. A library, really. Must have cost a fortune to bring 'em here. Why would anyone want that many books? I picked up the closest one and flipped through the pages. Some of them torn, all of them moth-eaten and molding. Old, old books. The language weren't even right. A feeling, not unlike the brush of scales against my skin, skittered up my spine.

"Now, I believe you wanted something from me?" Cody's raised voice called from the front room. Starting, I near dropped the book and went back out.

In his chair, Cody leaned into the soft leather, the long smooth skin of his neck exposed.

I cleared my throat and stalked over.

Cody didn't open his eyes. The only sign he'd heard me were a smile tugging slow at the corner of his mouth.

"I—what's so amusing?" I narrowed my eyes.

"It's really not funny at all, is it?" Cody gestured round the ransacked room.

"No, it isn't." *What were wrong with him?*

"So let us cut to the chase."

"Yes, let's."

"My uncle." His eyes flew open. And this time there were no drowsiness there. Clear as ice they were. "That is, of course, why you are here. Just leave it to Bastian to send a wide-eyed local instead of a University recovery team for help. That man really is as hopeless as my uncle said."

I raised my hands, taking a step closer. "I don't know nothing about your uncle, a University, or nothing about anyone named Bastian. That ain't why I dragged you in here."

He sat up bolt straight in his chair.

Good. "Like I said, I just want to know if you've—or any of you—has seen a girl. Or a man, big, white hair, black dog. They don't need to be together. I just need—"

"It's only me, I am afraid," he said. "Obviously, that is the problem." He gestured to the room.

"Well, that ain't my problem." I grunted. "But good to know."

Cody opened his mouth and then closed it. He blinked at me for a long time, trying to recalculate where he thought this conversation were going. "This girl you are looking for, who is it?"

"My sister, Bren."

"Your sister? Is there something wrong with her?"

You could say that. "She's been taken."

"Taken?"

"Are you just gonna echo back everything I say?"

"What, no." He looked around, eyes big, as if Bren were about to pop out of the fireplace. "Sorry, let me get this right. You have a sister named Bren and she is missing. And you think *I* somehow know something about it? That I know who took her?"

I fixed him with a glare. "Not missing. Taken. Like I said. And

50

yes. I see it as a distinct possibility." The South had money . . . but brains, that were clear optional.

"And just to be sure, you are *not* here about my uncle or me or his research? And not about what we were looking for out on the Fl—" Cody cut off abruptly.

"The Flats?" I finished for him. "Ain't no one got business out on that ice. Only ones out there are treasure hunters and dead men." Usually they were one and the same.

Cody shifted in his seat. "Right, well. No. Not on the *Flats* exactly. That's his area of research you see. Out there, past the ice and . . . you know . . ." Seeing my expression, he trailed off.

"Know what?" I asked. That Rover clear had business out there too. I took another step closer to him.

"Other places," Cody finished lamely, waving his hand.

It took all my willpower not to reach out and smack it.

I crossed my arms. "Look, Cody, you got problems, I can see." I put on my best smile. Like Bren would've told me. "But those problems? They ain't my problems. I just want to know if you've seen my sister. Or the Rover who took her. Big, white hair, goggles, runs with a nasty black wolf."

"A wolf?" he asked, going suddenly still. A strange note to his voice, high and low all at once. Like it weren't really a question. "Big one?"

"You could certain say that."

Cody stood up abruptly, and walked over to the desk, riffling through the loose papers that covered it, mutterin something I couldn't hear. Finally, he picked up a single sheet, letting the others flutter to the floor at his feet.

"Did it look something like this?" he asked, holding the page toward me.

I rushed to take it. Even from paces away there weren't no mistaking it. That were the very likeness of the beast. Right there on the page. My skin prickled. Whoever had drawn this had certain seen one. Not a coincidence, it couldn't be.

"You draw this?" I asked, giving all the papers another glance. A disconcerting image of Bren's charcoals flooded up inside me. Pictures and drawings littered the floor around us, like pulled pages from some fancy book. They showed all different types of animals and plants I ain't never seen. Bren would have loved them. I scowled.

"Well, not all of them," Cody said. I eyed him up and down. "It's more of a hobby, really. My uncle, Walter, he's the real naturalist. He drew most of them; I am not nearly as good. But I did, however—" He swallowed, indicating the page I held. "I did draw that one. Here."

My eyes went wide. He'd seen it. Or good as said so. No other way about it. "Your uncle and you, where did you . . . ?" I trailed off as the pieces slipped into place. *Oh you're an idiot, Jorie. A right drowned fool.* How could I have not seen it sooner? The two Southerners. Of course they were here together. The man and his nephew. The man and the Rover. I looked quick at Cody, a flash of something dangerous to pity flaring in my gut.

"Where is your uncle, Cody?" I asked. But of course I already knew the answer. In my body shed.

A thick stillness filled the room. The slow hiss from a dying fire and the thunder of my panting unnatural loud. It were the first time in my life I didn't want to be right. Please don't let me be right.

"I don't know," Cody said, running a hand through his hair.

"You do not know." I stared at him. That pity twisting ugly tight inside me.

"Why else do you think I was drinking? To drown it all out of course." He said it strange, eyes fixed on the far wall. Not looking at me. "It's because—"

"Because why?" I asked real careful like. It weren't a question.

Cody blanched, his breathing hitched. "Because he's dead. And it is all my fault."

CHAPTER 8

Death and Reclamation

———— ⋅ ————

Y our fault?" It was my turn to be surprised. I didn't know all that much, but I knew this boy weren't no killer.

Cody's brows knitted together. "Well, good as."

And now I knew I should have hit him. "What do you mean *good as*? Either you did or you didn't, Cody. There ain't much room for in-between." My words came out hard, but inside I were crumbling. He didn't know anything about Bren.

Cody's hands clasped at his side. "He's been missing for days. Just disappeared. Which he wouldn't do—he just wouldn't. But no one around here seems to care. No one listens and no one can be bothered to tell me anything." His tone bitter. "What other conclusion is there to draw? And it's my fault."

"Stars, Cody!" Least it explained the state of him.

"He left everything." Cody spread his arms wide. "His life's work. Everything he's ever read or thought or drawn is here. He would never abandon this, *could* never abandon this, not if he were still alive." His voice trailed off, as if the last words were a feather in his throat. His eyes shot to the floor. "I should have never let him leave that night. I knew something about the deal to get us out into the Flats was not right. The way he had been acting, keeping odd hours, not telling me where he'd been. For my own good, he'd said. And he got like that sometimes: anxious, quiet. So I dismissed it, or tried my best to. Marked it up to stress. But when he walked out . . . I didn't stop him. I didn't know." Cody dipped his head. "I never even said goodbye."

"Tell me, Cody, your uncle, did he have reddish-brown hair and blue eyes?" I knew, but I had to be sure.

Cody's head shot up, a sickening hope blooming in his expression. "You've seen him."

"I have." I wish I hadn't. It felt suddenly as if our roles were reversed. Cause maybe we both had something the other wanted. I didn't think that a good thing.

"Bless the stars. You don't know how much this means to me, that he's here and you've seen him. I've never been so happy to be wrong in my life. Come on, let's go right now," Cody said. Jumping up, he began to rummage through one of the smaller trunks, tossing silks and books onto the floor before finally pulling out a glossy blue-and-silver coat. I eyed it warily as he put it on. Fingers dancing along the bright silver edges of the heavily embroidered coat. Buttons closing. "Take me to him."

"I don't think that's such a good idea," I hedged.

Cody looked up, genuinely surprised. "Why ever not? If your place is close, surely it cannot be that much trouble. And if my uncle is hurt, I can help. I've learned all about triage and am good with—"

"You won't be able help him." I cut him off.

He paused at that. The conversation, my tone, finally sinking in. He looked at me. Just looked at me. And I knew in that moment I just had to say it. Like setting a break in a new fractured bone, there weren't no use messing around. Besides, I'd never seen any point in sugarcoating bad news. Just hurt worse later. I were practical. I weren't cruel.

"He's dead." I said it fast. Fast enough he blinked at me for a long time as it sunk in. When it did, his shoulders slumped, the jacket slipping ever so slightly down his arms. All the buoyancy of the new hope spilling out around him.

Silent, he moved to the fireplace. Face grim. "How?"

He were greedy or stupid or both. But I didn't say that. Instead I took a breath and stilled my impatience. "Shot." I grimaced a little at the coldness of my tone. "In the back."

"Shot? You mean I let him walk out of here alone, and he was— he was *murdered*?" Cody picked up a long metal poker and began eviscerating the inner bodies of the rapidly dying logs. "And here I've been worried about him getting lost out in the snow or at worst a fall on the ice. . . ."

Crackling sparks, like wayward stars, flew up and into the flue. Outside, the shutters moaned with the run of the wind. He stood for a long time, just staring at the flames. His shoulders taut, face unreadable. Tension running clear as a river through his bones.

"Are you certain it can't have been an accident? That we are talking about the same man?" Cody finally asked, sliding his hand into the pocket of his coat.

I nodded, but he did not look at me. Just stayed staring at the hearth, his fingers rubbing over whatever trinket he had in his coat.

"I should thank you then, I think. For telling me." He ran a hand through his hair, sending the floating embers that had settled there dancing into the air between his fingers. A few landed like gray snow on his sleeves. "At least I know."

"There ain't nothing to thank me for." *And you're gonna right hate me for it in a minute. If Cody had what the Rover wanted . . . I had to try.* I took a deep breath, forcing down the last flicker of pity in my gut. I weren't here for Cody. I were here for Bren. And I had to know. No matter what. Back straight, I strode over and stole the metal fire poker from Cody's hand.

"What in the—" he started.

"Where is it?" I brandished the poker.

"Where's what? What's wrong with you?" Cody tilted his head, disbelief written clear as the morning light across his face. Confusion, and then a slow dawning of realization. He let out a brittle bark of laugher. "Or was this what you meant by helping me? You are going to kill me too?"

"Hardly," I scoffed. "What kind of girl do you think I am?" *The one you are pretending to be*, a little voice inside me whispered. *The one holding a poker to his chest.*

"Then what?" he asked, all the tension flooding out of him. "What does it matter now, anyways? You can take whatever you want. You wouldn't be the first one to try."

"So you admit the Rover has been here?"

Cody gestured, sudden angry. "Someone has, clearly."

His anger stoked mine. "Well, either you get to talking or I get to making you talk. Your choice." I threw poker down onto the hearth, where it landed with a huge clatter. I leaned my face into his, stopping close enough to feel the warmth of his breath across my cheek.

"Whichever way works the same for me. Just because your family is dead don't mean mine needs to be too."

Cody's eyebrows shot up, cheek muscles flexing with disapproval. *Good. Get mad. Angry men talked.* When he took a step backward, I curled my lips into a wide smile. "So you better start tellin me everything you know. Beginning with exactly why you're here and where the stars his notebooks are."

Cody cleared his throat, spine once again tall. "The body. I want to see the body first."

"The body?" I took half a step back. "Why?"

"That's my condition. I'll tell you everything—I will—but I want to see him first. You said he was murdered. Shot. Well, I want to see it—him."

"Why?"

"He is my uncle, okay?" His eyes blazed with suspicion. "And you will show me where he is. Now. And then I'll tell you what I know."

If it weren't so irksome I would've smiled at that. This boy might be worth more than he looked after all. Good. If he were gonna make it out here, he would certain need to be. There was something of the dying fire in that look he'd fixed on me. Something hot and angry. A wild animal, sad and bright all at once. Surrounded by chaos and loss . . . and me.

It hit me then, like a bolt. The fact that he were very much alone. What he loved sudden and forever gone. At least we'd that in common.

He'd called my bluff. I may not be past riling him up, but I weren't gonna actually bruise him. Swallowing my irritation, I put up my hands.

"Deal." If I weren't gonna get answers here, I'd get 'em somewhere else. So be it. I gestured to the door. "If it's what you really want, I'll take you. But I warn you, Cody Colburn, it ain't gonna be pretty."

"Just show me." Cody swallowed, hard. But didn't back down.

I knew that there were worse ways than fists to hurt a man. And the way determination mixed with fear on his face, I didn't think he'd ever seen a dead man before.

Well, he sure as stars was about to.

CHAPTER 9

These Scattered Scars

———◆———

M e in front and Cody trailing, we trudged on through the town's high snows. The only other footprints were those left by the smallest of animals. Nimble, scattered prints of birds and mice, scratched into the ice. All of 'em lives just waiting to starve. Look as I might, there weren't no trace of any wolves, or their thieving owners.

I glanced behind me every now and again making sure Cody followed close. Each time, his head were down and his hands clenched in his coat. Over my shoulder, Shadow Springs began to disappear. A rotting smudge on the horizon behind us. Good riddance.

The snowbound road, lined as it were by rickety black buildings and the rusted lines of the defunct rail system, soon gave way to the boughs of massive evergreens. Great timbers, most without needles, stood like matchsticks in the snow, suffocating in white. Fitful rumbles filled the cold as great sheets of ice slipped from the laden evergreens, crashing to the forest floor. A noise as lonesome as it were beautiful. And deadly.

Turning us down a small path, we coiled deeper into the winter-bare woods. The smell of the cold pines sinking sweet and welcome into my lungs. Chill biting at my nose. The wild rushing over my skin. I near to closed my eyes with the welcome relief of it.

"It's always been all about him," Cody said at my side.

I started a step. When had he gotten so close?

"The rest of us all just came in second to it, really. Nothing more important to Walter than his great works." His tone wasn't bitter, just resigned.

I gave him a sideways glance, his square, clean jaw lit just right by the evening light. Something in the lonesome of his words caught at me, snagged down deep. I opened my mouth and then closed it right quick, scoffing at myself. What was I gonna say to him? Sorry? That didn't right cover his loss. Not even the start of it.

"Nothing was too much of a sacrifice; nothing was too much to give for knowledge. Unearthing the unfound. Academic discovery. That was the world—his world. Knowledge and truth above all else. Including family. Including me."

I frowned, walking quick and trying not to hear. Even if I said something, if I tried, why would he care? I'd only look the fool for trying. When you didn't know what to say, it were best say nothing at all.

Undeterred by my silence, Cody rambled on. "That's why we were sent up here, you know. Well, not sent, not really. He volunteered us. If it meant proving his findings, he'd run us anywhere. But he was always like that, really. Just ask my parents. Though you'd have to move a ton of collapsed ruins first." His words swirled out into the cold, his breathing hard as he caught back up falling into step at my side.

"It could have been worse I suppose. Growing up at the University. With my uncle. It's not like I was alone. Not all the time." Cody glanced up at the night sky, a slow smile lingering on his lips. "After all, out here we are never truly alone, not really. All you need to do is look around. This world, these places. Life. Always there, if you know where to look for it." He gestured with one hand toward the world. To the ice and trees and stars above.

"Is that so?" I said, the words out of my lips before I'd meant to.

A genuine smile bloomed across Cody's face and even in the dying light of late evening it were clear something truthful and unguarded. *Kind.*

With exaggerated focus I brushed the flakes from my shoulders and upped my pace. Reminding myself kindness weren't kind. Not out here. And not directed at me. What did I even care, really? *Sad boys and their kind smiles—those types of stories never end well. Not for you.*

"Aren't the stars beautiful? Swirling up there in the ether, fighting against the blackness of night. Antares was his favorite, you know. Lira was always mine. Every night we'd climb the stairs of the astrology tower. And every night I'd fall asleep counting them, not that I'd done that in years. Not since . . ." Cody hasty cleared his throat, exhaling a thin mist into the darkness. He didn't continue.

Around us on the path, massive snow pines stood sentinel at our sides, their long branches swaying in the cold air, shaking the ice clinging to their needles.

"None of that matters now, does it?" His voice, like his shoulders, slumped.

I let the question go unanswered. Out here, that is just how it were. Cause we were *all* alone. All of us. And no amount of tears were going to fix it. Out here, sadness were weakness and weakness got you killed. Only emotion got you anywhere were anger. At least it kept you warm.

In growing stillness we trudged on, the snow turning to ice as we left the shadow of the winter pines and the last of the solid ground behind us. My throat sudden tight as the front of my house came into view. Tiny crystallized teeth, icicles clung from the porch. Snow smothered the shuttered windows.

Oblivious, Cody walked past me, eyes wide as the blackness between the stars he were waxing so poetic about.

He cleared his throat. "This it?"

I didn't answer, frozen. No new footprints. I shook myself. What were I expectin? For this to all be a nightmare? For Bren to run out? For none of this to be real. I wavered ever so slightly on my feet, my hand catching on the cold wood of the fence.

With a snap, I forced myself forward. And ran right into Cody's back.

"Don't just stand there," I growled as he righted himself, dusting snow from his pants where he'd fallen. "We go in that way." I pulled rough at his sleeve, forcing him to stumble or keep up.

"Tell me this isn't your house."

"Maybe it ain't what you're used to, but if you're done gaping like a fresh-caught carp, I'd thank ya to keep those delicate legs moving," I snarled. "I don't need no judgment from anyone. Let alone some spoiled stargazing nobody from the South."

Cody looked at me, hurt flashing across his face.

"Come on." I motioned for him to follow and marched away without him. Cause even though it weren't much, this house was ours. Me and Bren and our parents. And it were everything I had left of them. No one got to make fun of it. No one.

The door to the body shed was cold under my gloved hand. I yanked hard, snapping the crystal film of ice over the metal. The door groaned open.

A waft of stale air curled out of the shed, mixed with the sharp tinge of sulfur. I stepped inside. Everything was a mess. I tiptoed over a large uncoiled length of blue-and-silver rope and kicked aside a small pickax. Cody followed in my wake.

I strode over to the bodies. He let out a small gasp. I smiled a little unkind as I turned a particularly rough-looking one onto its back.

"Bears gotta eat too."

"Who—who are they?" he said, the warmth of his body at my side a flash of summer against the cold. I shuffled a few steps away, stiffening.

"Fools. Fortune hunters. People like you."

"Like me?"

I gave him a long sideways glance, sniffing against the cold leaking down the back of my throat, and gripped the shoulder of the last body. "Yeah," I said. "Men just . . . like . . . you." I turned over the last of the frozen figures.

Only it weren't who it was supposed to be.

CHAPTER 10

Bodies Burning Bright

No."

I let Cody's single word hang. Not cause he were wrong. But cause he was right. The body. It wasn't the same. It weren't his uncle's.

I ran my eyes over all the others, counting, feverishly hoping there'd be one I'd missed. As if it might stand out, a blazing light against the frozen ground. But I hadn't lost one, and I hadn't miscounted. Walter Colburn were gone. Just gone. Vanished right and proper.

"What are you playing at, Jorie? Where's my uncle?"

"Stars, I don't know. This ain't the body I drug inside. I—I ain't never seen this man before. Never."

Instead of blue eyes flecked with green, these ones was a deep russet brown, their covering not the milky white of a frozen death, but clear as glass. I took a deep swallow. This man ain't died out on the ice. The man might've been new, but the coat . . . it were the same.

I suppressed a deep-down shiver. There were somethin real wrong here. Someone had put Walter Colburn's coat on this body. A fresh body.

Cody took a step closer, bending down to my side. He gave a sharp intake of breath and shot back, rocking on his heels. I narrowed my gaze.

"You know him?" I asked, suspicion rising.

"I—I can't be sure." Cody shook his head.

"Ain't sure or ain't looked." I crossed my arms.

Cody's face hardened. "This is not my uncle."

Obviously. I opened my mouth to say it, but Cody's expression was all kinds of wrong.

"That means my uncle could still be alive, right?"

I snorted. He ignored me.

"Alive and lost. Alone somewhere out there on the ice . . ." Cody's last words were near silent; he reached out and ran a hand along the collar of the dead man's coat. Walter Colburn's coat, I corrected myself. Though I suppose it didn't matter who wore it now.

"Your uncle is dead, Cody."

Across the body from me Cody's eyes flashed with a painful sort of light. Frantic. Edged. The kind of look made me feel I were missing some link, some piece.

I surveyed the shed, looking for anything out of place, but the way the Rover had left it made it near impossible to tell. I looked at the body and then Cody, tilting my head. "You sure you don't know him?"

"I might have seen him, once."

I advanced on him. "Might have?"

"It was dark. I was not supposed to be there."

"Where?" I asked, taking a step closer.

"With my uncle, I think. Only that was weeks ago. Before . . ."

"Before what?"

"Before he said he'd finally found someone to help. Before the Rover. Before he disappeared." Cody's expression were ashen. A look that were quick replaced by something distant. Slack. As if it were the first time he realized where he really was. In a stranger's shed. Full of dead bodies. For the first time he looked as afraid as he should have been. And he wanted out. He took a step back toward the door.

"You stop right there, Cody Colburn. You ain't leaving till I get what I brought you for. Cause whoever this man is"—I gestured to the body—"it don't change the fact that your uncle's good and dead. And it certain don't do you no good to think otherwise." I looked at the stack of bodies. "I may be many things, but I ain't no liar."

"But that is *not* my uncle." Cody stared straight past me, eyes focused on the stranger. He crossed his arms. And if I weren't mistaken none, jutted out his lower lip. At me.

"That might not be his body, but where do you think that coat came from? My closet?"

Cody shook his head, but slower this time, throat bobbing. I narrowed my expression. Closing the space between us, I slunk in behind him, blocking his exit.

Cody cleared his throat. Face careful neutral. "Where is my uncle?"

I tossed up my hands. "How the stars would I know? Ain't like I'm used to bodies just getting up and walking out of the shed."

Cody turned, only half facing me. Lips pressed thin. "Let's just say for the sake of argument I choose to believe you. That you've told me everything you know and that my uncle was here. Then what the stars is all this about?" Cody gestured at the dead man. The coat. The lack of his uncle. "Your idea of some joke?"

"My what . . . ?" I followed his gesture and started. A lick of something white stuck out from the side of the man's coat. I'd not seen that before. Moving swift round Cody, I bent down and pushed aside the torn flap of the coat.

And hissed in a breath. I jerked back. Stars above.

Nailed through the man's chest right between his sternum and his heart was a note, bloodred wax seal unbroken. Fingers unsteady, I pulled out the piece of parchment from atop the man's chest. The paper brushing rough against his cold flesh. A hunk of metal slid out from the coat, hitting the ground.

"That . . . that is my uncle's watch." We both blinked down at it. Silent.

But the watch, it weren't what disturbed me. Frowning, I rolled the thick paper in my hands. Dev had been right. Whoever this man was—associated with Walter Colburn or no—whoever Cody were, they were as mixed up in this as could be. And the Rover were done tolerating it.

I cleared my throat and broke open the wax seal. Inside, a single demand hovered lonesome in a backdrop of white.

Bring it to Nocna Mora.

My body went stiff and I flipped the paper over, looking for more. But nothing. As I read the words again my heart gave a sideways jolt, buckling my knees.

Nocna Mora.

Bile filled my throat, hot and painful. Cause if any place was worse than Shadow Springs, that were it.

A once-prosperous mining town near to seventy leagues west. In the very heart of the Northern Territory. A place long ago swallowed by the winter-strangled mountains from which it had once been dug.

It weren't a good place. And then there were the rumors. Told by the outlaws and Rovers that used it, ones that made even your bones go cold. Stories of hungry beasts of snow and ice, their teeth lingering in the expanse, just waiting. And of men too long gone mad with the cold to take care. My heart plummeted. Nocna Mora weren't a place a sane woman went. I looked at the note. Someone had left it. And there it was. Right there. Resting in plain sight.

The Rover had come back. And I—all the air rushed out of me as the realization hit—I had missed him. To run after some nothing in town. I let the paper flutter from my hands.

I spun on Cody, cinching up the distance between us in one strike. Grabbing his arms, I began to shake him. Cody's eyes went wide, his face drained of color. He ripped one arm free, putting a hand up as if to block a blow.

"No more bullshit, Cody Colburn. No more stallin. You tell me what that Rover wanted with your uncle. You tell me now, or you ain't gonna live long enough to freeze when I toss you out onto the Flats."

Slithering out of his coat and my grip, Cody skidded to the ground, leaving my white knuckles gripping nothing but his stupid, useless silver jacket.

I tossed the thing aside and reached for him. Cody dodged. Stumbling to his feet and near tripping on the mess of ropes and debris the Rover had tossed around at the base of the shelves. He put up both hands in front of him.

Panting, I stared, wantin to scream, cause his eyes, his face. It were like watching the tide drain a barren shore. He knew. He knew all along. The rotten, low-bellied . . .

"It is all true then. My uncle's really gone. Dead. Murdered." Cody leaned his head back onto the wall behind him, eyes downcast. "It's all do with that cursed letter.. That's when it started"

"What letter?" I asked sharp.

"An inquiry about an arcane book of sagas, one called *Aurum et Glacies*—the other *Urbs de Aurum*."

"Aurum?" I frowned. "Don't that have something to do with gold?"

"Indeed." Cody gave me a tolerant smile. "Those are the texts my uncle had dedicated his life to, worlds and words he knew like the back of his hand." Cody let out a long breath. He ran fingers through his hair. "And from them he made a map. That's what the trade was for. My uncle might not have been used to the cold, but he wasn't reckless enough to think we could make it out there alone. We needed help, and the man wanted the map."

I raised brow. "Why would a Rover care two licks about some man's moldering old map about the South?"

"Because it isn't about the South, it's about this." Cody gestured. "All of this."

"What this? Ain't nothing up here but the dead and snow," I snapped out reflexive.

"And exactly why is that? It's because of what lives here." His eyes shot to mine. "What waits in the lost city of Vydra."

"Vydra." And it's fabled treasure. Was that what this was all about? My sister was missing because two soft-skinned academics from the South wanted to play heroes? My lips curled. "Vydra don't exist, except in children's stories and snow-fever dreams. Nocna Mora isn't some great hiding place built atop a lost city of gold. Those mines collapsed and ran dry generations ago. Nothing left out there but desperate men telling desperate tales."

A flicker of an old memory, of Ma and me and Bren gathered round a fire warm and happy, Bren drawing and Ma spinning stories from her own childhood. Before Ma had gotten so sick and—I shoved it back. Didn't do to dwell on what I couldn't change. No matter how hard I dreamed it otherwise.

And besides, I'd stopped putting stock in those tales long ago. I weren't about start now. Certain not for some untried boy from the South and his delusional dead uncle.

"What of all those stories? They cannot all be false, surely? Even in the tallest tale there is something of the truth. Some piece of history waiting to be uncovered. To be learned."

"There's nothing out here to fill your dreams but nightmares, Cody Colburn. And the screams of dying men to tell you about theirs."

"Surely all those people cannot be liars."

"Why not? If you don't think a man will lie when it serves him, you're more a fool than you look." I scoffed.

"But what then of all the recorded accounts? Generations of them, passed down from parent to child. And the chronicles in the Library—"

"I can tell a tale about killing a rabbit, but that don't mean I ate supper."

Cody were undeterred. "The creatures then, even you've seen one of those." I opened my mouth to protest, but he held up his hand. "That picture I drew. Massive wolves too large to be real, more snow and ice than tooth and fur. Or the winter maiden who lures men to an icy death, and if caught scatters to nothing but snow. There are more, too. Recounted and complied in book after book. Each of them a warning of what lies waiting in the Flats. Guarding the golden city of Vydra and the Ice-Witch." His went eyes bright.

"Only real monsters I know about out here, Cody Colburn, are men."

He waved me off.

I scowled. It were like tryin to reason with a snow bank. "Belief is all well and good for some people, but no matter how hard you pray out here, ain't no god gonna save you from the blood freezing in your veins when you fall through the ice. Fill your belly when you run out of food." And no gods to bring your parents back to you, no matter how hard you'd been taught to believe.

"But the map *is* real. My uncle had the pieces, but he needed a guide. Someone who knew the Flats, who could help him find it. Our first attempts had all been dead ends. People would listen, agree, and then simply take the money and never show their faces again. He was getting desperate, I think, to get out there."

I snorted. "Seems about right."

Cody grimaced. "So this time he didn't just offer money to the next man who said he had been that far north. I think—I think he showed him the map, or the part of it he had with him. The man agreed to help. Only, I could tell something was off. The more they met to plan, the more nervous and secretive my uncle became. Said the man would only meet him if he was alone. So I followed him, just the once. And I didn't see the man, but I saw that . . ." Cody trailed off. He cleared his throat. "And that is why we are here. To get to Vydra. You asked what the Rover wanted from my uncle. It was that map. Only if the Rover doesn't have it, and neither you nor I have it . . . ,"

"Then where is it?" My heart fell.

"My uncle had it with him the night he disappeared. I guess it could be out there, somewhere in the ice." His voice trembled.

He looked earnest. I wished he didn't.

"I would give it to you if I had it, I swear. I know what it is to lose the people you love. What's some piece of paper compared to that?" he said, looking at me and then the dead bodies. Then quick away. "Family is always worth fighting for. Always." He near to whispered it.

A stillness filled the room that had nothing to do with the cold.

The lure of treasure, or at least the lure of swindling a pair of rich Southerners and leaving them to die out on the Flats? That did sound mighty like a Rover. Cody began to pick through the things on the shelves—his uncle's things. Only trouble is the Rover, he didn't get what he wanted. And now he thought I did. And he had taken Bren for it.

"So, Nocna Mora," Cody said. I started.

"What about it? It's real enough, but it ain't like *you* need to worry about going out there with me. Unless you've plans to turn outlaw I don't know about, which would be as like to get you killed as anything else. Rovers ain't exactly the asking kind."

"You believe that and you're still going?" he asked, surprise written clear across his face. "Even knowing you don't have what he wants?"

"Belief don't got nothing to do with it. And I don't see as I got no other choice. Unless you happen to have the map right handy?" I asked. Cody crunched his brows. "No. I don't suppose you do." Hand slipping into his pocket, Cody pulled out his uncle's broken watch, fingers tracing the swirls on the surface.

"You're not the only one he hurt, you know, Jorie." His eyes took on a hard glow, something feral in the deep greenness of them. That look were something I recognized. Something I weren't sure was going to be helpful.

Cody took a deep breath, pocketing the watch, and stared up at me. Determined. Whoever I had first met at the bar—that boy was gone. "That man killed my uncle as sure as I breathe. And I'm not going to sit idly by. Because even up in this lawless wild of a town, this isn't right. No one murders a man and gets off free."

"A pretty sentiment, Cody Colburn. But out here, that's about all it likely is. Only justice you're like to see here is what you can take with your own two hands." As much as I wished otherwise, justice didn't tend to stop too long in Shadow Springs. Turning my back on him, I walked toward the house.

"Well, that settles it then. I'm afraid I don't see any other choice. There is nothing else for it." Cody cracked his knuckles. As if something had snapped inside him. It were a sentiment I knew all too well.

"Ain't nothing else for what?" I asked, dread filling my gut.

Cody fixed his gaze on mine.

"I'm coming with you."

"Stars you are." I blurted the words out and they just hung there, as frozen as a beaver's ass at midnight.

Cody's lips got thinner, knuckles whiter.

He followed me into the next room. Ignoring him, I stalked over to the pantry, taking stock. I gave Cody a stare to freeze a bear's balls and started pulling things down. Come first light, I'd be gone.

It weren't much, our stores. A few handfuls of berries, some pots of a waxy rendered fat, salted deer and not near enough cured herring. It weren't enough. But it was all I had. My heart gave an uncomfortable beat against my ribs. There was a big chance I wouldn't ever see any of this again. No matter what I took.

You can't think like that, Jorie. You are gonna find Bren and bring her home. You have to. Cradling the meager supplies in my arms, I glanced over my shoulder. Cody sat silent, his face unreadable, his body naught more than a silhouette in the growing darkness of the kitchen. Not my problem. *He was not my problem.*

Shutting the door with my heel—and a touch more force than were strict necessary—I plopped all of my pitiful stores down into a pile on the table.

At my side, Cody cleared his throat. I ignored him, concentrating on the edge of the frost-covered windowpanes. It'd be hours yet till I could leave. Hours for Bren to get farther and farther away.

Least I knew one thing about my plan were good enough. Dev's dogs—that team could run through anything and back. I only hoped Dev would forgive me for stealing 'em. After all, Fen had been Pa's once.

"Jorie, please listen to me. . . ."

I blinked up. Cody was standing next me, too close.

"I *can* help you find her." Cody lifted his arm toward me.

"And how would that be? You, your uncle, and whatever you've got mixed up in is the reason my sister is gone. The reason I don't know if she is dead or alive. How could you possibly help now?"

"Jorie, I—"

"No, you listen. If you think for even one second that I'm gonna to let you come with me, you're dead wrong. You couldn't last three leagues out there. Not three."

Cody looked down, his head low, lips pinched into a tight frown. I didn't like that look. I was being rough, I knew. But I'd no room for sympathy. He'd just get me killed. Get himself killed.

"Have you ever even been out on the Flats? Do you know even the first thing about surviving out here?"

Cody shook his head.

"No." I scoffed. "That's what I thought. An ignorant man is worse than useless. He's dead. And anyone fool enough to be with him is too. And I for one ain't gonna die out there cause of you. And let's get some things straight between us right now." I held up a hand, counting. "I don't care one lick about who killed your uncle, I don't care about some stupid fairy tale, and I most certain don't care about whatever it is your kind of stupid thinks is worth dying out there for. The only thing out there I care about is Bren."

I stormed off, more angry than I'd a right to be. But the Rover weren't here to scream at. Cody were. And if he hated me, then he'd leave me alone. A pang of something close to guilt yanked at my stomach. He had lost someone too.

Down the hall, the door to my room had been near to ripped from its hinges. The doorknob an unwanted metal eye pulled from its socket. I stepped inside and took a breath.

It still smelled of her. As if she'd just gone out to get firewood.

From under my collar, I pulled out what Bren had dropped in the snow. The ice-stone rested in my palm, the warmth of my hand creating a milky fog across the sparkling surface. Swirls of white crossin the stone's face, almost as if it were breathing. The stone unnatural cold in my hand. There were only one thing I wanted. I wanted to find Bren. I wanted it more than anything in the world. I shuddered back a breath. And for the first time in my life I knew it. A wanting so deep, a girl could die from it.

Dipping my head, I slipped the necklace on. Cold burned at my chest where the silver-set stone nestled under my coat. A hesitant tapping came from the doorway. I ignored it, and making my way to the back of the room, stepped over moth-eaten pallets and opened the wardrobe.

Deep breath Jorie, you can do this.

The pack lay at the back. I pulled it out. Burlap and sealskin, the thing had clearly seen better days. But it was what I got. I set the kit bag, which had been Ma's, on top of my pallet. The leather cords dry but not brittle. I ran them through my hands. The smell of rosemary and cedar and everything else that were the soft smell of her floated up to me.

Grunting, I pushed aside my pallet, revealing the wood flooring underneath. Running my fingertips over the split between the boards until they came to a rest on a slight imperfection. The panel came up slow, bits cracking along the edges where years of hungry wood beetles had eaten to their little guts content.

Underneath sat a small box. I pulled it out, carefully setting it down next to me, and reached back in. Groping, dropping to my chest, I dug around the hardpack earth until my fingers brushed an edge of cold, smooth metal. Pa's hunting rifle.

I pulled it out. Along with rounds of ammunition and a short but wicked hunting blade. I set them all next to the rifle. Sitting cross-legged, I ran my fingers over the delicate silver scrollwork decorating the carved oak top of the box. Inhaling the earthy smell of it, I opened the lid. Three leather bags nestled inside.

A white, a yellow, and a black. Each one tied sure and tight against light and air. For good reason. I, for one, enjoyed my flesh very much still attached to my bones.

I tossed the white one, the lightest of the three, in my palm. Quicklime. Ground from the bleached bones of long-dead sea creatures. If you found yourself caught out in the storm, it were worth its weight in gold. Maybe more.

The black one contained iron ore, which when mixed with the sulfur from the orbs made fire. And explosions. The last one—the yellow—was by far the smallest of the three. It were the one that contained some sulfur and all the wealth I owned in the world. No more than a beggar's savings, I didn't bother to turn out the coins or pitifully thin flakes of gold. It weren't near enough to bribe a Rover. But nothing I ever owned would ever be. I tucked them all into the kit bag, making sure to wrap it in extra furs. All I had. Weren't anything close to enough. Only it had to be. *I* had to be. I plunked down and pulled the furs over my face, burying myself in their warmth.

Out in the hall Cody's knocking had finally stopped. I glanced at the bare closed door. A wide gray shadow leaked in under the gaping frame. Well, if he were going to play the waiting game, he were welcome to wait out there long as he wanted. Sniffing, I curled up onto my side and tucked my knees in tight to my stomach. And when I opened my eyes the only thing there was Bren's empty bed. I reached my arm out to where she should have been. My hand hanging in the cold air, useless and alone.

"Hold on, Bren. I'm coming. Just hold on." I whispered it. Soft as the brush of a fox's fur against the night.

CHAPTER 11

Trails the Night

W hen I woke, the outside world were just sipping in the very first hints of light, a dull buzzing green and blue against the horizon. Not that I had done much sleeping.

Nightmares had riddled my dreams. Dark and mute and falling. Chasing and being chased. Twisting my hair back into a tight bun at the base of my skull, my neck sticky with the last flush of my dream, I stood. Breathing for a long moment, thinking—and trying not to think—before shaking off the night and gathering all my kit.

When I opened my door, the hall outside was empty. I looked both ways and gave a little grunt. Least Cody knew where he weren't wanted. I hitched my bag higher on my shoulder and gripped the gun. Well past time to get the stars out of Shadow Springs.

The trip into town took no time at all, my only companions the echoes of hungry birds and the gentle trickle of falling snow from overloaded pine boughs.

When I got to the inn there were naught to see. Dev's place were shut up tight. Not a man or light in sight. Still, I set a long board across the back door, just in case. I leaned the gun against the porch railing. The runs before the dog kennels were empty. Not a footprint dusted the snow. I walked over to the feed bucket.

Cracking open the lid, I grabbed what I could only assume was a back leg of a winter hare in one hand and its half-rotted spine in the other. I unlatched the dogs' run.

First thing came out into the cold were a nose. Then two, then three. Pretty soon, half a dozen furry muzzles were sticking out of the den, sending a clean white mist into the air. I smiled. I had run dogs since before I could remember. Pa had taught me.

"Come on out, Fen, breakfast." I tossed the hare's leg into the snow.

The alpha stuck her head out. Fenrir was beautiful. All sleek black-and-white fur and fierce as anything out on the Flats.

Sharp yellow-and-blue eyes fixed on mine, ears alert, she gave a little tilt to her head before coming all the way out. Every step filled with deliberate purpose. The kind of walk that had meaning. It were all control. Fen padded right over to the leg, gave it a single dismissive sniff. I tossed the spine. It skidded to a stop at her feet. This time she didn't even look down. Typical. My lip gave a twitch of a smile as Fen padded over to my side. Behind her, wet noses jostled disembodied in the darkness of the kennel. The sweet, heady smell of warm canine bodies drifting out on wafts of curling air. As did a low whine or two.

Fen's perfect head came up to the middle of my thigh. I stayed quiet, letting her smell. Which she did with intense focus, stalking around me, showing me my place. She would take as much time as she wanted, and I would sit and stay. I smiled wide enough to feel the cold burn against my teeth.

"We haven't got all day, you know."

Fen ignored my protest, busy smelling my left shoe. Finally she gave a loud snort and sat back on her haunches. Expectant. She tilted her head up at me.

"Alright, alright already. I should have known." From my pocket I pulled out a small strip of dried caribou meat I'd been saving for my breakfast. Fen caught it, a perfect snatch out the cold air.

Tail wagging, she swallowed the offering whole. Reaching down, I ruffled her ears. Eyes dancing, Fen gave a short, sharp yip, and in no time flat the entire kennel was plunging out toward me. A jumblin mess of wagging tails and furry bodies, they spooled out, tongues licking, faces bright. They were ready.

Fen gave another bark, and the gang settled itself down. A little. Boz, the other lead dog, sat himself down next to his mate, while the other four busied themselves with the offerings.

By the time I had all six of them harnessed, the lead lines gathered, and the sled loaded, I was springing with more anticipation than them.

We made it near two leagues out of town before we found his body.

CHAPTER 12

Shadows

———◆———

Cody's face was freezing cold.

Fool. Idiot. I didn't have enough words for this kind of stupid. In fact, as he gave a weak, raking cough, I considered that the whole world hadn't enough words to string together for how stupid he was.

What he'd been thinking didn't right matter. I didn't have the extra hours of sunlight to run him back to town. And he didn't have the time, or the abilities, to walk back. I squished an uneasy feeling in my gut.

I rocked back on my heels. In front of me, Cody's trembling arms fell palms down from his chest. He gave me a weak smile and pulled himself up to full sitting from where I had set him against the pine tree at his back. Behind us, a black-jawed vole scuttled off into his icy crevice. The sky overhead was clear as ice.

"Stars, Southerner," I cursed. "What in the world possessed you? The Flats? Alone? Or ain't it avenging your uncle you're after anymore, but just flat-out dying?" I cocked an eyebrow. "Cause if that's what you want, I can certain set you back out where I found you."

Cody blinked up at me, giving a half-hearted smile, lines of ice cracking across his lips like splinters of white against the blue of his cheeks. If he were trying for charming, he certain missed the mark.

I tugged at my coat. Cody gave a sad little cough, pulling his coat around his face.

I slid a hand into my pocket and pulled out a small metal flask. For a heartbeat I stared down at him. But only one. Twisting off the cap, I handed it over. Leaving him here would be leaving him here to die.

Cody turned his face to mine. I'd only what I'd taken from Dev. But right now, Cody needed it more than me. I let out a long sigh, shaking the liquid.

"Go on, take it. It'll help." He blinked up at me. "Promise."

He eyed the drink for a long moment before reaching out. He took a deep pull. Followed right quick by a sputtering retch. But the drink had done its job. A flutter of red were already creeping into his face. The tension drained out of him.

"Th-thanks. I think," Cody stuttered out the words, handing back the flask.

I studied him for a long time. At the end of the reins the dogs turned restless. Eager to go. The pack's barking shook around us, splintering the ice in the branches above.

I turned to leave. Cody, unready, stumbled to his feet, slipping in the snow. Cursing, I passed an arm under his and with effort drug him to rest against one of the trees. Panting, he closed his eyes and leaned his shoulder into the rough bark. I looked at the sun and scowled. He wouldn't make it back. Not like this.

From the top of his coat pocket the shine of something caught my attention. I reached down and plucked it out. He didn't open his eyes. It was a picture, all bent up, the corners soft and fraying from wear. My gut sank. Cause there were no mistaking who it was.

In it a small boy with tousled red hair and green eyes stood proudly, a spyglass clutched in his hands. Only he weren't alone. Three adults stood delighted at his side, one of them I already knew. This was his family. All of them now dead. A bead of heat pulsed raw up my throat and I glanced back at the face of the freezing boy at my side.

"I found him last night, you know," he said.

I went dead still, the picture cold in my grip. "Who?"

A twist to his lips. "My uncle. I went looking for him after I left your house."

Relief flooded into me. Of course that were who he'd meant. Relief that were quick replaced by guilt. I knew the look well enough. It weren't a kindness, learning the truth for yourself. Learning that last shred of hope you held deep inside were gone. Out here hope were easier to lose than hate. I scanned the road ahead.

"They didn't even try to hide him," Cody said. "Just dumped him. His body twisted out on the ice, like he didn't mean anything. Like his life didn't mean anything. Who does that?" Tears, bright and freezing, edged at his eyes. He coughed again.

"Rovers. That's who," I said. He were lucky dumping him were all they'd done. It were a message, plain and simple. Not that I needed any more of those. The unknown dead man he'd left us and the note were plain enough. A message that the Rover could take whatever he wanted, from whoever he wanted, whenever he wanted. And he'd do it again and again. Nothing were sacred, not even death. Not till he got what he were after. What I didn't have.

"I'll bury him. I swear it." Cody's face turned to mine. Hurt and fear and anger plain across the hard angle of his jaw. Real and raw and cold. For a moment I were uncertain who he meant. The Rover or his uncle. It would honest do for both.

"At least he's covered now, even if it is only shallow snow," he said.

The picture fluttered in my hand. I stared down into the face of the boy, frowning. Decided, I held out the picture. Cody hesitant slipped it back into his coat, eyes downcast. I eyed him up and down, yanking my gloves on tight. That were the problem with people. Everyone were something to someone.

"Well, come on then. Enough socializing," I said rough. "Get your snowy rear over here before I change my mind and really do leave you out here to freeze. I ain't gonna wait round all day."

Cody's eyes flew open. "Really?"

"Really."

His smile split wide, green eyes earnest. Something got uncomfortable tight in my chest. Grumbling, I looped a steadying arm under Cody's. Together we managed to stagger him to his feet and toward the dogs. With a mighty groan, he half fell, half sat onto the bucket of the sled.

"You won't regret it," he said, puffing slightly with the cold.

I gave him a flicker of a sad smile. Those were the usual words people said—right before you did. Taking this untested Southerner with me were probably the single dumbest idea I'd *ever* had. But I was doing it. Stars help me, I was doing it. Ahead of us, the dogs pulled on their harnesses.

Cody rolled slowly onto his side. I began rummaging around in the bags.

"What are you looking for?" he asked, shifting to see. "Can I help?"

Not really. A light fluttering of snow floated down from the pine boughs as the wind shook them. I wiped a few stray flakes from my eyes and leaned over where Cody rested.

He froze, shoulders tense.

I near to rolled my eyes. "You always this jumpy?"

Cody gave me an embarrassed smile. He ran a hand over the breast pocket of his coat. "Only since I met you."

Now I did roll my eyes. *Southerners.* Yanking aside the bearskins, from under my kit bag I pulled out a single black orb. Warm and smooth in my gloved hands. Despite myself I gave a little sigh.

"Hold out your hands."

"Why?"

I slipped the orb into his upturned palm. Surprise washed over his face, settling into satisfaction. Content, he leaned back, nestling into the basket of the sled. "Cause the stars know why, but apparently I ain't gonna let you freeze to death."

"Ready to get out there whenever you are, Jorie," he sighed.

"Is that right?" I grumbled. For someone near to dead not half an hour past, he certain were pleased with himself.

"Yes," Cody replied, oblivious to my tone, eyes fixed out on the Flats.

I pulled my scarf up over my face, the warmth of my breath a sweet echo under the wool against my lips.

Ahead, the dogs were clear ready, impatient whines, tiny puffs of misty protest swirling up and out of their throats. You couldn't let them rest too long out here or believe it or not, they'd get too cold to run.

"Hey, watch it!" I said, just catchin most of the kit from getting pushed out over the sled. A beaching whale is what he put me in mind of. A helpless, beaching baby whale. "Those packs might be soft, but they're most of the rations and all of our heat, so don't go knocking 'em off."

"Sorry," Cody said.

With maybe a little more force than were strict necessary, I pulled out one of the bearskins and tucked Cody in tight.

"That feels wonderful." He gave a little a moan, his face naught but a set of bright green eyes above the warmth of the furs. Something in my belly went uncomfortable warm. Out in front Fen gave a yip, the rusted bell on her harness jingling.

"Alright. Alright already, enough crowing. We're leaving," I called, pinching the long leather leads in my hand. Securing my hood down tight across my brow, I stepped up onto the slim footboards. Time to go.

With only a slight clumsy, out-of-practice flick of my wrist, the dogs lunged into action, the world around a whirl of cold.

It weren't long before the stooped, shrouded figures of cold-stunted tree boughs caked heavy in snow and ice became first thin, then near altogether gone. Another few hours and it weren't nothing but a vast plain stretching out far and fast as your eye could see. A horizon of white. Blindingly cold. The Ice Flats burned with it.

I took care to stop and water the dogs, making sure they were all well enough. Cody too. Successfully avoiding his attempts at conversation. Each time, I checked the dogs over real careful. Even the smallest of injuries could break out catastrophic when you least expected.

Out here, cautious were smart. And smart weren't dead. I glanced at where Cody, having gotten back in after our last stop of the day, nestled in tight into the furs. A twinge of unease nipped at my spine. I flicked at the reins and pushed the dogs on.

Hours passed. Every once in a while I'd squint up at the position of the sun and count 'em. Marking the hours as they whipped past in sweeps of bitter air as we ran. One turned to three, and then five, and then like nothing at all. I ran the team on.

Here and there slender fingers of land wound their way out under the ice, the last vestige of some long-slumbered volcano. Staying close to these were both a blessing and a curse. Land meant the world were less like to sink unexpectedly under your feet, to swallow you whole. But land also kept hold of what little warmth there were out here. And more warmth meant more melts. Great frozen rivers of shifting glaciers surged next to these tendrils of land, their waters only crusted with ice.

A delicate balance. I gave a shiver and in the dimming light took care to skirt the largest of these underground crystal rivers as I drove us farther and farther out into the cracking heart of the Flats. The world one great, ever-expanding plane of white.

But it weren't all so flat. Along the western edge of the horizon sheer walls surged from the broken, icy waters like sets of rocky teeth. Vertical faces that served as perilous nesting sites for garrulous kittiwakes and crested puffins. Gray rocks teeming with dark wings as birds darted in and out of climbing mists.

Then there were the Stone Forests. Massive clusters of what had once been evergreens, but that now resembled a true forest about as much as the carcass resembled the deer. Trees stretched for miles gunshot straight out toward the western shore.

Rumor had it that nothing lived inside those forests, nothing grew or moved. That even the storms were afraid to enter. Blizzards died to nothing but a whisper as they hit the petrified trees. But every year desperate trappers would tell you another story.

Tales of trees that rippled with sunlight in the night, branches humming with the echo of lost voices, leaves rattling soundless against the sky. Nothing but nonsense stories born of ice-fevered minds and lips too drunk to know truth from lies. And knowing the difference between myth and reality? Between story and fact?

Out here, that's what kept you alive.

As the day lurched on, we did indeed pass by the rim of one such grove, no more than a league or two off.

"Can we get closer?" Cody craned his neck, eyes wide.

"Not a chance."

"But I've read about them. The Great Northern Petrified Forests." He leaned over the edge of the rail to get a better look. "They are supposed to be full of all sorts of interesting animals. Ice foxes. Blistered bark beetles that have adapted to eating stone rather than fiber."

"Petrified? You mean like scared? Well, one of us certain should be."

He had spun a bright smile on me at that. A flicker of heat snapped at my throat. I frowned. Didn't know what were so funny.

"But don't you think they would be *interesting*? My uncle, he has this theory about how the trees up here turned to stone. Patches of them, anyways. The ones that didn't freeze straight away when this land became an everlasting winter. He hypothesized that it has to do with the adaptations of the xylem. A special kind fluid to prevent the ice from bursting the trees. He reasoned it wouldn't be in the sap itself per se, but a very particular substance that developed from . . ."

Something massive, ivory body glittering bright as cut glass, darted between the black boughs of the trees.

"Did you see that?" Cody said, awed. "Is that what I think it is? They *are* real! Can we—" But whatever it were we could do was lost as he leaned out over the rail.

The sled pitched violent to the right. His weight tossing at just

88

the same moment as the rails snagged on a ridge of snow. I'd not even the time to curse as the rails lifted dangerous off the ice and we were thrown to the side. Ahead, the dogs were yanked sudden into the air, startled cries tearing from their throats as limbs caught in the lines.

I slammed into the ice. The world went bright and then dark. Ringing filled my ears. I don't know how long I lay there, but then hands were yanking me to sitting. A wave of dizziness washed over me. I put my hand to my mouth. The world were a jumble of white. I swayed a little and tried to rise.

A hand fell on my shoulder. "I don't think you should try and stand."

I blinked. A face came into focus. "Cody Colburn."

Cody frowned worried down at me. "Yes. We crashed and you've hit your head pretty hard I think."

The dogs were barking. The dogs. I jolted to my feet. Nausea swept through me. I swallowed it down. Shoving at Cody, I staggered to the dogs. Limbs and lines were tangled everywhere.

"Please." I knelt down at the first harness. Boz licked at my face. With shaking hands, I stripped off my gloves and undid the ropes. I ran hands over every furry inch. But Boz were fine. He weren't even limpin. I looked up. All the dogs lay quiet, tongues lolling, eyes watching me, as if to sayin *hurry up, there's snow to run*. Dazed, I freed each one by one. They were all fine. I near to laughed with relief.

Cody were pacing by the sled. He'd already gathered up all the supplies, stacking them neat against the overturned sled.

"Come on then," I said. "Help me tilt it back up."

Righted, I steadied myself against it, near to panting from the effort. My head ached something fierce, like there were a spike burning just behind my right temple. But the dogs were fine. Cody were fine. The sled weren't damaged. It could have been worse. We could've been dead.

"I'm sorry, Jorie." He fussed about my side, putting back all the furs. "I didn't know the sled would do that. That we would pitch over like that."

"Which is exactly why I didn't want to bring you in the first place." I walked round, putting my gloves back on. "And if you ever do that again, you ain't never getting back on my sled. You hear me?"

"Yes. Sorry, won't happen again." Cody, his green eyes wide, gave me a dip of his head.

"Just get in before my head stops ringing and I smarten up enough to change my mind."

"No problem." And quick as shot got himself settled back in the bucket.

I glowered. My head hurt something fierce, my vision still blurred at the edges. Nausea whirled in my gut. Waning as I placed a hand on my temple. A concussion—mild, bad enough to be worrisome, but not the worst I'd ever had. I'd be right in a few hours. Still, I groaned, head throbbing. I knew he would be trouble.

Cody, furs tucked up tight under his chin, offered me a smile.

One I didn't return as I placed slight, shaky legs onto the sled. Even if them stories weren't real, this was a not place a girl wanted to get hurt. And fool Southerner didn't know enough common sense to make sure we stayed safe.

Leagues past the Stone Forests, patches of buildings began to appear. Flaking black bruises along the edges of the Flats, they were places that had once been working farms. Someone's home. Even as near back as when I were a little kid. I'd memories of this place. But then, like the towns and settlements farther out to the North, they had simply died. Some said they'd moved on. Others spoke of a hungry white curse that had leaked out from the most desolate reaches of the North. Places people had left nothing behind save the memory of their bones.

I'd always thought it were the remnants of folks too poor, too starved to run. Too fearful to leave, who'd just got caught in the ice and storms. Which happened more often than not. Weren't nothing uncanny about it. And certain no Ice-Witch to blame. Just bad luck.

It were near an hour past dusk, and my head finally ebbed to a low dull ache, when our destination came into focus and we could finally halt. A small outcropping of crumbling rocks and spindled trees making the narrow throat of the once prosperous town. I guided us deftly between them.

This were as far out as I'd ever gone. After this, there weren't nothing I knew. The shadow of a massive great horned owl passed noiselessly overhead. I drove us into the shelter of the fallen buildings, shaking off the sensation we were being watched. At the end of the widest lane, I spied a like enough refuge for the night.

I pulled us through heavy gates and past what must have been stock pastures. The barn ahead were not much, but unlike near all the other buildings I'd seen, it had a roof. Or least most of one.

As we pulled in, a rustling came from behind. And with it the sensation of rippling cold washed over my skin. I tightened my grip on the reins, hip nudging the rifle at my side. But when I scanned the corrals, weren't nothing there left to move. *Don't be ridiculous, Jorie. Who's the jumpy greenhorn now?*

Parking at the back of the dilapidated barn, I began unloading the sled.

Cody, restless in his sleep, gave a little moan, sending the few black sulfur orbs about him, like burned-out stars, clinking. I left the bearskin tucked in tight. He'd be right enough in the basket of the sled tonight. I'd no inclination to deal with him any more than exact necessary. And it were best to let him sleep.

To be honest, I were surprised he'd stayed up as long as he had. Cold did that to you, especially if you weren't used to it. Flats could take the energy out of even the hardest of people. I glanced at him and away. At the very least it'd give me some much-needed quiet.

I saw to the dogs first. Their rations—melted chunks of ice with globs of fat and strips of dried meat—were quick enough to heat before I staked out their chains. Each one a perfect three paces from the last.

Boz finished up the last licks of his dinner. I walked over to my kit by the sled. I'd a tent—a small canvas thing that were gonna be close quarters when we'd need it—but tonight I were just too exhausted to get it out. Taking some of the furs, I trudged over to what had once been some kind of animal stall.

I shuffled the hay with my foot. The rushes were a discomfiting black—which usually meant mold and rot had set in—but they smelled fresh enough, and more important, they were dry.

It'd suit me well enough. Especially when Fen curled up at my side. I ran a hand through her coat, feeling the downy undercoat of her fur. The necklace at my chest warm.

We'd just gotten snugged in when a low brush, like reeds over stones, bristled against the night. Fen sat bolt upright at my side, motionless. I rested a hand on her side.

A few heartbeats later and a cry echoed high and shrill from somewhere outside, springing up the hairs on the back of my neck. My every nerve were on fire as all of the dogs stood up. Perfect and still. All of them waitin.

I were all too aware that the gun were tucked tight against the sled, twenty paces too far away. Shivering, I snuggled in closer to Fen at my side.

The owl's cries didn't come again.

CHAPTER 13

A Memory of Ice

T here is something about the night. About that lonesome whisper of blackness.

Makes even your best memories into something wrong. Something that wakes you in the dark. Nightmares that don't leave, even when you open your eyes.

With a head pounding fierce enough to feel in my jawbones, I rubbed at my wind-burned eyes. My limbs and back and everything hurt. By the time I straggled out of my makeshift den, Fen were up and wandering.

Cody, on the other hand, were still sleeping in the sled. And had to be shook awake. He muttered something near to coherent before turning over. Too bad it were time to go. I were therefore entire within my right to yank the bearskin right off him. He began cursing as he rolled himself up from the ground, eyes blinking with unspent sleep. I distinct heard the words *intolerable* and *regrettable*. I smiled big. *Indeed he were.*

After a short meal, we loaded up the sled and I took my place on the rails. Cody back in the bucket.

All these frontier towns, they was laid out the same. Main roads ran east to west to best catch the sun and avoid the worst of the winds, so least I knew in which direction we were starting. Twelve leagues. That were what we had to cover today. We could do it if we were lucky—and fast.

Hours passed. Near to most of 'em in merciful silence. But more than I'd care to admit, I found myself caught staring out at the whiteness of it all—the nothingness—lulled into a hallow calm.

A sudden gust of wind tore at the corner of my collar, slipping down my neck. I swallowed, shivering as I tried and failed to not recall the stories of people who stayed out too here long. The ones that kept you up at night, worrying about the things that could crawl out from under your pallet and gnaw on you in the dark. Like the ones about the god lights. The white glowing eyes of men and women snared by the old magic of the North, by the last whispers of fallen gods. Souls hungry for their stolen lives that stalked you in the mists, following with songs that lured travelers to their deaths.

As we pushed on, my world were consumed by the unending vastness of the Flats. One horizon bled into the next. Till it was hard to tell what was real and what weren't. Whether we had even made any progress at all. As if . . . my head drooped and I started, near to dropping the reins.

"Bloody stars," I cursed, righting myself on the sled's rails. Had I fallen asleep?

I blinked, focusing on my hands. After another league or so I were doing it again. How close were we to nightfall? In the sky the sun were well past its zenith. Late enough. And as good as time as any to break for a rest. Ahead there were a dip in the landscape. It looked tall enough to give us at least a little break from the winds. I guided us toward it.

When the sled came to a halt, I took stock of the team. They all looked fresher than me. Good. I pulled out the bowls to melt an ice block.

From the basket of the sled, Cody lumbered out and stretched. I glanced at him from the corner of my eye, and quickly away when he caught me lookin. Ignoring him, I poured out the water for the pack. When they was done, I handed the bowl to Cody. He took it.

"This place." Cody cleared his throat, his voice raw from cold and disuse.

I grunted. Cody took a long drink before handing me back the water.

"My parents used to tell me these stories about it before they died. They were always some of my favorites."

"Humph." I grunted, looking round. "I don't know what they told you, but this sure as stars ain't most people's idea of favorite."

"They were mine. I believed in them." Cody looked over my shoulder. I followed his stare. But other than air so cold it burned shimmering on the horizon, there were nothing there. "Stories where the glow of the northern lights never dims and the wilderness is so vast a man could lose himself, shed his deepest fears in it. Of the wild at the top of the world. And"—he turned his attention back to me—"of the monsters that drink the wind. Creatures that hunted in the darkness between stars, and the heroes that rode them. And most of all of the Witch made of winter, in whose veins runs the very unchecked power of that wild North."

"Why? Why do you care so much? They aren't even your stories."

He gave me a lopsided grin. "Because a world like that one, Jorie? One with no Scholars to impress, or people to please—where being brave and good and kind are more important than status, connections, or wealth—it would be a paradise. My whole life, I've wished more than anything for a place where just one single worthy heart could stop the world from breaking. A place where someone who has been overlooked their whole life, where they mattered. A place I . . . I mattered."

I kept my eyes firmly fixed straight ahead.

Cody rubbed his hands together, shifting his feet. "But then I went to live with my uncle . . . he studied the histories, so I asked him about that wild, but all he would talk about was the research. The facts," he said low and bitter. "Only then he stumbled across something in his studies that made him pause. And then it was him asking me about them. And saying that wild world of myth is all really real. Vydra is real." Wonder raw tinged his voice. "Don't you think it's magnificent?"

Yes. No. I didn't know. I swallowed hard, fighting the urge to be away, anywhere but here, away from the too-close memories I didn't want to look at. From the coil of emotion dangerous close to sympathy spooling in my stomach.

"Jorie?"

I didn't reply. Cody turned to me, smile serious.

"What?" I grunted. A tremor as if I were about to step out onto a fresh edge of ice flashed through my spine.

Cody looked down at his hands. "Never mind."

The silence went on long enough that it started to get awkward. Something of that feeling twisted painful in my gut. I should say something. Anything. I cleared my throat.

"If it makes you feel better, Bren always said the same thing. That it was only me who weren't looking at it right—" I flushed. *Don't be a fool. Cody don't care about you or Bren, not really. He's only here for his uncle. You are the means to the end. No one is nice for nothing.*

But then Cody's eyes flashed to mine and he smiled. It were quick as the flash of silver beneath the sea. Beautiful bright and unexpected. A sudden thrum of heat twisted though my chest. "You might think it beautiful out here, but this wild? It ain't kind. It'll eat you alive if you let it."

For the barest of moments, his smile faltered. Only to redouble, blinding sharp. "Danger and beauty are not always so different, you know."

I looked away. Looked anywhere but his face. Feeling like that, it weren't for people like me. For girls that had to survive. A stone weren't hard because it wanted to be, but because it had to be. Else it'd be nothing but sand.

"Sentimental and dead ain't always so different neither."

Cody only beamed at me, brilliant and happy, as if I'd said some great joke.

"That ain't a compliment," I said. "A wolf might be beautiful, but if you think she won't tear out your throat when she's hungry, you've got more than a few bloody surprises coming your way."

His smile widened, crinkling the edges of his eyes. I tossed up a hand. He were impossible.

Cody turned his auroral gaze out to the molten glow of the setting sun. "But the greatest mystery of the North is, is *she* real?"

I frowned. "Is who real?"

"The Ice-Witch, of course."

"What? No." I stared, incredulous. That were certain an unexpected turn in conversation. And an even more ridiculous one than the last.

"Oh." He flicked his eyes to mine. "I just thought, since you've lived up here and you, well, you know"—he waved generally—"have survived well enough, what with you bringing in all those bodies, that maybe—"

"Well, you thought wrong," I snapped. "And I ain't all alone, I've got Bren."

Cody had enough decency to look chagrined.

Good. "So I'd thank you to do your own thinkin and leave me to mine." I had one job, one girl to save, and I wouldn't be distracted. It were better this way. It were.

"I'm sorry, that was rude." He placed a hand gentle on my arm. "But I would really like to know what you think. I've only read about this in books. But you, you've lived it." Cody's lips tipped up in a grin. A tiny echo of warmth rose inside me. Aching.

I jerked my arm away and rubbed the spot where his hand had rested. *Who was this boy?* "It ain't so great as all of that," I muttered.

"But you know them," he said.

"They are just stories."

"Aren't they just." Cody's face crunched down and he went silent. For a long time.

"What's that supposed to mean?" I asked. Rather than answer, he turned away to study the dogs.

"How far can they run in a day?"

I tilted my head at the question. His attention were bouncing all over the place. But I didn't argue. No more talk of Witches were well and good with me. "Depends. But if we don't hit too much trouble, twenty to thirty leagues in a day ain't bad."

"As far as that, huh?" Cody, more troubled than before I'd answered, wandered over and in silence helped pack the sled back up.

The trip turned too rough to keep conversation going, which suited me just fine. We made decent enough time, but the wind soon grew to a near constant headwind and stunted our route. By the time the sun set and it had become too risky to continue, we'd not made it to the next town.

Some luck held out, as I spotted a promising-looking outcropping of rocks. It weren't much, but with the ice becoming more and more unpredictable the farther out we went, I weren't about to run the team at night. In the dark there were no one to see you fall. Cody didn't protest as I'd pulled us up into the meager protection of the rocks and told him to get out.

Below us a harsh golden glow strummed across the ice. Sunset igniting the world at our feet, as if we stood upon a river of fire running through the glacier's veins. Maybe it were a little beautiful after all. Not that I were gonna tell him that.

Cody cupped his hands over his face, blowing out heat from his lungs. "How much longer till Nocna Mora, do you think?"

"Takes what it takes." I rubbed the light caking of sweat that had settled into my eyebrows.

Though the rocks displaced most of the wind, the temperature were dropping fast. Cody pulled the bearskin tighter around his shoulders. I busied myself feeding the dogs. After a moment Cody came up beside me and reached down.

"I wouldn't do that if I were you. Fen don't take kindly to outsiders. Specially when the pack's eating." But my warning came up—as usual with Cody—a bit too late.

Cody had already stuck his hand out, his palm about an inch above the sled dog's raised hackles. But to my surprise, that were all she did.

Instead of snapping or pinning her ears, Fen gave Cody a curious sniff and a sharp tilt of her head before trotting off to join the rest of her pack.

"Nice dog." Cody smiled, walking over to my side.

I shot him a quick look. Like me, *nice* weren't something Fen were usually called.

"Funny thing to name her though, wouldn't you say."

I grunted.

"Fen. Short for Fenrir? Monstrous wolf who ate a distant god," he said.

I snorted, hefting off some of the kit from the sled and setting it into the snow. "Not too far off then."

Cody must have mistaken my comment for interest in his opinion, and he went on. In bloody verse, no less.

"Unfettered will fare the Fenrir Wolf, and ravage the realm of men. . . ."

I hunched my shoulders. For a tagalong who were about dead only a day ago, he sure had the energy to talk. A lot. The tent were in here somewhere. I dug in deeper, shifting the sulfur globes. More than a few were colder than I'd like. Thin cracks of ice forming at the stoppered end. Not useless, but used. And if they split open? Stink something fierce.

"You know, this would be a lot easier if you maybe helped. Start with not moving everything around in here. Basket's as stirred up as a marmot's burrow." I sniffed the canvas shelter, thankful it only smelled of old shoes and dried earth. I tossed it out onto the ground, where it hit with a burst of flurries. Cody ambled over to my side, humming. I shot him a sideways glance.

"Here. Make yourself useful." I chucked Cody one of the hinged poles. He caught it smartly and began unfolding it.

Only a few misdirections—including Cody tryin to put the center pole up 'long the side so that it looked half skewered—and we had it put up right and proper. Unlike last night, where we'd the shelter of the barn, out here this were it. The small canvas covering flapped lonesome in the cold. One tent. For the two of us. My stomach gave a funny turn.

Must be all the salt-dried food and not enough water. Cold didn't make you realize how much water you was actually losing.

Piling the pelts high, I glanced over my shoulder. The dogs were naught but little rolls of fur, faces and tails tucked in tight against the night. Wind blew past, breathing life back into the snow about my ankles, sending tendrils of cold up my spine. I snugged my fur coat tighter about my waist.

Overhead, billows of gray-green clouds poured in. The promise of frost in their vaporous hearts.

Taking the few steps over to the rocky overhang, I snapped off a couple of the more promising-looking icicles. Their cold bare registered in my hands as they slipped into my pocket. When I got back to the tent, I paused. Cody stood just a few yards away, back to me, coat wrapped tight about his shoulders. I called out, he didn't turn round. The dip of his head the only sign he'd heard me. Otherwise he just stayed eyes fixed out over the white of the ice, unfurled in an unending tundra around us. I didn't blame him. It were . . . a lot. Shaking, I ducked in and set myself into the tent.

The small space more comforting than confining in the cold. Lighting one of the few stubby candles, I placed it careful inside the glass belly of the rusted lantern and started thawing what little would amount to our dinner. A flush of smoke filled the air.

After a short time, Cody joined me, taking up the front half of the shelter. I scuttled as far back as I could. Even though it did feel sudden like he were all too close, least his body heat scattered the dull ache of cold. Pretty soon I couldn't even see my breath.

Aware of every motion I made, I handed Cody half what should've been my dinner. Slipping off my inner gloves, I arranged the bearskins under me, nestling in tight, and began the sad process of making more dinner. One eye never leaving Cody. I took a deep breath, pushing a little farther away.

He were just too close. My heart beating too fast for my liking, I ran a hand over my neck, feeling the weight of the pendant that hung there. *Don't be ridiculous, Jorie*, I scolded myself. What does him being this close matter any road? With what waited for us out on the ice, best get used to him now. Cause this were certain gonna get more uncomfortable before the end.

Cody didn't need telling twice about his dinner. Eager as the dogs to eat. Though eating were a generous term for what he were doing. Despite myself, a little smile crept at the edge of my lips.

"Slow down, Southerner, you're gonna choke eating it like that," I said.

Cody held up the strip of meat, looking at it as if it were some strange object he ain't ever seen before. "Are you certain you didn't mix up the rations with the leather reins? Please tell me this is . . . not supposed to be edible?" he asked real hopeful.

I grunted out a grudging laugh. "You gotta warm it first." I opened my hands to show my piece. "*Then* chew it. Unless you don't want your teeth."

Clear annoyed—I would be too if I didn't know how to eat—Cody did what I showed him, and with some persistence, were finally able to rip off an edible section.

Leaning across the small space, I held out the cup of water I'd melted for us when I'd seen to the dogs. Cody took it, his bare fingers brushing mine. I snapped my hand back.

"What is that?" Cody asked. And for a long moment I were

confused. Cody pointed at me. "It's beautiful," he added. Which only made me more confused, and a heat rose in my chest. I looked down. *Oh. Right.*

Bren's pendant swung at my neck. The ice-stone caught the flickering flame in its many facets, looking near enough to a beating heart. I shoved it back under my shirt.

"Nothing," I said.

Cody frowned. He slipped one hand into his pocket. "It didn't look like nothing. It is just that it reminds me of something my uncle . . ."

"It ain't mine. And I said it were nothing, alright? So it's nothing." I swallowed hard.

Cody held up his hands in surrender. Only they weren't empty.

"You swiped that," I said, more curiosity than heat.

"Yeah, sorry. But it is—was my uncle's. Though I suppose now it is mine." He blinked down at the compass. And real gentle he ran his fingers over the silvered surface. It clicked open. "He always told me he won it in a game of cards." He gave a little laugh. "Said he wasn't sure which had been more extraordinary: that he had won the game at all, or that the old man had handed this over. Some spun-up tale about it having held a shard of a fallen star. It was from the North country certainly, but it was just broken silver. Whatever else the compass once held, it had long since been lost."

I held my breath, but there were a great big nothing inside. "Just impressed I didn't see you take it is all." *What had I been expecting? The map? You'd seen it were empty before, Jorie. Don't be a fool.*

Cody saw me staring and gave me a sideways smile. He closed the case. I could just see letters running around the outer rim.

"What does that say?" I asked.

"*Sanguinem veritas stellis.*" His words were thin. A dusting of gloom chilled through me.

Cody cleared his throat, eyes meeting mine. "It means, roughly, *In the blood of starlight, truth.* Or close enough to it."

"But that don't mean nothing real, does it?"

"My uncle always did have a flare for the dramatic. Didn't make him many friends. Though that doesn't much matter to him now." The shine of water brimming in his eyes. He wiped it away. "I guess I have nothing now too." He said it sad, and slid the compass back into his coat. "Useless."

I opened and then closed my mouth. Comfort weren't something came natural to me.

We ate the rest of our dinner in silence.

Not that there weren't a lot to say. I gave a hesitant glance at the boy across from me. Only that the quiet had always suited me fine.

And so too did the cold.

CHAPTER 14

Echoes in the Snow

F rom underneath the ice a flash of silver that caught my eye. That made me stop.

"What is it, Jorie?" In the basket of the sled, Cody whipped his head around, searching for the danger.

I stared down at my feet. "A trick of the light. That's all." I waved my hand. But it weren't all. Not by a long shot.

I kicked the covering of snow from the sheet of ice, smearing the flakes across the blue surface. Through the frozen water, an unblinking face stared back at me. A young woman. Golden waves of hair suspended still about a heart-shaped face.

A silver necklace floating up and off her thin neck, pressed against the underside of the frozen lake. I fought back a deep shiver.

Below me, the girl's mouth was slightly open, teeth parted as if in prayer. And she weren't alone down there. More forms hung suspended in fleshy shadows around her. Men, women, horses, caribou. I refused to count them. There were too many.

The image of another blond girl, this one's hair back in fishtail braids, flashed up. My sister's face, perfect and pale and more scared than anything I'd ever seen, disappearing below the surface of the cracking ice. I had run. Sliding to a stop at the gaping brim of the ice, my body gone cold as I pressed against it, my fingers reaching....

We was just seven and eight. I had walked that floe a hundred times, if not more. The ice should have been solid for another month at least. But it weren't. I'd trekked out not knowing, and behind me, bluebell braids whipping in the wind, had followed Bren.

If I hadn't found her fingers with mine . . . if I hadn't held on . . . if Pa hadn't heard me scream. I pressed my eyes shut. Only this time when I opened my eyes the girl's face that stared up at me through the ice weren't Bren's. None of the people down there were. Not that anyone could save them now.

I stood there numb, clutching to Bren's pendant. Heartbeat after heartbeat, I felt naught but the swell of my breathing and the cold stone in my palm.

"That poor girl," Cody said, kneeling on the ice. "How terrible."

"And Winter swallowed them whole."

"What was that?" Cody tilted his head toward me.

"I . . ." *I didn't mean to say it out loud.* "Nothing."

He pressed his lips but didn't push. For which I were glad enough. Overhead the clouds parted and a dark shadow passed below us under the ice. "Do you see that?" Cody's eyes widened.

I did. The edge of a submerged building visible just under the body of the girl. And then another. It were a whole town down there.

"What happened here?" Cody turned to me. As if I somehow knew all the answers.

A wry twist of my lips, I turned to him. I suppose I did know this one. "Yesterday you were askin 'bout all the stories, the tales of what happens out here on the Flats. Well"—my breath came out short—"now you've seen one."

The ice under our feet gave an ominous groan.

"Oh," he mouthed.

Oh were right. "It's called Silent Lake." I walked back to the sled. I didn't turn to see if Cody were following.

Cody plunked down in the sled. "What is the story? If you don't mind telling me."

I hitched the team up. Taking the reins, I cleared my throat and stood next to the sled, one foot on the rails. "The Silent Lake was supposed to be a warning."

"A warning? What kind of warning?" Cody's gaze turned back over his shoulder.

A smile played at my lips. "A pretty stars-forsaken good one, I'd say." The image of the girl's face flashed up before me and my smile faltered.

"I'd say," Cody said. "I can add it to the Compendium."

I frowned. "What's a *Compendium* . . . no, never mind, I don't reckon I want to know."

Cody grinned.

"Alright, fine, but it ain't a pleasant tale."

"The best ones hardly ever are."

I gave him the crooked look that comment deserved. "There were a girl once. Lived out on the edge of ice with her brother and father. A small village of trappers and traders. But she weren't treated well."

"Do they ever treat them well?"

I ignored the interruption. "Well, one day, as it's liable to do round here, food stores ran low. And they sent the girl out in search of game. But it were late. The sun near to setting. And she got lost in the woods. Like any sensible girl she didn't right *want* to starve, but the snows closed in. Near to dying she stumbled into the night. Alone. But she weren't alone, not really. There was a woman there too. A strange woman callin herself Winter. She took the girl to her moonlit cottage and fed her and warmed her. Reminded her of a sister she'd once had, Winter said, before she was forced to live in the forest. All night she told the girl tales, all the while the world outside burned with cold."

"And then what?"

"Then the girl, belly full and heart happy, woke warm in her own bed. A rich fur coat white as snow spread atop her. Her father and brother were angry, and demanded she show them the woman, who they called Witch so they could steal her furs, her foods, her home. Tried to peel out of her where she'd been, who she'd seen. But the girl kept the Witch's secret. The punishments got worse and no one in the village would help her. Well, Winter, she didn't right like that. She'd saved the girl after all, who were so like her long dead sister. And who were these men to hurt what the Witch had mended?"

"I've a feeling this is not going to go well for those men."

I laughed, parroting his words back at him. "It hardly ever does. She saved the girl, set her up rich and warm and well. She buried the rest of 'em. Not just the family, but the whole town. Everyone who'd ever wronged the girl. Drowned them in ice."

"That's not so very nice."

"It ain't. I said it weren't a good one. Dev would tell it when we were being troublesome, interfering with the hunting or the distilling or the like. *Be careful now or the Witch will freeze you too.*" I frowned at that. "We'd laughed at him and run off, Bren and me. . . . He said you'd see an arm here, a head there, bits and pieces of people reaching out for help that sure weren't coming. And the ice were so clear you could see every frozen breath, the remnants of their screams still rising from their lips." I gave a heavy shiver. "The entire village eaten alive by the hunger of the Flats and the anger of the Witch waiting for them."

"Thank you." Cody blinked at me. I blinked a little at myself. It were the most I'd ever said to him at once.

I nodded brisk. Not sure what to say. At the front of the line, hackles high, Fen gave a shake, steam rising from her dense coat. Teeth bared and ears alert. The team restless behind her. This weren't no place to linger. I took up the reins.

"It's time to go," I said.

Cody scrambled to pull the sled's furs over him. "Yes, right."

When we were all loaded, I snapped the team into motion, glancing over my shoulder only once. Cause even though I knew we were alone, I were unable to shake the uneasy feeling that maybe we weren't.

Troubled, I drove us into the Flats. Big rolling walls of green-white clouds soon began pooling over the horizon. Pillowed forms dulling out the low sun, giving the world a hushed kind of stillness as we drove. Muted, expectant. Charging the world with a near-palpable current. A friction in the air. As if even the Flats were waiting.

A storm were coming for us and it weren't gonna be small.

CHAPTER 15

What We Cannot See

———◆———

Our stop for the night were far worse than expected.

A small frontier outpost used mainly by summer trappers and their crews, Dev had told me about it. Had said it were a backwater at best. And for a man from Shadow Springs, that were saying something. Heart sinking, I scanned the terrain. Knowin more and more why it were called Dead River. Cause if it had been not much then, it were even less now. There were barely anything left at all. It were Cody who spotted it, jutting out from behind a barrier of ice. I pulled the team round.

I jumped off the sled, Cody quick to scramble out of the basket behind me. This were as protected as it were gonna get. The structure had no roof and only three standing walls. One of which were made entire from a series of rotten hides and supported by what looked suspicious like a set of bones. Elk. Or caribou maybe? Something big, any road.

I took hold of a massive antler, longer than half again the length of my arm, knife-sharp at the tips. At least twelve points, it were twice what were normal.

Real, real big. Not a comforting thought. Cause if the prey were this big, what did that make the animals that hunted it?

Ahead of me Cody, who had already and efficiently taken out

the kit, had wandered to the front of the team and begun to unharness Fen. Who were leaning her canine body into his attentions, her tongue lolling and head butting his side. The very best of friends. *Traitor*, I thought without heat. I strode over to help.

The tent felt, if possible, even smaller than it had before. Which were in part due to it being black as pitch outside, combined with the fact that the tent's walls rushed in and out with each howl of the storm. As if we were inside some giant bellows.

I scrambled in the bottom of the kit for a candle. If I didn't much like seeing Cody during the daylight, not seeing him in the dark were worse.

"How bad is it going to get out there?" Cody asked, worried.

Where were the candles? "Well, it ain't gonna get better anytime soon." I thought I'd put them in here. . . . maybe in the other pocket?

"Will the dogs be alright?" Cody asked.

The question gave me pause. "I sure as stars hope so." At least I'd managed to get them settled in tight; the cover I'd made from the animal hides were good. Well, good-ish. "Fen and the team have seen much worse, Cody, they'll be fine. It's us we've got to worry about. If we can't get the light going, we won't be eating. . . ." I began searching every pocket I could find. Finally, my fingers closed mercifully around the stub of a candle in a pocket of my coat.

It were the whale-fat candle from the dead man's stuff. Cody's uncle's stuff. But if Cody recognized it, he didn't say. I lit the candle and began melting some ice. We ate in silence.

"I don't . . . what is that?" Cody reached toward the lantern, where a piece of something stuck out of the melted wax along the candle's side.

"No idea," I said, surprised. Yanking on the edge of the foreign material, I took care not to let the wick go out. Despite the warmth, it were in there firm. I tugged harder. And in a sudden give, a piece of paper came out. We both stared at it. A tingling cold spread out across my skin. I flattened it.

"A drawing maybe? Can't quite make out of what." I turned the page round and round. Squinting in the low light. "I think it's a circle and there's a bit of writing. . . ."

"It isn't a drawing, Jorie," Cody said, breath hitching.

I looked up from the paper. And I knew. I bloody knew.

It was a map.

My heart rose and then crashed as that realization hit me. I had what the Rover wanted now. But it also meant I had it then. If I'd searched better, he would never have taken Bren.

I looked up from the map. Cody was staying perfect still across from me. Waiting. I took a deep breath. You can't change the past.

But I knew something else too.

If I couldn't change the past, I were certain going to change the future.

"Cody, tell me everything about this map you know. Everything about Vydra." If it meant any advantage on this Rover, I'd have it. I'd have it all.

Nodding grim, Cody began to talk.

CHAPTER 16

All Good Things

———— ◆ ————

I pushed hard all the next day. Too hard.

If I kept us on this pace, it'd be only three more days. Three more till Nocna Mora. And Brenna. And now that we had the map, at least a chance. Slim as it were.

I'd felt a dangerous flutter of hope inside me that morning, even if I didn't believe half of what Cody had been saying. Stories from Scholars at the University about the great Northern city lost in the ice. Of the treasure it held, locked away and forgotten. And of the Witch who kept it that way.

I didn't buy one word of it. Not that it mattered if I believed it or not. The Rover did. And his greed for it was what had brought him to Shadow Springs. Just like Walter Colburn. Different kinds of obsession, driving them to the same place. And bad ends.

Sitting on the ice were not the place I wanted to be. Not when there were still light in the sky. My hands shaking with more than frustration, I growled and began to stitch the pieces of my broken reins back together.

It were all my fault. I'd been careless, right stupid. Fallen asleep. Only I couldn't figure out why. Cause I knew better. I *know* better. And I certain weren't tired now. But I *had* let the reins slip.

Let the leather get caught under the cut of the rail. Get clear cut in half in four separate places, slicing the harnesses useless. Grumbling, I picked up the heavy S-shaped needle and leather thread.

I weren't no good at sewing even when sitting by the fire, Ma and Bren at my side, warm fingers and a full belly. Which meant I sure as stars weren't good now, out in the middle of the ice, angry and hungry.

"Damn it!" I dropped the needle and rein, red blooming at the tip of my finger. I cussed again, kicking at the lead rope. I pressed at my finger. Blood pooled.

"Here, let me see." Cody held out his hand to me. His arm hovered in the chill between us. "I can help."

I narrowed my eyes at Cody. Putting all my frustration into that look. At him. Though none of it were his fault. I put pressure on my finger. The cold made you worse than you were. Clumsy. Stupid. Bitter. Least that's what it made me.

Only Cody didn't recoil. Instead, calm as you could wish, bent down to my side. I shifted away. I didn't need his help. I didn't need anyone's help.

Cody leaned in close, face near enough to smell the bright perfume of his skin. And with a hesitant smile, he picked up the needle and thread.

"Is this all we need to fix?" Cody asked, running his attention down the length of the leather, ungloved fingers feeling the rough cracks and broken edges of the caribou hide. And the clean slices of my carelessness.

His hair caught in the breath of wind, running over the soft skin of his cheeks.

I tugged rough on the edge of my scarf, stuffing it tight into the neck of my coat, and rumbled something along the lines of agreement. His smile got wider. And my scowl got deeper.

"Great. I think that shouldn't be a problem." Cody took the sliced leads and sat down on the sled next to me. Our shoulders touching. His breathing light as the brush of a fish's tail in the reeds, exhaling in rhythm with mine.

The rail gave a little bow under our combined weight. I held my breath. Within a few minutes, he'd sewed it up right. Cody pulled hard on the rein. It held.

"Where in the world did you learn to do that?" I turned the rein over in my hands. It looked near as strong as new.

Cody smiled big, running a hand across his scarf. "Not so useless as I seem, huh?"

Despite myself, I let out a laugh. "Maybe, maybe not. Verdict ain't in on that yet."

A shadow of exasperation passed across Cody's too-green eyes and I smiled. I took the rein with me. It would work just fine. Whistling, all too pleased with himself for my liking, Cody settled into the basket. And we were off. Just cause he were handy once . . .

Before we were over the horizon, a weight like the press of a hand pushed between my shoulders. I glanced backward. But there were nothing there.

I pressed one hand to my side, to where the map rested. It was making me paranoid. That were all. But for all the white emptiness, the press turned into an itch I couldn't right shake.

By the time we'd settled down for the night. My mind found a million reasons to stay awake. To not dream, to think about the girl under the ice, her face, her hair. What kind of life she might've had. How much she had looked like Bren.

I lay awake in the darkness, my eyes fixed on the fluttering of our tent in the night. And tried and failed to ignore the wind outside, the great sweeps that lashed across the Flats, trapping the world in frost and muted starlight. The eerie calls of bodiless voices echoing across the snow, dark cries that pressed the cold of the world ever deeper into my bones. Cries that had me wishing fervent they weren't real. My imagination robbing me of what little warmth my shivering body made. It were the worst night out here yet.

Sunrise came and with it the chore of digging ourselves out of three feet of fresh snow. The dogs of course were in heaven.

The sky weren't completely clear, but the world under our feet soon became hard packed and the travel brisk. It took me near to midday to stop hearing the wild of the night ringing in my mind.

I studied the Flats. All around us the world vibrated with gold. The sun, low on the horizon, shimmered with it. With the illusion of warmth. Far to the west, you could just make out a thin line of black pushing through the air. Sea birds. I smelled the air.

Brisk as ever. Only now it came with a hint of salt and briny decay. I kicked at the snow. A sheet of worrisome thin ice glistened back. The glasslike surface disrupted only by hundreds of air bubbles that had been trapped just under as it had froze. The more recent the freeze, the more air got caught. Struggling from the sled, Cody came to stand at my side.

We'd need more than luck from here on out. Not that we didn't need it before. Cody handed me the water flask. I took a long pull and handed it back. "We're gonna need to be careful now. Cause this is where the Flats start to get real tricky," I said.

Cody gave a sputter. "As in, it has not been hard up until now?" He wiped the spilled water from his chin.

"Not like this." I pointed out over the face of the ice. "Just look."

Cody's eyes followed my hand. "I don't—"

So impatient. "Just wait for it, Colburn."

Cody raised an eyebrow, knocking the snow from the treads of his boots. "I don't see what . . ." His voice trailed off as no more than fifty yards to the west a massive jet of water shot skyward. "What the . . . ?"

"The ice round here? Not so solid as it seems."

"Is it a geyser?" he asked, wide-eyed.

I shook my head. "Looks like it, but it ain't. That's the breathing of pods of animals caught in the ice when the rivers they use to go between hunting grounds froze ahead of 'em. And behind them," I said. "Happens every year. Trapped with no food and no escape for months at time, just waiting for the sun to melt them out."

"Melt them out? That's terrible." He looked around, disbelieving.

It certain were. "The rivers here all run to the sea, and salt water don't freeze like normal. So between the motion of warm bodies and the seawater"—I waved a hand—"you get . . . holes."

"That's . . ." Cody looked out over the maze of ice with a new understanding. "Very interesting."

"I hope it ain't *too* interesting, is all," I added, getting back to the sled's rails. "I enjoy being above the ice, not below it."

We pushed on, moving careful over the maze. Until there weren't no easy paths left. I pulled up the sled.

I squinted against the glare of the sun. Ahead of us weren't just thin ice anymore, but huge black lines. Cracks in the ice wider than I were tall. I turned to look back the way we had come. If we had to retrace our path, it would mean another day. Another day out on the Flats, another day to Bren.

I tied the reins, staked the sled to the ice, and stalked forward.

"Gotta be a way through." But I knew there weren't. It were

already too broken up, large cakes of ice—brash growlers smaller than floes—there weren't no safe way past.

"What about there?" Cody lifted his arm.

I shook my head. "See there." I pointed to where a long, thin collar of ice had risen from the ground, piles of frosted snow like flowers coating the surface. "That ice field still ain't right. Looks solid enough, but that ridge were formed by one sheet of ice mounting the other. Step on it and it'll flip."

As if to prove my words, the top sheet gave a massive crack, splintering the silence, and slid into the waiting waters below.

Cody swallowed. "Right. So that is a no."

I gave him a flick of smile.

To the east and west were massive fields of brine blooms. Outcroppings of sea salt leaking through the cracks in the ice and freezing. Beautiful crystal warnings that meant the start of the broken belt, an area of breaching sea ice miles wide. A place deadlier than the kiss of the rifle at my side.

North were also no good. Row after daggered row of stories-high shards of ice impaled the landscape. And if you somehow made it through, there were a massive swath of an impassable glacier, waiting.

"Stars help us, the only way is south." Back the way we'd come. In my haste I'd missed the right path. Cursing myself for a fool, I turned us round.

Six hours. It took me six hours to find it. The place where we had started. A whole day gone. But weren't nothing I could do about it but keep on. You always kept on. My teeth were clattering something wicked by the time I got the tent staked out, and I near fell to my knees with the ache in my bones. Rough didn't begin to cover it. Tonight, even the dogs were tired.

"Grab an orb or two from the sled, will ya," I asked Cody, pretty sure my nose were as blue as my fingers. And my stomach as empty as the Flats.

Cody pulled us both out a black orb.

"Near empty," I noted.

"Mine too," Cody said.

I rolled the orb in my palm. It were too light to last much longer. But it was warm enough. I breathed deep as the buzz of feeling crawled cross my skin.

Sighing, I pushed open the tent with my shoulder and ducked inside. Cold breeze at my back told me Cody were right behind.

I spun slow, sitting down on top of a pile of furs and put the orb between my knees. My lap grew . . . lukewarm. Time, I think, for a little something more than dried caribou meat for dinner. From my kit bag, I took out two of the hide-wrapped bags.

"Cody, would you quit fussing and just sit down already. You are worse than Bren." I winced a little at my words.

"Right. Sorry." Cody stopped fretting and took up an awkward half-sitting position. Real delicate like, but without complaint, he rubbed at the blue tips of his fingers.

Grunting I tossed him my orb. He caught it without fumbling and gave me a grateful smile.

Undoing the ties on the dwindling rations, I frowned. The hunting weren't good up here. Most anything either too big or too small to be worth the effort. It weren't like I could just dive down and eat what the whales and seals were eating. But maybe I'd be able to find something, maybe find part of a bear's discarded kill. Cause even at this rate we'd make it there, but it were the getting back that were gonna be the issue. And then we'd have three mouths. . . . I rubbed my hands together.

I suppose we could chance across a winter hare tucked up in its den, but this far north it weren't likely. And counting on chance usually meant the only thing you'd be soon counting were your last breaths.

"Jorie, I was wondering . . . well, you know. You've never really said. I mean—what I mean is . . ." Cody paused.

"Hmm?" I weren't payin him much mind, but Cody swallowed hard. No caribou left. I counted the dried strips of fish.

"Well, about your sister."

My attention snapped up quick. "What about her?"

"Well, you've never really talked about her and about what happened to you both the night she was taken. I know it can be hard . . . and I was simply wondering if you needed to, you know. I mean, if you needed someone to talk to about it, I'm here," he finished lamely.

"Why would you think I needed to talk about it? Cause I don't." My entire body gone stiff. "Bad things happen to good people all the time."

Shifting a little where he sat, Cody stared down at his hands. His lashes batting softly in the low light. "It's only that I can hear you at night." A tick began at the corner of his right eye. "I hear you crying in your sleep. And it's not—not something to be ashamed of—I did it too for a long time. After—after my parents died." His voice cracked.

"I just wanted to let you know that you aren't alone. That I know what it is—to lose everything. See your world ripped away from you in a heartbeat." He raised his eyes to mine. "I know what it is to stay up late at night wondering what you could have done differently, only to wake up to a world you don't want or know. To have it all come crashing down around you. I want you to know that I'll do everything I can to help."

The silence stretched. And stretched. Numbness, sallow and familiar, bubbled up inside me.

"I'm sorry if I said the wrong—"

I bit back the sudden hot flash of salt running down my throat. This weren't Cody's fault. It were mine. And noble as he were trying to be, I didn't think that were the conversation I needed to be having right now.

"You ain't got nothing to apologize for," I said quiet. "Not to me, any road."

Cody flushed, running a hand through his hair, causing it to fall across his eyes. He brushed it aside. My heart ached in a way I ain't felt before. But I couldn't let it. I had to stay hard, not let the what-if failure overwhelm me. For Bren.

"Sorry ain't gonna bring my sister back. Or your uncle."

"I know. I just wanted to say I'm here. If you needed me." He finished high and awkward.

"Cody Colburn, I don't know much, but I know we can't any of us change the what-ifs. But we can stay alive. Right now I'm hungry, so you just quit thinking about that and get to helping me with dinner."

Cody gave me a real wide grin.

"And quit smiling. It's distracting."

Cody's smile only got bigger. Dipping my head to hide the rising heat in my cheeks—I handed Cody a long strip of white sinew and fat. Little bits of black dotted the old meat. A side effect of the curing process. It weren't nothing to worry about, but it did look downright awful. Not that it tasted any better.

He held the food out in front of him, looking it up and down. "Not that I am complaining, Jorie, but what precisely was this?"

"Haddock."

"Not to doubt you, but this does look . . . rather unappetizing." Cody tried and failed to flick off one of the black spots.

"As is your personality, so we're both making sacrifices in this tent. You'll take what I give you and hush your mouth about it." There were no heat in my words, and he beamed.

Frowning at this sudden familiarity, I pulled out two small steel mugs, one slightly bigger than the other, and shoved them in the space between us.

Careful, I untied the white bag I had taken from under my pallet back home, and taking a handful of snow out of my pocket, I plopped it down into the larger of the two mugs. I stuffed the smoked fish down into the smaller one. Three cubes of salted fat followed. From the white pouch I took a pinch of the quicklime. Too much was as likely to burn a hole in the metal as warm what were in it.

The reaction were as immediate as it were intense. Steam rose and the scent of melting fat and fish meat filled the tent. My stomach growled. It smelled near miraculous. I stirred the contents of the cup, reaching out and plopping a strip of meat on top of the mix to soften in the steam. When the food were done heated, I looked up. Cody were right there, his fingers dancing in his furs. His lips pressed tight against the same pit of hunger that were nestled snug in my gut.

"Here." I passed him the cup. He took it, expression right ravenous. "Just don't eat it. Yet."

"Uh, okay." His mouth forming a perfect little O as he curled his fingers around the warm metal cup, his eyes soft. Amazing how it were the smallest things that mattered. Warmth. Water. Food. You only realized their comfort when they was gone. What made you feel human.

I unstoppered the half-dying black orb and with care poured the boiling quicklime water into it. The low hiss of mixing chemicals filled the tent. The hint of yellow-smelling sulfur from the orbs filtered about.

I got up and collected a few cupfuls of snow. It melted fast. I poured the excess, cup by cup, into our flasks. We would need it later.

"Right, hand it back. Please," I teased, sitting down and reaching out my fingers toward him. Wiggling 'em, worms on a line.

Cody passed the cup back to me. I mixed the two equal portions into both. Cody stretched out and took his share. Making the soup were a little bit of a luxury. But between the low rations of the last days and the failure of today, I reckoned we needed it. A whole day. Just gone. Like it didn't matter.

The hot liquid slipped in and slid down my throat, warming me to my toes. I let out a little moan as the soft warmth of the soup bubbled in my gut. Across the tent from me, Cody's cheeks turned a summer-rose red.

"Jorie, what do you think about if we—" Cody began. My heart gave a sharp tug in my throat, but I were saved from hearing what he were about to say as a deafening bellow rocked the canvas of the tent around us. We both froze.

The cry were followed right quick by sharp, short snorts. Rusty breaths and heavy, crunching footfalls. The promise of a quick death at the mercy of hungry jaws. I listened stiff, neck twisted.

Across from me, Cody bare breathed. The only motion were the rapid beat of his heart pulsing in the crook of his neck. A pace near to match mine.

Then from one beat to the next everything turned impossible slow. One moment I were eyeing Cody, wondering if we were about to be eaten by a snow bear or worse, and the next—the whole world broke loose.

CHAPTER 17

Breathing Like Dying

The world turned to chaos. The dogs barking, going wild. Snarling.

Gasping, I rolled to my side. Pressure twisted at my legs. I kicked out, scrambling to sit, my heart beating fast, breaths burning in my chest. But it were only the tent, the thick canvas snaked like seaweed about my limbs. I slid free along the ice. The scene that greeted me were madness.

A milk-white musk ox swayed his massive head, heavy half curls of steam pouring from his flaring nostrils, curling around eyes black as pitch. Fen, her coat covered in snow and blood, had her jaws sunk deep into a foreleg. Boz and Addy were circling wide around the dueling pair, teeth snapping fierce.

Fen darted in and out, weaving between the beast's massive legs. Biting, tearing.

The other dogs were caught, straining desperate against their harnesses. Feet whipping the earth, heat and snow erupting into the space around them. At my side, Cody too scrambled to his feet, the soles of his shoes slipping in the slush that was our belongings, furs and kit scattered everywhere in the snow.

"Cody, the team!" I screamed it, only certain it came out when Cody stumbled toward the dogs. My gun. I needed my gun.

Trouble being, I couldn't find it. Anywhere.

More snarls ripped the air as Cody freed the team. But it were too late. Fen weren't fast enough. With one wide thrust of his head, a wicked yellow horn caught her along her side. So hooked, the ox tossed a snarling Fen clear up and over his back. Slashes of gleaming copper red filled the air, cascading down on the beast. Behind it, Fen landed rough, a limp pile in the snow.

I started toward her, but the musk ox were now between us. He turned his massive head to me, eyes fixed upon mine. Red discolored the whites of his eyes. The animal must be crazed. With a roar the ox reared skyward. Shards of ice scattering from his coat. Front legs clawed at the air. He roared again and again. I clasped my hands over my ears.

With a violence the ox landed, dangerous shaking the ice underneath him, his stare locked on me. The beast took a step. Then Boz and Addy and all the rest were there. Pulling. Biting. Saving.

Cody staggered to my side, near falling over, rubbing wicked at his eyes.

"What is wrong with you—" I clipped my words short. His eyes burned with red. The skin swelling, blistering. Something had got in them. Something like—my gut sank—sulfur from broken orbs.

I reached down and with a bare hand grabbed a handful of snow. Quickly I scrubbed it into his eyes. Handful after handful. Until my fingers dripped with melting snow. Cody hissed, but finally the redness began to fade. Relief passed over his face. His eyes were far from clear. But they were better.

I cupped his face in my hands, turning it back and forth. "Can you see me?"

"Yes." Cody swallowed the word, but at least he could see. I helped him to his feet. He rested some of his weight on me.

"You okay?" I asked, setting him to standing on his own. Handing another fistful of snow over.

"I think so," Cody said. The swelling near to already gone. That were one thing down.

The dogs and the unnaturally snow-white ox were a tangle of limbs and teeth I couldn't right tell apart. Or tell who were winning. But Fen mercifully had managed to pull herself sitting, and at her side Boz stood teeth bared, tail lashing, while the pack kept harrying the attacker. Good dog, Boz. Fen had Boz. I needed my gun.

I darted over to the remains of what were once our tent, skidding to my knees and tossing through the ruin of our possessions. *Come on, come on.* I pulled torn and useless furs, empty and ripped bags, clumps of snow, and—and nothing.

"Where the stars is it?"

"Jorie—I think we should move. Like now." Cody's voice was close, and it held more than a note of concern. "It's getting closer."

"Not yet, we need—this." I grasped the cold metal of the barrel. I raised the gun and aimed . . . only nothing happened. Not a thing. "Stars below!" I fumbled frantically at the bolt, but between my shaking and the frozen metal, it weren't gonna move. Not one inch. The bolt was jammed.

"Jorie!" Cody jerked on my shoulder. I brushed him off and hit the butt of the gun on the ice. Something inside gave an odd metallic clunk.

"No, please no." Still focused on the gun, my body was jerked backward to the right. Cody's fingers slipped across my left arm as he were chucked back hard onto the ice and I were pulled free of his hands. I glanced up. Too late.

The musk ox had caught the corner of my coat with one massive blood-tipped horn, and in seconds I was airborne. The rip of splitting fabric filled my ears. The thick steam of animal breathing filled my eyes. My bones shook with the bellows erupting from the ox's red throat. I looked down. Except for the beast and me, the entire world simply ceased to be. Muted out.

Below me was the back of the ox. Unmarred muscle covered his spine, thick bones braced with tendons, body rippling under his snow-white coat. The sway of his head, thrusting his huge body in arches and turns. Me dangling like ragweed from his horns. And buried deep against his neck, a twisted vine of black-tipped green barbs, like tiny inverted teeth, dug deep into the thick hide. Little specks of dried blood clinging to all the long white hairs. A collar. Only who in the world would want this beast for a pet? And if it were someone's, did that mean . . . ? But then my body was tearing weightless through the air. Untethered.

I hit hard. The icy ground hurt fierce as my body slammed into it, ribs and elbows landing first. The wind chucked itself painfully out of my chest, ripping away my screams. And then I weren't alone. The ox were above me, eye to eye. A long drip of drool curled down through the space between us, salty and cold.

Blood welled up along his leg where the dogs had gotten teeth in, frozen slashes of red across his white coat, leaking heat.

Up this close, the smell of the wild were overwhelming strong. Reek stole what little air there were. I tried desperate to raise an arm, to block. But it fell by my side, useless, numb from cold and pain.

Lowering his face, the ox let out a rumble. I swear it sounded like laughter. Black eyes rolled back in their sockets as horns turned straight at my belly. Turned for a killing blow. The end. This were it. Cody were screaming. The dogs howling. But it didn't mean much.

After everything, I failed her.

I'm sorry, Bren. I'm so so sorry.

I braced tight for the final, impaling shock.

CHAPTER 18

No Good Deed

———————

But instead of the squelch of my guts spilling into the snow, it were a gunshot that roared out. Loud and true.

I opened my eyes. Tiny flakes of snow rained down onto my exposed face. Lingering green moss, dirt, and blood caked the ox's fur. His heavy body looming above me. Suffocating warm.

Another shot rang out. The ox roared and staggered to his side. Snuffing hard. He began shaking his head, swaying violent like. Angry. And hurt.

Pressing their advantage, the dogs darted in. Between the ivory of dogs' teeth and the gunshot to his side, he didn't know which way to turn.

Addy snaked in, biting at the ox's hamstring, fangs sinking into flesh, the crunch of teeth across bone. The ox thundered with rage, kicking out wildly, shaking his horns. Fighting even as he stumbled on the injured limb. Staggering, the beast pawed at his face, forcing me to roll or be trampled.

A gunshot tore through the freezing air. I looked up. Red poured down the ox's side, fresh drops scattering into the snow. A crimson bloom on the ice.

Gritting my teeth against the spreading pain in my side, I drug myself to my knees and stared. Ox were stumbling away, three of the dogs worrying his every limping step. And there were Cody. My useless, untrained Southerner. Only here weren't useless no more. Head high, he stood tall. Right and strong, legs wide, my gun pressed to his shoulder.

The beast's snow-white form disappeared into the horizon. I near collapsed with relief. Cause if for nothing else, he had earned every piece of fat, drop of water, and useless hours of talk he had cost me.

I struggled over to the camp. Or what were left of it. Which weren't much.

My ribs gave a mighty cry of protest. I sucked in a hard breath against the pain.

"Jorie, here! Are you alright?" Cody skidded to my side, tossing the rifle down into the snow. I shivered. He offered his arm, placing his own furs over me. His eyes looked clear, his skin no worse than a bad sunburn.

"I don't need ... you're hurt." It weren't a question. A slow pooling of deep red curled at his wrist. Another wound wept out from just under his torn shirt. Cody looked at his wrist and frowned, pressing his sleeve over it to stop the flow of blood.

"It's nothing."

"Don't look like nothing."

He winced. "Looks can be deceiving. I fell is all. Landed awkward when that ox tossed you." He looked up at me, fear plain as day. "The real question is are you certain that you are alright? That was wild, Jorie," he said holdin out his other hand. "I thought I had lost you."

I gave him more of a grimace than the smile I tried for.

"That were some nice shooting, you know." I owed him my life. Hurt as my head and ribs were, I would be fine. "Where in the world did you learn to fire a gun like that?"

Cody pressed his lips tight. "You are looking the colligate skeet shooting champion, three years running. Best shot in the University. My mother always said I needed a useful hobby. I suppose I just proved her right." He paused, leaning over to pick up one of the bearskins and the gun from the snow.

I let out a rough laugh, the motion sendin pain across my cracked ribs. Done gasping, I rubbed at my side. "Well, Cody Colburn, you tell me if you have any other hidden talents. And next time promise to tell me *before* we near get killed by a rabid animal."

"Promise." He crossed his heart and laughed. When he were done wiping his eyes, he looked right up at me. My breath caught. "But Jorie, if I had missed that shot. I don't know if—"

The spike of a pitiful yelp cut him off.

Stars, Fen. "Fen!" I ran to where the dogs circled her, every breath a hitch of pain in my side. Be alright, Fen. I pushed between Addy and Boz, expecting the worst. I would never forgive myself, never. But I shouldn't have worried. Fen rushed over to me.

"Let me see, let me see." Fen, skeptical, submitted to my ministrations. Quick survey told me it weren't fatal, but it weren't good. And that I'd have to see to it later. I threw an arm around her; she licked up at my face. I nuzzled into her fur. I'd need to check them all over. I turned to find not Boz but Cody standing there. Staring at me. As surprised as if he'd just caught me doing something he ain't ever seen.

"What?" I asked.

"Nothing." Cody's smile faded, his eyes a quick mask of flashed hurt.

I turned away. *Good.* If you don't let people in, if you don't care bout 'em, then they can't hurt you. I'd clear forgotten it. But I remembered it now.

"Let's go." The map. I slid my hand into my pocket. Empty. I searched the snow. Frantic. On my hands and knees, I threw piece after piece of our kit to the side.

"It can't be gone. It can't be." But search as I did, the only bit I found were a small piece ground near to pulp in the slush. I coughed hard. A spike of pain, searing up my side.

Cody knelt helping me search. But it were useless. Everything hurt.

"Jorie, it's gone."

Slumping onto the ice, hands in my lap, I clutched at the small, useless piece of what had once been the paper that meant my sister's life. One breath. Two. Three. My spine hardened. My muscles went cold. Because we—Bren and me—we didn't give up. I raised my eyes, looking right at Cody.

"Save what ya can. We move out as soon as we're able."

"Jorie—"

"We leave as soon as we can." Cause no matter what happened, you picked yourself up and you went on. You had to. Pity? Save that for the foolish and the dead.

Troubled, Cody agreed. Together in silence we picked up what little were left.

A long whip of freezing wind ripped past, sending snow and scraps twisting into the air. Setting my teeth to clattering. We may have survived the ox, but if we didn't get out of here soon and find some shelter, it wouldn't much matter. We'd be dead from exposure before sunrise.

"Where did that thing even come from?" Cody asked, tone careful neutral as he picked his way over what had been a blanket, but which were now no more than thin strips of the once plush pelt.

I near wanted to laugh, but even the shake of bitter mirth had my ribs aching. I ran a hand across my brow, pushing away stray hairs. "Wouldn't be the first time an animal had done that out here. Not by a long shot," I said, fingers shaking. I stilled them on the warmth of the pendant.

Cody glanced over the horizon where the ox had fled. "Right."

Didn't sound like he meant it. Behind him, the pack were trotting toward us.

Fen was up, the bleeding mostly stopped, and she weren't limping too bad. The rest were tired but no more worse for wear. Not that the dogs had anything left to pull. Our sled, like near all the rest, were crushed.

Right. First things first, I need something to clean and wrap the gash on Fen's leg and the slashes to the side of her chest. She was lucky. The wounds, while wide and looked something awful, weren't too deep and nothing were broke. I knelt at her side, torn cloth in hand, and pushed around at the wounds. Fen never let out more than a little whine.

Across from us, Cody were sifting through the remains of our gear. Leaving Fen with a pat, I walked to Cody's side. I kicked over one of the furs. Maybe, if some of this blood would rub out, it'd be okay. I picked it up and wrinkled my nose. Maybe not.

Some of our stuff were still useful. All of the dogs' rations for one, and maybe less than half of ours. Least the dogs could eat. A black ball caught my eye.

I brushed the snow from it. And then another. Three of the orbs had made it unbroken. I handed them to Cody, who tucked 'em under his furs.

When all were said and done, there were enough left of the sled to cobble a littler one together. A narrow sling I fashioned from the shattered sled's rails and the remains of our tent. Not a ride for either of us, but it could take Fen while she healed; no way were we leaving any one of us behind.

As Cody finished clattering the boards together, I turned to our own transportation.

No sled meant a slow journey. It also meant we needed something for our feet. It took me no short time, but by bending the now-useless metal of the side rails, I curled them into snowshoes for the both of us. Not great, but we wouldn't sink. Least not too deep.

Stars it were cold. My teeth rattlin in my skull.

Get it together. Ain't no one here to save you but yourself.

Tightening the reins with shaking arms, I lumbered to my feet— hissing my breath in against the stiff pain of my aching muscles— and tested the shoes by jumping. Hard. Sunk into my ankles. At this point I were sure even my shadow hurt.

I didn't much like the idea of traveling by night, but there weren't much choice. No tent to speak of, no nearby shelter, not even a bald rock face. I stared out at the blackness of the horizon. It just weren't fair. It weren't.

Only instead of letting that desperation drown me, I let it burn. Stoked it till it warmed my tired muscles. Till I near to glowed with the heat of it. Cause we were going to get out of here. We were going to make it. Grinding my teeth, I straightened my spine. And we sure as stars were going to save my sister.

Cody stumbled to my side, his eyes bleak, his entire body radiating exhaustion. Quiet, we stood shoulder to shoulder, arms touching ever so light. The silence of the landscape swelled around us. Shifted and moved as overhead the first flicker of the great northern lights, green and gold, marveled into life.

With only the icy breath of the Flats at our backs and the light of the heavens above, I walked us into the great expanse of ice looming before us.

CHAPTER 19

Red Dawn Rising

S ometime in the very early hours, the stars came out.

Little echoes of light in the dark, they hung bright and lonesome against the night. A midnight map scrolled across the world, just waitin to be read. To the north, the eye of the Great Bear were the largest. High and luminous light, it shone merciful brilliant, blinking down, guiding us on true. Toward Nocna Mora. Toward Bren.

The shimmer of a false sun hung in the horizon. A mirage. There were still hours till light, real light, would rise. Pressing my hand to the ice-stone pendant under my coat, which had gone cold, I kept us walking. One foot then the next. One, two, one, two. *Just keep moving.* Hours and hours passed with little other than the beating of our hearts to mark our progress. One foot then the next.

When the aching white flatness finally broke, it weren't good. A massive cleft cut across the ice. A gaping dark wound, it split the horizon wide. There would be no going round. Not for leagues and leagues. Time we didn't have. My only hope were that somewhere along its icy grin, it were narrow enough to jump. Not a happy prospect.

I inched closer, dropping the litter. I leaned over real careful like, unsure if the ledge could support me. From the depths a gust of cold air raced up, stealing at my breath.

Sheer walls of blue ice plummeted hundreds of feet down, their path eaten away by the rushing of a massive river. The churning crystal blue of a glacier-born water. A sinking dread filled my gut as the growlin waters reverberated from the down deep. I shuffled back from the edge. Racing water, I knew, would flow all the way to shore. Cause water always found its way. I just hoped we would too.

With care, I guided us along the most stable section of the western edge, searching for a way across. For some lone strip of ice not yet pulled under by the river below. It felt like hours passed before I found one strong enough. Like a frozen strand of impossible silk, the narrow bridge of ice spanned the fathoms-deep fissure below. Just wide enough.

"Stay close," I called out. Cody and the dogs came to my side as the first stretch of sunrise were just beginning to break over the edge of the ice. In it, Cody gave me a grim but determined look.

I unhitched the dogs, taking the reins. I gave Fen a pat on the head and were rewarded by a slow wag of her tail as she stood. Tiptoeing my way out, I tested the bridge. Mercifully, nothing broke. Or cracked. We'd just have to see. Swallowing, I took a full step out onto the strip of ice. And stopped. Listening for shifting. For that slow creeping that filled your gut with fear. Just before the whole world gave way beneath your bones.

But there were nothing. I tapped my heels. Solid enough.

Behind me, the dogs began to whine and crowd at the narrow start, jostling for position. Ice groaned under my feet. I put up hand. But too late, as Addy ran into my legs, knocking me off balance. The world spun; my feet slipped. I didn't have time to scream. Snow scattered off the ledge, falling free into the turbulent waters below as I caught my balance. Inches from the edge. When my heart quit lurching, I settled my breathing and walked Addy back. Properly chastised, she sat with the rest of the pack. Cody walked to her side. Taking a deep breath, I turned away from his still-worried stare and back to crossing. There'd be time to think on it later, how close that had been. I tested the bridge near to all the way middle. Again it held. I walked back to Cody's side.

"We'll have to go single file," I said.

"Or else what?" Cody's face had drained of all color. His hands dug in deep into Fen's fur. Knuckles white. The dog gave him a worried twist of her head, but didn't move from his pet.

"We all fall. I'd thought that were pretty obvious."

"Ah, right. Yes, got it."

"You sure?" I shot Cody with a look.

"I'm not great with heights." He grimaced. "But I'll be fine."

I frowned at him. "Just try not to get too near the edge. You'll be alright. Just do what I do and keep close."

Cody didn't look too convinced.

"Dogs first, I think." I whistled and gestured over the bridge. Lightest, they'd the best chance to get over before Cody and me cracked it with our weight.

My brave Boz walked out first out. He slipped a little, makin my heart thump out of my chest. But he didn't seem troubled. And finally, after Boz had made it, the rest of 'em, in a great show of running, crawling, and scrambling, made it across. I turned to Cody.

"Ready?"

"Ready."

I stepped out onto the ice bridge. Cody, a step behind, followed.

Breathe, Jorie. In out, in out, one foot in front of the other. Breathe, pause, and walk. Breathe, pause, and walk. It were like a dance. Measured and exact. The world narrowed to just the very act of moving. When we at last took our first steps onto solid ground, every nerve in my body were buzzing bright.

Behind me, Cody stumbled onto his knees. "As fun as that was," he gasped out, clutching at the snow, "I vote we do not ever do that again."

I held out an arm. He took it without hesitation and I lifted him up.

His hand held mine a heartbeat too long before he let go. We were so close. I took a step back and brushed my hand off on my shirt.

"Stars, Jorie, it was pitch as night down there. It felt like"—he ran a hand over his face—"like I was walking over my own grave." His face so serious, eyes wide.

He weren't that far from wrong. I patted his shoulder. "Don't you go getting any ideas, Cody Colburn. You ain't getting out of this that easy."

Cody gave me a slow smile, tension easing from his bones. "Banish the very thought."

I smiled back. I couldn't help myself.

If we were hoping for a break after the crevasse, it weren't a wish that got answered. The glacier on the other side of the rift turned out to be extraordinary slick. And the going were slow at best. But at least it were firm enough. Ahead of us the horizon were a golden band of rising sun. Squinting into it, I oriented toward the northeast. And walked.

Hours passed, and finally the glacier's massive ice sheet ran up against an immovable face of what looked like granite. The promise of stable ground.

From the erupting rock, heavy threads of ice hung one after another. They didn't interest me. But the small opening in the rock . . .

that did. I pointed. Cody followed my direction. Shelter had arrived.

The closer we got to the cave, the more everything hurt. All my adrenaline from the ice bridge crossing had finally faded, leaving me nothing but pain. At the base of the rock Cody tripped. Pack slipping from his shoulder. I reached out, my muscles screaming in protest.

"Cody, I—" A scuttle of pebbles fell from the white cliff overhead, raining onto my shoulder. I looked at the fallen stones. All of them were coated with a thick red clay. I froze. There weren't no mud around here. The hairs on the back of my neck stood up. I put a finger to my lips.

In the silence we waited as the muted crunching of rock filled the air. From behind me, the dogs let out a series of low growls. Slow, I reached for my gun and scanned the ridgeline.

One, two, ten minutes and still nothing came. My arm grew tired and eventually the dogs lost interest and began to whine. We needed to move out of here; I had to get us safe. Without thinkin, I took Cody's hand and pressed us forward, walked to the cave with one eye on the ridge behind.

The cave tunneled deep into the rock. Far larger than I'd thought it'd be from the outside. Not just cause it were wide, but because it kept going. Rock walls twisting away into darkness. I went to tug up my collar and were met by resistance. Cody hadn't let go of my hand. And I hadn't let go of his. Hasty, I dropped it and took a step away. A flash of hurt crossed his face and I turned, avoiding the deep green of his eyes. I itched the palm of my hand against my chest and scowled. I were tired, that were all.

I forced my attention to the dim of the cave around us. Which might not have been as abandoned as I'd hoped.

Along one side, a ring of charred rocks circled the sandy floor.

A firepit. Surprised, I walked over and brushed my foot over the remains of a what had clearly been an old fire. Deep strands of ash feathered into the air. I sneezed.

Beneath the old coals, a little stick of white peaked out. A chunk of broken bone. Rib, if I weren't wrong. Little teeth marks nibbled along the edges where someone or something had chewed away the hard outer bone to get to the sweet red marrow within.

Outside the wind picked up, a well-timed screech rattling the ice. We both turned, but there were nothing, no walking shadows out of stories. No myths at all. The silence built, but no one and nothing came. Half an eye on the entrance and the other half on Cody, I picked my pack up from the ground and shook out our supplies. Warmth. We needed warmth.

Only a few false starts later and I managed to breathe flames into the old pit's meager excuse for kindling. The fleshless bones catching, snapping with newborn heat. Heat that were something merciful against our skin. Flickering waves of light, yellow and blue and green, lit the cave, dancing off the walls and sinking into the sands.

With a huff, I joined Cody. The dogs had already curled up in tight little balls along the far wall. A little edge of rock dug into my back, and it took a few movements to get comfortable. Cody gave me a half smile. I looked at his profile. And hoped I didn't look near that ragged. Cody and I traded the water flask back and forth, sitting quiet for a long time. Outside snow began to fall.

"Can I ask you something, Jorie?" Cody said, turning a half-opened eye to me.

I leaned my head into the wall, my legs and toes finally warming from the fire. "Sure."

"I've been thinking."

"Good for you. Never too late to start."

He gave me the flick of a look. "I mean about all of this. About the Warders of Vydra."

I started a little at that. "What about them?" I asked real slow. Not many people talked about them. Stars, not many people thought they were real. I'd never heard anyone even say the name. They were supposed to be human, but only just. Their lines forged by generations of people sworn to the city, bound by the cold. An otherness fused into their very frames. And as ice-touched as they came.

That were the real curse. People died out in the Flats not by magic, but by madness. Their stories all twisted up wrong inside them until they thought cold were warmth and death a mercy. Till they couldn't believe nothing their minds told 'em to be true. Across from us the fire, burning low and warm, sent light flickering over the sleeping dogs. Black shadows swaying on the far wall, forms distorted and strange. As was everything out on the Flats. It could get to you, that. If you let it.

"Just hear me out. If the Tracers are real, if Vydra is real, it follows its legendary guards are real too. Doesn't it?"

"Does it? Cause of the few stories I've heard, I really hope they ain't."

Cody dipped his head, as if I'd agreed. I suppose I had. "And Nocna Mora?"

"What of it?"

A pensive look passed over his face. "Is that where the Warders are from?"

"No."

"So then where *do* the Warders come from? Where do they live?"

Cody stared up at the ceiling, face thoughtful. "And what about the Rovers?"

I scoffed. "Ain't no use wastin time on thinkin about it." I rolled my neck, a knot piercing painful at the base. "Cause where we're going, we don't need no more terrible men to add to it."

"But—"

"If you think anything stuck way out there in the ice needs any more protecting than what the Flats themselves already provide—well then, that's just plain stupid. How many people you seen here just walkin round for the fun of it?"

"Then what about the Witch? Surely we need protection from her? That is what they are for, at least in some of the stories."

I laughed. Just how many questions were lodged in that head of his? "You mean the Ice-Witch that brings the storms and the ice and the snow? The one that don't exist?"

Cody frowned. "But don't you ever wonder about it? That there could be something bigger than us out there? That this life, that it isn't all there is? That there is something . . . more out there waiting for us, something different and real and wonderful?" A note of something desperate sad were in the question. I thought of that picture in his pocket. Of the bright-eyed boy in the sun. And his parents, smiling down at him.

"No," I said, surprising gentle, thinking how to explain. It weren't my strong suit. "Cause this is it." I gestured around me. "We only got one life, Cody Colburn. And it's us that's got to make it enough.

"The North ain't something you can learn in books, sitting in comfy chairs. This ain't some dream, some adventure you have cause you're bored. This is it, what you see. And it's real and raw and painful. No matter how many stories you tell yourself, no matter how hard you think about 'em, there ain't nothing that's gonna save you from this." An ache began to build down deep in my belly. "No matter how hard you try, this place, it kills you. Year by year. Takes everything from you one aching breath at a time. And I can tell you, Cody, there ain't much adventure in that."

Cody were silent a long time, face real pensive like. "But you live here. Surely all those books I've read, all the lectures I've heard—my uncle's research, it can't all be wrong, can it? Legends have to start somewhere, Jorie. Why not here? After all, most of our own histories seem impossible if you stand far enough away. What are stories in the end but the truths we hide from ourselves?"

I ran a hand over my face, scrubbing at the cold. How else could I tell him? When you weren't sure where your next meal was coming from or who were gonna die next, you stopped askin silly questions. Quick. Curious ain't ever something I'd had the privilege to be.

"Just take those people we found under the ice," he said.

I side-eyed him. "Can't say I'm inclined to."

"They were real. That story you told me, it *was* real," he said, a note of awe in his voice. "That has to mean something. It just . . . does."

"It don't." I gave Cody a half glance. "Sometimes stories are just that. Stories. And the truth is that someone were bored and wanted to scare or cause fear or get people to give over their coin. Silent Lake is real, but it's not because there is some avenging Ice-Witch out there punishing foolish men, it's because men were foolish enough to try and live out here."

He opened his mouth.

"Enough speculating." Irritation bloomed. I were tired. And hurt. "What's real is right now. It is those wounds on your side, your wrist.

143

What's real are the cracks in my ribs. The ox and the ice and wind. That were real. The people who listen to all them stories you love so much? Those are all the bodies layin dead out there in the Flats. Them, your *uncle*." My Pa. I began to shake. "They all listened, just like you. And look at them now. Those stories only ever kill people, Cody Colburn. So I stopped listening to them years ago." You can't be hurt by what you don't believe in.

Cody were silent a long time. Long enough I thought he'd fallen asleep. But then he turned his eyes to mine, so that we weren't bare a foot apart. "I'm sorry, Jorie. About all of it. About your family, my family. Your sister. And the Rover, the map and . . . everything."

My throat felt sudden hot. I turned my eyes away.

Cody placed a gentle hand over mine. "You know, Jorie, I can make a new one."

I stared at where our bodies met.

"A map. I can draw a new one. It might not be perfect, but—" He looked down into his hand over mine, shy or sad or both. "But the Rover won't know that. You haven't lost her yet. Not if I can still help it."

"I . . ." I didn't know what to say. *Thank you. That means everything.* But instead of sayin it, instead of reaching out, I pulled my hand from his and stood up.

"Great." I walked over to scoop up a piece of burned scrap wood. I tossed it on the fire, where the tender flames ate it eager. I glanced at Cody's expectant, beautiful face. Throat seizing tight. "I—I'm gonna go get more kindling. Stay here."

"Oh—okay," Cody murmured.

Feeling like a thousand kinds of stupid, I stumbled past him, turned away into the comforting darkness of the cave.

But dark weren't all that were there. A path had been cut through the sandy floor.

Snatching up a low burning stick from the fire, I followed the heavy animal prints as they mixed with those of what looked like sets from two different people. One large and heavy, a man's, and the other lighter and smaller. Like a child's. My breath grew fast. A man and a child. Like maybe a girl. Like Bren.

I ran. At the back of the cave, the walls tapered tight. But it didn't end. Protecting the light ahead of me, and laying flat on my belly, I slid through. Finally, just as I began to panic I'd get stuck, the tunnel erupted into a massive cavern. Stalactites and stalagmites ruptured all around me like sets of giant teeth.

I kept on, following them until I couldn't. The cave dead-ended. I spun in circles at the far wall. My heart sinking. Cause though there were two sets, they not only went into the cave, but out of it too. There weren't no one else here.

I stared blankly at the wall in front of me. The wall stared back.

I reached up and took out Bren's pendant, running a cold finger over the smooth silver chain. Over and over until it were shinning so bright it were practically glowing. I must have been more tired than I'd thought. Frowning, I slipped the pendant under my coat and turned away. A flash of motion caught my eye.

I froze. No, not motion. Not exactly. I lurched a step backward. The wall. It were shimmering. A trick of the light, surely. I reached out a hand; the stone rippled warm under my skin, and I snapped my hand back. There weren't no water.

Slick as silt my fingers brushed over the stone. The cold solid stone. I glanced down at my hands. Warmth spread from them up my arms, into my chest. Thrumming.

I fell back from the wall. But the heat scorched through me. Burning. I couldn't stop it any more than I could stop the blood pulsing through my veins.

My home flashed into existence, blotting out the darkness of the cave. I blinked and blinked, but nothing changed. I could *feel* the flicker of the fire over my skin, the brush of Bren breathing next to me, smell Pa's cooking. The weight of the warm hand that fell on my shoulder.

"Tell me again," I heard myself saying. "The one about the Witch and her pieces."

"Really? Of all my stories, that's the one you want to hear?" My mother raised a brow. "Haven't I told that one enough for you?" But she were laughing.

I pressed in tighter to her knees, nestling. She dropped a warm kiss to my head. I yawned.

"The girl had not always been a Witch. She was once a girl like you."

I smiled up at my mother, but her eyes were far away. "She had a mother and father and sister. And then one winter, a strange sickness ravaged the village where they lived. People and livestock fell sick, most dying. But not the girl's family. The surviving villagers began to whisper. To call them unnatural. Dark magic. And so what appeared good luck soon turned to a curse. Desperate and scared, the villagers marched on the one family that did not suffer." My mother paused, her breathing steady behind me. "They attacked the family's home."

"That's not nice." My lips moved with the words. "They shouldn't have done that."

"No. It is not, my darling." She ran a hand through my hair. "I think that's enough for—"

"No, please, Ma, keep telling it." Bren yawned from by the fire.

Ma gave us an indulgent smile. "Very well." She hugged her arms across her chest. "Desperate, the girl cried out. For anyone who would hear. She would trade anything to save them. To protect them. And just when she thought she was most alone, that no one were coming, something answered. Old and long forgotten, it lurched out of the raging sea below their burning home. The villagers ran, but it was too late. The girl's family was dead.

"Grief cracked at the girl's heart. And so she made a bargain. The power twisted half-truths and fancy promises into the girl's heart. Those villagers had shown her family no mercy. Why should the girl show it to them? Surely she wanted vengeance? The power curled about the girl, drinking in her warmth, soaking in the beating heat of her heart. The bargain was struck. A mortal life for an immortal power. And magic, like burning moonlight, poured through the girl's veins, pooling in her heart. The villagers tried to run, but the girl was hungry and would not be settled. In her body, the powers grew more and more wild with each villager. Until there was nothing left inside the girl but the bitter cold vengeance beating in her heart.

"The remaining few villagers, weakened and thinned, made one last stand. They may not have been able to kill the newborn Witch, but they could hurt her. And so they wounded her where she was weakest. The girl's already cracked heart. They were lucky. They stole the seven pieces, bound them in the Witch's own blood, and hid them away. Piece by missing piece, the Witch grew too weak to fight back. Until there was not enough of her left to hold together. The villagers tricked what was left of her into a prison of ice. Sealed the way with bones and silver, not dead but no longer living. The villagers bound themselves to the prison. Pledged to watch over her always. Just as trapped by the ice as the Witch, who was left injured and raging inside. . . . "

Sudden as plunging into the sea, I were thrust out of the vision, near drowned to breathlessness and aching alone. The cave the only reality around me. I scrambled back from the wall. At my feet the last burning ember of my light sputtered out.

Fear sunk inside me. I turned and ran. Ran until the darkness of the stone had faded into nothing behind me. Until I were once again tethered strong. Here. In this cave. A silhouette in the darkness shimmered. *Weren't I?* A thread of doubt, a real one, began twisting at my roots.

When I got back, Cody were fast asleep, body curled up in a little ball. He looked so peaceful. So quiet. Trying not to cry, wishing fervent I weren't going ice-touched, I slid down next to him and wrapped the bearskin tight. Letting the deep, warm living breath of the boy at my side wash over me. Let the steady solid warmth of him beat against me, let it lull me.

My nerves slowed. I breathed in the crisp, clean cold of the coming storm, and the hard cold reality around me.

Bren, Ma. Their faces soft in firelight, their voices warm. The happiness that fluttered inside my chest. Aching. I remembered it all. I did not move to dry my tears. Because I thought most of all of the sister I hadn't been able to save.

Cody's words echoed inside me. *What are stories in the end but the truths we hide from ourselves?*

Truths hidden in myth just waiting to swallow us whole.

CHAPTER 20

Shallow Graves

W e traveled without rest for the next day and a half.

I tried and failed to shove the night far into the back of my mind. I pushed us harder than I'd ever run before. As if, in the sweat and strain, I could outrun the memories in my bones. It did little good.

Cody didn't complain. In fact, he'd begun to not say much of anything at all. Getting so quiet that I had started to worry. And slow. But with the rest came new worries.

Wild Falls. That were the last place I knew of that existed before Nocna Mora. But hour after hour, nothing. Nothing but more snow and ice. Maybe I'd led us wrong, swung us off course. I'd check us against the path of the sun, and between Cody and me, we were more than good enough with the stars at night. We should've been enough. There should've been a town. There weren't.

I could have sworn I kept seeing it, just shining over the horizon. Only when we got there, there weren't nothing but snow. So we carried on until at last Cody and I both collapsed against the only structure we had found in days.

A massive black rock wall erupted out of the ice. We'd seen it from leagues off.

I imagined, stupidly, that this were what it looked like at the heart of a long frozen mountain.

The more I studied the rock, the stranger it were. Near to three stories high, it were also massive wide. Deep indentations like the press of some giant fingers shaped it. As I got close to it, it radiated heat, warmed from the sun. It wasn't the town, but it were large enough to block the wind.

I panted to my feet and set about seeing to the dogs, who were busy biting at the rim of algae at the rock's base. I knelt down. Sure enough, little bright green specks dotted the surface, like lichen. Only it didn't grow out here, and—as I scrapped off a bit into my palm—it didn't tend to *glow*. Still, it were the first sign of anything other than snow and ice and death we'd seen for a long while. It were welcome enough.

Lettin out a groan, I got up to prep for the night. As I passed him, Cody gave a weak cough, pulling himself into the lowest cove. I didn't like the wet of that cough.

Taking off a glove, I pressed my palm to his face. Cool enough. No fever. I'd have to check again later, when he were warmer. I stepped back, turning away. Motion, quick and sharp, flashed out of the corner of my sight. I spun.

And when I looked at Cody, I near to started. Cause there were two of him in the nook of rock. I rubbed my eyes and looked again. Only one Cody waited for me this time. One boy and his reflection. I must be more dehydrated than I thought.

Frowning, I put my glove back on and walked over to the kit. I were certain not thinking straight lately.

I blinked, trying to shake the cold grip of memory. I was standing, though I do not remember doing it, and staring down at the small pile of my earthly goods. Right. I forced my body to move.

Starting with a bowl of melt water. If I were dehydrated enough to see double, bad as we felt now, it would be a hundred times worse tomorrow. The eerie cry of an owl echoed out across the snow, though by rights there shouldn't be any birds this far out. I swirled the snow in the bowl. While it melted, I worked on blocking the curve of the rock where Cody sat. A combination of the broken canvas, reins, and piling up the snow in front to seal it in.

When I were done, I took a long drink, my lips cracking and raw. Rousin Cody, who were having trouble stayin awake long enough to take a deep pull, the whites of his teeth chatterin against the metal.

I slumped down by Cody's side. The white world rolled out before us. In the silence, Cody extended his furs. With hesitation, I pushed close.

Sighing, Cody leaned in, the warmth of his body an unfamiliar comfort against my side. Overhead the owl's cry echoed in the dark. I ran a hand over the back of my neck. At my side. Cody's breath settled into the regular pattern of sleep next to me. Warmth against the cold. I pulled the furs over our heads.

It was easier to be close to him like this. When he were sleeping. When I could watch the slow rise and fall of his chest, the flutter of his heartbeat and not worry. Not think on how I moved, or what I said, or if I said it too hard or too cold, too everything people had always told me I were. I didn't know what that said about me, that I were better with people when they weren't conscious.

Careful, I pushed the loose strands of hair from his face. He looked so fragile there in the cold. As if I pressed him just right, he'd shatter. It weren't fair. None of this were. For any of us. Everyone needed someone, didn't they? Cody, he didn't have no one left to hope for him. At least I had Bren. Even if I died trying, I would find her. But if Cody died, if he got lost out here in the Flats, there would be no one left to mourn him.

An unexpected spike of heat pierced at my throat. We all needed someone. And right as I could figure, I owed Cody.

"I won't let you down, Cody Colburn." I pressed a soft hand over his heart. "I promise."

"Jorie," he whispered.

I froze. But he didn't say no more. Just let out a long breath and tucked his face into my shoulder. I snapped my hand back to my side. But he didn't wake.

I cussed my foolishness.

It were always easier to make promises when no one were listening. I slid his head off me and curled deeper into my furs, uncaring that a pit of something dangerous had begun heating inside my chest.

Or maybe, as I leaned back into the smooth black rock, it was that I were simply too tired to know the difference between what were exhaustion and what were sadness.

Tucked up together in the warm hollow of the rock, sleep were surprisingly easy to come. This time, it weren't wakefulness, but the ache of the nightmares that were impossible to avoid.

It were my shiverin what woke me first.

I tried to open my eyes, but all there were was blackness. My heart skipped a beat before I knew what were wrong. The furs had slipped off my face, and my eyelids froze closed. I must have been crying in my sleep. With care I peeled the ice off, lash by ice-covered lash. I let out a long sigh.

Cause it weren't like the sight that greeted me were any better than the nightmares, dreams of Bren stumbling alone out on the

Flats, of Bren calling my name, trying to tell me something important, to warn me. And when I ran, I never got closer. A phantom in the snow, always just out of reach.

I shoved my way up onto my feet, furs falling to the ice beneath me. I began packing up. Behind me, Cody stirred.

Ignoring him—weren't no kindness to wake him a moment sooner than needed—I forced my cramping muscles up. I had to see to the dogs. When I'd finished, still something itched at me. Like the cracking of sea ice under my skin, my nerves felt like they were splitting.

I hugged my arms about myself. The quivering weren't stopping. Cody placed a gentle hand on my arm. I blinked. And dropped the ice-stone. *When had I even picked it up?* A sensation, not unlike the lingering trail of a finger, passed down my side. I shook out my arms. I turned from Cody, cheeks flushing.

"Jorie, I—I don't think that is such a good idea." Cody tugged at my sleeve.

"I weren't going anywhere. I ain't stupid."

"Jorie, that's not . . ."

Nostrils flaring, I spun back round on Cody, only Cody—he weren't looking at me.

CHAPTER 21

The Color of Death

It were a man.

Covered all in gray furs, the hooded figure were like a ghost made real. A specter of dawn rode astride a sled, calling out a rhythm to the team pulling it. The largest pack I'd ever seen.

Rough winter-coated beasts—black and white and burnt-forest red—three times the size of normal dogs, they tore across the horizon, lean bodies catching in the low morning light. The pack ate up the sky in front of 'em with every stride, one for every three my pack could have taken. A shiver ran through me.

"Please tell me you are seeing what I'm seeing?" Cody asked.

"Sure am," I said, tracking the huge canines over the snow. But that were a lie. I knew what they were.

Though I had denied it when the Rover and his beast had stolen Bren, there were no mistaking it now. Tracers. That were a whole team of Tracers.

Boundless northern beasts of legend, they were supposed to be wolves twisted by the wilds of the ice and snow. Wolves that had been formed into something more. Something strange, unreal. Some said unnatural. And big. Wolves that thrived where nothing else survived. Wolves that lived with Warders.

A gust of wind tore across the Flats, filling the entire world with a blinding white. Disappearing the wolves and the man, as if they were naught but spirits in the snow.

"Are they gone?" Cody asked.

"I ain't never been that lucky," I said. "Look." Like running shadows, gray bodies formed out of the snow. They were heading right at us.

I pulled us back, forcing Cody behind me. Tucking us into the shadow of the rock face. Against the wind, the driver snapped the reins. The lead animal let out a mammoth growl, massive claws tearing into the ice, straining at the pull. My heart lurched as the gray hood fell, revealing the driver's profile. Cause I were wrong. It weren't a man.

Behind me, Cody whistled in a breath as the woman's halo of golden hair whipped about her head. They were coming closer, closer. I forced us back into the shadow of the rock. Deeper and deeper. But the driver, if she saw us, gave no cry.

The team made an abrupt turn. They passed within fifty yards of where we stood. Without even a glance our direction, the woman pulled rough at her coat, whipping her furs over her head, and pushed on.

And then they were gone. Like a storm kestrel skimming the ocean. Testing the waters. Seeing what lay beneath.

Hairs stood up all over my skin. My hands fell to my sides. This was no man's land and I'd be stupid not to be mighty curious what she were doing out here. More to the point, where she were going in such a hurry. With Tracers. Cause in my experience, there were only two reasons to run like that. Either you were running from something or you were running *to* something.

"Cody, I got an idea."

"On it." Before I could say nothing more, he were already moving, gathering up the dogs. On the tiny piece of what had once been our sled I put all our pitiful goods. They weren't enough. Two more nights like we'd just had, it wouldn't matter what was living and dead out here on the Flats.

I took up the litter and I smiled. Cody's face practically burned with determination. Now that was a kind of stubborn I could work with. This was worth a shot. Stars, it was worth all the shots. If it meant we lived long enough to make it to Nocna Mora.

Gloved fingers gripping tight against the leathers of the litter, I pulled us into a run. Those animals may have specters straight out of nightmare, but the woman? She had been real enough. And for good or bad, people meant food. And shelter. And maybe, just maybe, the chance to hear about a girl and a Rover.

The day wore on and the trail began to fill, disappearing as flakes of snow slipped into the ridges, washing them out. Dusk began to hum along the horizon. A new night chill spiked the air. And still we marched on and on.

Until a shift in the wind brought the thick aroma of coal fires and ash. Ahead of us a long line of smoke, like the curl of an eel's tail, swirled into the sky ahead. The smell were barely strong enough to cover the heavy foulness of human and animal waste that also came as we got closer. The dogs began to whine. I suppressed a cough. We had certain found something. What that meant, I didn't yet right know.

"There aren't supposed to be any towns left out here, except Nocna Mora," Cody whispered, coming up next to me.

"There ain't." We stalked closer, keeping low as we could.

Thick green rusted metal wire wound between a series of silver spikes set at perfect intervals around the perimeter. Beyond which sat a maze of tents. Well-worn paths wound haphazard between them. The biggest were at the center, with smaller, clear rougher looking ones ringing around them. The sets closest to us looked nearly deserted.

Thin folds of unmoored flaps snapped in the wind, no hint of movement within. Here and there strange pockets of color could be seen, but try as I might I couldn't tell what they were. A flash of gold or blue. A line of some kind ran along the side of the one of the low white tents. On it, like a chain of broken teeth, dead black birds swayed.

"Don't like it, Cody." I crouched lower to the snow.

"Me neither. There is something very"—he paused, looking around—"dreamlike about it, as if I've seen it before. Or that I should have." He furrowed his brow. On the far side of the encampment red sparks danced in the smoke, until glowing flames licked high above the tents. The sickening smell of burning fur filled the air. My stomach lurched.

"Nightmarish is more like it."

"True." Cody said. "There is something about it though, almost as if . . . what's that?"

The fires sputtered. A flash of darkness against the horizon. A sharp cry.

"I need to get closer. Stay here."

"Jorie, is that such a great idea?"

"No, it ain't. But I'd rather know what's out there before we turn our backs on it than after."

Cody swallowed.

I stood and striding no more than a few yards stopped. I kicked at the snow at my feet. "What the stars?"

"What's wrong?" Cody asked, rising quick to my side. Looking down at the snow, not seeing the trouble. But I did. Stars I were a fool.

"The tracks, Cody, the tracks. They aren't right."

He eyed me, confused for a long moment. "The tracks?"

I brushed my foot out over the snow. "How many sets do you see?"

He blinked. "I don't see any, what's that—?" Realization snapped into place. "There aren't any."

I nodded. "We followed that woman right to this very entrance. I don't think we were as unseen as we thought we—" I spun around. And cursed. Four fur-cloaked men strode out of the camp. Straight at us. Guns glinting at their sides.

Reflexive, I took a step back. And stopped. *Show no fear.* I stepped back to where I had been. Even if we'd been inclined to it, it were far too late to run. It had been since the moment the woman had passed us by the rock. There weren't no coincidences out on the Flats, only trouble.

"She wanted us to follow," Cody said, coming to a rest at my side. His own back straight, his hands balled at his sides.

"We may have taken the bait. But we ain't the kind of prey they're looking for."

"Definitely not." A wry twitch at the edge of his lips. His hand wavered toward me ever so slight. Touching, but not touching.

A head taller than the others, one leading figure raised a fist. Those behind her fell back, eager fingers straying to their sides. I let out a little growl.

A flick of motion and the woman's gray hood fell. A blink later and she were in front of us. The fires raged out behind her. A smile quick and sharp.

My only warning. A set of strong arms snared me from behind, pinning my limbs against my sides. I screamed out. At the pressure or my own stupidity—of course there are more of 'em—I weren't sure. Both like as not. I kicked and bit hard as I could. Next to me Cody were doing the same.

Tossed face-first in the snow, I sputtered. Flakes catching in my teeth. Pain shot through my back as my arms were curled behind me. Ropes wrapped my wrists. I couldn't move.

A second later, Cody were thrust down next me, red pooling at his temple. Eyes fluttering, a low groan pressing from his lips. Alive. But not conscious. My heart gave a sideways lurch. I fought down a surge of panic. *Not again. Not again.*

I thrust my elbow out hard as I could. There were little give to the ropes. Not enough. I connected. The man holding me bare grunted. Growling, he grabbed my arm, rolling me to my side in the snow. He pulled a long piece of cloth from his coat.

"How dare—" The gag were shoved into my mouth. I bit down. It tasted of smoke and the damp. I cursed out every swear I'd ever learned. Little good it did. He dragged me to my knees. My head swam. I forced myself to focus, counted the long pulls of breath through my nose, anger and air welling inside in equal measure. *How dare they.* More men, Tracers at their sides, appeared. And before I could reason, fast as adders, they ran past us. I whipped my head round. Cries filled the air.

"Fen!" I screamed, but the word lost to the rotting fabric in my mouth. Man holding me chuckled mean, as one by one the others began chasing down my pack.

They pinned my dogs to the snow and snapped collars around their throats, muzzles over their snouts.

Anger hot and boiling split through my veins. Cause if these bastards so much as damaged one hair on my pack's heads, they were dead. All of them. A growl came from Fen. A moment later she broke free of her captors, man cursing and holding his bleeding hands.

Good girl. Run. I wanted to scream it. I lurched on my knees. Only to be jerked back. With a sickening laugh a rough woven bag came down over my head.

The whole world went dark.

CHAPTER 22

So Brings the Dawn

———— ◆ ————

With a massive heave, the man repositioned me over his shoulders. There came another set of footfalls. Heavier than the man's who were carrying me.

"Reckon they're worth something?" the man carrying me asked, a heavy hand falling on the back of my knees. Hard enough that a fresh bruise were already blooming.

"Well, they gotta be worth more than the dogs."

"But dogs eat less." Both men let our rough laughs. Hard laughs. The kind of laugh a girl weren't too keen on hearing if she wanted to make it out alive.

I choked back saliva as I ground my teeth and kicked. The man holding me let out a grunt of pain as heel met rib cage. The man's grip tightened.

After a few minutes, our abductors once again began bantering back and forth. If I hadn't been so angry, I would have been red-faced. Stars above, is this what men talk about?

In the darkness of the hood, I tried to tune them out and instead strained for any sign of Cody. And were rewarded by a low, breathy moan from beside me. Just one. But it were him. He were alive.

The scuffing of leather against wood marked a sudden transition from cold to warmth across my skin. My body prickled with the new-born heat.

Then without warning I found myself dropping through the air, ass first.

I gave an involuntary grunt as I hit the frozen ground. Gasping for breath under my hood only swirled my head with the unwelcome taste of dirty smoke. I spluttered, coughing. A second later, Cody were tossed down next to me. His breathing labored. He slumped against my shoulder, shivering against me, the ragged pulse of his heart beating against my side. He murmured something I couldn't understand.

"Be okay. Please be okay," I whispered. He didn't reply. Pain flashed through me that had little to do with where we were. Echo of words I'd whispered into my sister's ear not so long ago, it weren't lost on me.

I tried to roll, to move enough to maybe see him under the edge of my hood, but unbalanced, fell instead. Hissing through my teeth against the pain that shot up my shoulder. Heavy-booted feet came to stop in front of me, the slit of vision I had under the edge of hood just enough to see a set of leather shoes. Bloodred, they stood heavy in dirty slush. I took store of all the shoes, keeping their sight to memory. Just in case I ever got the chance to repay them.

"Enough of that," the man grunted. Amused. And hit me. I bit back my cry. I'd not give him the satisfaction of my pain. Grunting his clear disappointment, the man strode away.

The trail of conversation ebbed as the men left the tent, and with them went near all my strength. I puddled to the floor. It were as if someone had let out the plug. Every ache, bruise, welt came flooding into my body. All at once. Fighting against the tide of pain and exhaustion were like fighting the break of an avalanche. But there were Cody and the dogs. I needed to stay awake. To stay alert, to stay—

Snow-burned hands grabbed at my shoulders, yanking me to my knees. The hood ripped from my head none too gentle.

I blinked hard against the sudden light. A second later the tent flap opened and three people strode in. Like three huge gray wolves prowling toward us in the snow. The two behind quickly thrust weapons to their sides, locking the barrels close to their chests. Closing the flap, they stood sentinel at the entrance.

The one in front lowered her hood; this close, the tops of tattoos peeking out from under her collar were clear. But more eye-catching was the wicked scar that ran, ropy and red, from one side of the neck to the other, just over the jugular vein. A killing cut, like a memory of a promise left undone. A twisted echo to my own. Unyielding. Cold. Determined. Just like me.

Like everything I'd ever taught myself to be. Everything I'd ever made myself be. Stars, what I *wanted* to be. And yet . . . despite my best efforts to the contrary, I couldn't shake the basic fact that I *cared* about people. My family, Cody, Fen and Boz and all the pack—I cared about them. More than I cared about me. And this woman, whoever she were, I didn't think she cared about nothing more than her own skin. Whatever I were, I weren't like her. I burned with that certainty.

The woman studied me, tilting her head as a smile, wide and feral, split her face. I stared right the stars back. And her answering expression left no doubt why she could command a pack of Tracers. She barked out an order and turned from me. As she did, a single ruby pendant on a long silver chain slipped out from under her collar. Just like the Rover's. Just like the one Della had seen.

The woman, either not caring I were there or not even notic-
ing she were doing it, ran it along her cheek, slow and steady as all
around her the men scrambled.

From somewhere they produced a rich-looking table and solitary
chair. When the men bowed back, the woman moved—*stalked*—
toward it, tossing her coat over the back of the slatted wooden chair.

Time slowed as she sat, running black-tipped fingers slowly
across the surface of the table, nails catching in the flaking yellow
grains, tracing but not touching the deep insets of silver scrollwork
that flooded the wooden surface. Deliberate, as if she didn't care one
way or the other, the woman turned her notice to Cody and me.

I went stock-still. Her eyes. Gold-flecked cotton gray, they was
sharper than any steel. Without meaning to, I pressed my palm to my
chest. The stone beneath shocking cold.

With a quickness that weren't natural, the woman's stare
snapped to my hand. A look of calculating hunger flashing cross
her face. Startled, I dropped my hand.

"Now, exactly what would a good God-fearing Northerly girl
and a weakling Southern boy be doing out all the way out here all
by their lonesome? I do wonder what could lure them oh so far from
home." Her nails scrapped hard across the table. "Not lost are you,
pigeon?"

I glared. The blond's eyes flickered with amusement.

"You never would've made it. Scrawny things like you—they
never do. Little pigeon, you'd be dead by dinnertime." Whip quick,
the blond let out a low, deep-chested laugh. Her body shifting as she
did, exposing the flash of three guns strapped tight to her side.

"Doing you a right honest favor. The emptiness out there, that
really ain't a pretty way to go." Her glance darted between Cody and

me, calculating. Of what, I weren't exact sure. Nothing good. "Yet somehow, I don't think I need to tell you that, do I?"

She certain did not. But for the first time, I wondered. If these people *lived* out here, maybe not all those I drug home had died from the beasts or the cold.

"Not many reasons to find you out this far north that don't keep most honest folk awake at night. And we here don't take too kindly to stupid or to thieves. Which one are you, I wonder?" She tilted her head expectantly.

I bit out a string of curses against the rag in my mouth. The men in the tent let out a long, raucous chorus of laughter. Only the blond weren't laughing.

I exchanged a glance with Cody, who were clear as anxious as I should've been. Only I weren't. I were mad. Real mad. We'd bare had enough to keep us alive, bare made it wherever this were—and here were some woman trying to bait us? I snarled, anger reverberating against the back of my teeth. We were poor game for anyone's catch. And if this woman thought otherwise, I would make her regret it. Even the weakest animal out on the ice still had teeth.

The woman growled something to the man at her side, who scurried out of the tent. Turning, she fixed me with a considering gaze.

"Now, don't you go thinking on it girly, I've seen that look plenty times before. Even the hard ones give to begging in the end." The drumming of her fingers against the table her only outward sign of tension. I narrowed my eyes. There was nothing for her to be worried about. Though if she untied us, I could certain give her one.

"Last traitor we found round here is buried three feet deep in snow. Well, least his bones are. The ones the wild wolves didn't see fit to carry away for the marrow." She said it so calm, like we was talking friendly. A pleasant chat over drinks. "And that ain't the way you want to go, now is it?"

From outside the tent, a piercing series of howls erupted. The wolves. The unworldly chorus went on for a long time. Long enough that I grew more and more uncomfortable as the woman sat in silence smiling. As if she weren't just listenin, but understandin. Who was she? Rack my sluggish brain as I could, I didn't think of nothing else but—Warders.

I ground my teeth, my anger coming out as little more than muffled noise. She laughed and looked around the tent.

"What do ya say, boys? Should they see the same send-off as good old Reeves?" The blond ran a hand over the gun at her side. A revolver slid into an intricate raven-embossed leather holster. "Or should we play nice?"

Reeves. Holy stars, she had said Reeves. This was where the Rover had come from? My thoughts spun. Had she said *traitor?* What had he done? But more important, why did this woman clear think him dead?

"Been a little while since we had us some good and decent runners. Maybe a little predinner sport, or—" But the woman was cut off as the tent flap snapped open.

A man strode into the tent.

Next to me, Cody sat up, eyes wide as mine. Stars above, we *knew* that man.

CHAPTER 23

Be Not Afraid

D ev?" It came out nothing more than a raw rasp against the fabric. So quiet I didn't reckon anyone could've heard me.

Dev missed a half step, his cloak just open, hand raised to the caribou antler buttons on the front. His pupils widening in recognition for the briefest of moments. Ignoring me, he strode over to stand behind the blond. Right behind her. Hand on the back of her chair. Like he were meant to be there.

"Been a while, Devlin. Thought you might've stayed away for good this time." The woman's smile weren't friendly. "Any longer and I might've started to worry you'd gone and turned Rover on us."

Rocking back in her chair, the woman laid a proprietary hand on Dev's. Dev didn't move. He bare breathed. "Should've known better."

It weren't clear who she meant. Herself or Dev. Going by Dev's face he weren't right sure either. Finally, the woman gave one pat and let his hand go. "But bygones are bygones. And none of us can really stay away that long, can we?"

I didn't understand. I'd known Dev all my life; he lived in town. He weren't one of these people, he couldn't be. I tried to speak, but it were useless, the gag too tight.

"So." The woman spun her attention back to me. "This is Harrow's ilk then, is it, Devlin? Don't much look it. Though why should they? Runts, as I'd expected. Harrow never did have good choices in men." The blond eyed me, running her fingers over the smooth walrus ivory handle of the gun at her side. "Shame, really."

Harrow. My Ma. It didn't right register. That name on her lips. Not for a long moment. Then the world lurched below me. This woman, how did she know Ma's name?

Dev walked round to stand at the blond's side.

Her smile turned vulpine. "Well, that's the deserters line settled then." She gave a bark of laugher. My chest contracted painful. "As empty as my grandmother predicted it would be." She turned to face Dev. "Unless there's something else I should be aware of?"

Dev's fingers flexed at his side, eyes flashing to mine. "No. She's it. The only one."

"Good. Always have preferred a clean ending. Don't you think? Much simpler for everyone that way."

Dev made to take a step toward us. Then stopped. Didn't open his mouth. Didn't raise a single objection as Cody and me were picked up rough, bodies tossed like rag dolls over the guards' shoulders. I hissed and kicked out, struggling against my bonds. Anger and fear mixin inside me.

Next to me, Cody were doing the same. Pink-tinged saliva from where he were biting his lip fizzing at the corner of his mouth.

"Maybe not so shameful after all." The woman were laughing now. "Spirit like that, she'll certain make it farther than the last one. He didn't get more than a league 'fore Rill set those rounds into the red of his spine. Isn't that right?"

The man holding me chuckled. "I give 'em three leagues, Bass. Less if she keeps hollering like that."

She really was going to kill us. Just like that. Desperate, I shot my pleading glance at Dev, but he didn't meet my eye.

Dev pulled out a large piece of paper, smoothing it down onto the table in front of the woman. "Galle's found a breech along the eastern face of the rock, and more bodies. On top of that a good number of the markers are clear broken in half. It might be from the shaking, but it—"

"The creature's been getting stronger." The woman's eyes sparked eager. Hungry. Dangerous. Like she wanted it.

"Or someone else has been trying her bars," Dev said troubled.

"I would like to see them try." Bass mused, fingers running along the edge of her jaw. "But true or not it won't matter for long. The stars know all we need is one more piece and I'll get my shot; finish this once and for all." The woman knocked her hand on the table. A moment later and a map appeared in the hands of the man behind her. She studied it, frowning. "Get 'em out of here. I've a war to finish." With a single wave of her hand, we were dismissed. "Devlin, I am gonna need you to take Rig and go see to the tunnels in town. I've had reports of strange fires—"

Her words cut off as we were pulled up and out into the night. But my mind were clean stuck. This woman had known my Ma.

CHAPTER 24

Without Cause

I t were hours before I knew anything but the cold press of the floor where the men had thrown us.

I flickered in and out of sleep. Startled every time I woke to be lying in the same place and not getting dragged out over the ice. Despite the hood keeping the world in darkness, I tried to stay awake. But it weren't no good. The hunger and cold and pain were just too much and my eyes closed.

At first I thought I were dreaming. Cause what I felt were a loosening. The breaking of the ropes binding my hands. Then the flush of a blade, feather light and freezing against my wrists. I hissed against the back of my teeth, my eyes shooting open. Pain from muscles held still for too long spasmed up my arms. A million tiny pin pricks up my skin.

"Don't shout," the voice behind me hissed, "or you'll wake camp. We don't have much time clear."

The bindings fell to the floor at my feet and I kicked them away, spitting the cold taste of copper from the inside of my cheek to the floor. That were when I turned. And looked up into the face of the man standing over me.

"The stars are you playing at?" I growled.

Tossing the rest of my bindings behind him, Dev grunted. "I'm sore sorry about back in the tent with Bass."

He were trying to change the subject.

"Is this what you meant when you told me I shouldn't trust no one?" I stared at him, struggling up to my feet. Legs felt like they was made of rubber. Dev offered a hand. I batted it away. "Don't need your help."

Dev winced as if I'd struck him. "You've every right to be angry with me, I won't say you don't. Stars knows I certain would be if I were you. Your ma would be."

Still glaring, I stood. Body shaky with the effort. Stretching the tender muscles of my arms, rubbin where the bindings had bit at my wrists. We'd been thrown into some kind of storage tent. Broken tables and boxes stacked up against one another in a far corner, packs in another.

"Dev—or should I call you Devlin," I let the name snag, pull. "You tell me straight. Were my Ma mixed up with these people, with Bass?"

Dev hesitated. A hitch no longer than a breath. My heart sank. Ma had never told me where all those stories had come from. Or where she had come from.

"Bass don't know what she's saying. We don't tend to take too kindly to the children of deserters round here, you understand."

"My ma weren't no deserter."

Dev sighed, his eyes heavy. Troubled. "Your ma were different, Jorie, even from when she were young, anyone could see that plain as ice."

I opened my mouth.

"Don't," Dev cut out. "I can't say more, not now. It'll just make it worse for you. Just know that your ma, whatever else she were, she weren't like Bass, not in the way you're thinking." The answer were fast and hard.

"Then what was she?"

"Your mother. And a good woman." His tone brokered no question. "And she deserved more than the shake she got in this world, I know that. Whatever else she were or weren't, don't matter now. That hurt is a story best left for another time. . . ." *If there were another time.* The unfinished statement threaded the air between us. Finally, Dev held up his hands. "I ain't given you much, and I'm sorry for it. But I swear I ain't never lied when you asked."

"Maybe, maybe not. How could I know? What I do know is that it's easy to lie to someone when they don't know to ask the right questions."

"Leave it, please." Dev's eyes flashed with an emotion I didn't understand. "I ain't lied to you, Jorie. But if we don't get you out of here, truth won't matter one way or the other. It'll already be too late."

"What does that mean?"

Dev shook his head. "Never you mind. Only know that if I could change the past, I would. But even here there ain't no one who can do that. Your parents were good people. They were my friends. Not bringing them back to face Bass were a choice I made long ago. It were the right thing to do, no matter the consequences." He fixed me with a look. "Just like getting you out of here what's right. And if the consequence is that it interferes in Bass's plans, all the better." When his gaze returned to mine I near to took a step back. "I can help you, at least. Let me do that."

I scowled. But there were something in his voice. A pleadin desperate tone I ain't never heard him use before. Like he were drowning. A man reaching for the last knot in the throw line over the rail, the sea ready to swallow him whole. And in that moment I made a choice. The past were the past. But right now—right now I needed help. And Dev were offering.

"Fine, but that don't mean I have to like it," I grunted out. "Or you."

"No, you don't." Dev gave a flicker of a smile, proud if I didn't miss the mark, and began unbinding Cody's wrists. Once the ropes were off, Cody were quick to jump to his feet. Fighting rope-bound legs, he stumbled to my side, his expression tight. A wicked set of black bruises already forming under his eyes. I'd enough concussions to know that look. His head likely felt like it were gonna explode.

Dev gave the pair of us a once-over. By his face, he must have seen it too. Whatever he had been planning on saying, he swallowed instead. I didn't like secrets. Especially not when they weren't mine.

"Can I ask you one thing?" Dev asked, slipping his knife under his belt.

"Depends," I said.

"Can you just tell me why you're out here," Dev said. "I don't need to know everything, but I do need to know what you think you are chasing."

"What we're chasing?" *Not who.* "That's a mighty strange way to phrase it." The words were out, belligerent like, before I could stop 'em.

"Running, that's what. And one hardly expects to find their *innkeeper* mixing with your kidnappers in the middle of a frozen death trap. So I am certain you'll excuse us if Jorie doesn't answer you."

I stared at Cody as if he were a stranger. Maybe that concussion were worse than I'd thought. But he didn't look out of it. Gone was that fuzzy look; in its place were something cold. Firm. Something that looked just like me. I weren't entire sure it were a good thing.

Cody were glaring at Dev. And Dev were staring at Cody. I took a step between them. Enough. Enough of this. Dev were right. We needed to go. And we needed help. His would be far preferable to what I were sure Bass were gonna offer.

"Bren. Dev, for stars' sake, it's Bren we're after. That's the why and the who of it. We're chasing after Bren."

To his credit, Dev looked surprised. "Tell me."

I hesitated.

"Stars, Jorie, please. I know what you must think of me, and I deserve it, deserve every last curse of it. But please, tell me what's going on." Dev ran a hand through his hair, gaze sweeping between Cody and me. "Let me help you. It is the very least I owe your family."

I looked over at Cody.

"Your choice," he said.

He were right. This was my choice. Everyone had secrets. Didn't always make them your enemy, though knowing them didn't always make them your friend either. Dev may not have told me the truth, not all of it, but neither had I.

I straightened my shoulders, squared my jaw.

So be it. Breathing deep, I told Dev most everything, or near enough to it—the dead man that night at the house, the Rover, the note. Only thing I faulted at mentioning were the map. If they knew the Rover, the less Dev knew about what I had, the better. My confidence only went so far. Yet with each word, with each detail, Dev's scowl grew deeper. His expression beyond troubled. As if I were confirming more than just what he already knew. As if all this made some kind of horrible, awful sense.

That made one of us, at least.

"The fact that you are trying to save your sister and not interfering in her plans won't make Bass go lighter on you none. She don't take well to strangers, even ones she should be abiding," Dev said. He started to pace. "The sooner we get you two out of here the better. Your parents were good people and even better friends. And stars above, no matter what happens next, I ain't about to let their daughter get hurt out here, not if I can help it."

Cody, who had been standing at the back fiddlin with something on one of the stacks of boxes, walked over to my side. Hands slipping into his pockets. Our shoulders bare touching. I stood straighter. Taller. I weren't the only person out here looking for their family. Or what justice were left for them.

"Tell us what you are not saying," Cody said. "Tell us who you are."

Dev stopped his pacing. "Take too long to tell it, honest. Most of it you're better off not knowing. Stars"—he ran a hand over his beard—"most things I would be better off not knowing."

"But you aren't just average criminals out here, are you?" Cody asked. Before Dev could answer, Cody turned to me. "These people, Jorie, they aren't Rovers. They're Warders. This is a Warder camp. It fits, all the stories, all the tales. We've been taken hostage by Warders." His voice went all over strange. Some mangled mix of awe and anger and fear. Don't know that I could blame him.

"Hostage? It ain't that simple, and you ain't that lucky," Dev said gruff.

"Tell me I'm wrong. That if Jorie or I walked out of this tent, Bass would just let us go," Cody demanded.

"It ain't like you've got a lot of choices out here," Dev said, visibly trying to control an uncharacteristic flash of temper. "You wouldn't understand."

"Try me." The two of them stared at each other.

Sudden as a storm, realization struck me. "Dev, Walter Colburn, the man from home. What do you know about him?" I darted a glance at Cody. That were what was bugging him. His uncle. Cody thought Dev knew his uncle. Or, I furrowed my brow, were it the other way round?

"You don't know what's your messing with," Dev said. "It's complicated."

"Then uncomplicate it," I said. Cody's eyes flashed grateful, my stomach dropped. I turned back to Dev, smiling wide enough to show the white blaze of my teeth. He might be right, but so were Cody. "And make it quick."

"All I know for certain is that Bass don't have what Walter were killed for, she never did. She wouldn't need to. He were just flat-out wrong about that. He should've known better than to keep pressing about it." A deep sadness swept over Dev's face. "I'm telling you the truth, as much of it as I can, you need to believe me, Jorie, please. For your parents' sake, you need to trust to me, it ain't safe for you here."

"I—" Next to me, Cody sucked in a long breath, but just as he did, raised tones cut the air. We froze. The voices grew closer. Louder.

The eager braying of wolves—*Tracers*—joined the fray. The scar on my face began to itch. Fear, real fear, flashed cross Dev's face. Same as it pitted in my gut. The time for talking were done. Believe him or not, we'd only one choice.

I stepped up to Dev's side. "Then let's get the stars out of here."

"You can start by taking these." Dev handed me two guns. A silver-and-ivory revolver and a lean barreled rifle. Both of 'em had seen better days. "They aren't much, I know. But I've never seen Bass not get what she wants. May take her days or weeks but she'll find you. And I don't know what she will do when she does." He placed the guns in my hands before striding to the back of tent. Lifting up a flap of canvas, Dev pulled in two large packs. Both stocked with heavy furs and food. He cinched the tops closed.

I slid the revolver into my pocket. The other I handed to Cody.

"I know it ain't all you need, but it's all I can get. I got some of the things Bass's men took. Put them at the bottom of that pack." The faintest trace of wetness appeared at the corner of his eyes. He wiped it quick away.

"What about Fen and the pack?" I asked.

"Already taken care of. I don't forget my own," he grunted. He shifted, tugging at the edge of his coat.

I studied him. I had so many questions that needed answering. But only one I really cared about deep down. And if these were Warders and they knew Rovers . . .

"Dev?"

"Jorie?" Dev furrowed his brows.

"Do you think she's still alive?"

"Aye, I do. Girl like Bren is worth more to a Rover alive than she is dead." A troubled look passed over his face. *You know that sure as I do.* "So you get her back, Jorie, you hear me. You get Bren back. There ain't much I can say I am proud of in this world, but knowing your family were one of them." He looked me straight in the eye. "And so are you. Your parents saved me once. And it's high time I returned the favor."

"I . . ." I didn't know what to say. And so, stupidly nodded. "I will Dev, I will." I placed a hand on his arm. His mouth set in a firm line as he placed his, callused and cracked, atop mine.

"I know you will," he said. "You aren't Kit and Harrow's daughter for nothing."

The howl of wind outside filled the stretching silence with a strange anticipation.

"Right." Dev gave a sniff and rubbed his nose. "You, Southerner, grab those bags and let's get you two the stars out of here. You've got a sister to find."

CHAPTER 25

This Midnight Sun

————◆————

Dev were more helpful then he gave himself credit for.

"Nocna Mora. Now that's two days northeast. If you take the straight line, there should be only one ice stream that crosses that path. It's breaking up real quick, but I were out there not two days ago and it is still passable. If you push it, you might just have a chance," Dev said.

"Got it," I said.

Cody emerged from the tent. A funny look on his face. I didn't have time to worry on it as Dev pressed his hand to mine.

"And I pinched this back. Fixed it for you too. Just in case," he said, taking his fingers away and leaving Cody's silver compass in my palm. "No one should get lost out there."

"Thanks, Dev." I slid it into my pocket before settling the new pack on my shoulders. It were a little too big and I had to tie the shoulder straps together across the front to keep it from slippin. I took a deep breath. Each cold inhale of air filled my lungs, each pump of blood rolling through my veins, clearing my head.

"Ready," I said.

"Good. Cause to outrun Bass, you're gonna need to be. If she wants to find you, Jorie, she will. She's as tied to this land as the snow. Your only hope is that you can move faster than she can hunt. Those wolves of hers aren't called Tracers for nothing." Dev spun on his heel and strode away. He didn't look back. Not once. I didn't blame him. It was always easier that way.

"You ready, Cody?" I asked, turning.

"Ready as I'm ever going to be," he said, staring off to the north. A muddled whiteness was beginning to blot out some of the stars. Another storm were coming. Fast.

"That's not good." I pressed my lips thin, eyeing the vapors. Even for the Flats this were getting ridiculous. We'd bare a break from the last one and now more were building fast over the horizon. It were like breaking waves out at sea. The closer they got the shore, the faster and more furious they came.

"Can we outrun it?" he asked.

No. "Yes."

He looked me over. He heard the lie. A twitch of his lips as he ran a hand over his face.

"I shouldn't have followed. I've only slowed you down. It was selfish. I didn't . . ." He stared out at the bleak white, at the gathering storm. "I didn't understand what I was asking of you, but I do now. And I'm sorry."

I waved a hand. "Maybe that were true at the start, Cody. You know finding that Rover isn't just about Bren for me, right?" *Not anymore.* I were as surprised by my words as Cody were. Interesting.

"You mean that?" he said, eyebrows high.

"What's done is done. Besides, you ain't been all that useless. If you weren't here, who else would I have to tell to stop talkin?" With a twitch of a smile, I took out his uncle's compass, flicking its face open. East of north. Nocna Mora. "I said I'd help you, Cody Colburn, and I still mean to. We'll find that Rover. For the both of us." *Together.* I placed the compass in his hand.

He took it and gave me a grin, a little rock of a thing, but it were from the heart. Raw. And that were enough for me.

To say the going were rough were an understatement. The soft undulating rises we'd covered on the way here soon became steep walls of slick ice. More than once, both of us had either slipped or fallen through what should've been a stable ledge. Legs bursting into a dark hollow of ice below. Right unnerving. All the while the sunlight grew lower and lower.

If the dimming stillness alone weren't bad enough, there were the other things too. Snaps and creaks and whispers that weren't really there. Voices that brushed across your skin when there weren't no breeze. More than once I shot glances over my shoulder. Searching. There were never anyone there. We were alone. Nothing but our own tracks filled with the echoes of starlight rolling over the snow. Right unnerving.

Worse though were the aurora tipping over the horizon. The farther we went, the more the verdant glow of the northern lights overhead shifted, changed. At first I thought I were hallucinating. But soon there were no denying that the comfort of the once soft greens and blues were gone. The night sky burned with red. As if we were walking not into the night but into the heart of a raging fire. As if, just over the curve of the world, great flames raged. And the brighter it became, the darker the red in the white snow bled under our feet. The world began to take on a wicked, menacing feel. Nothing felt . . . right.

As if the very world had begun to bleed.

I lost track of time as the sky raged in that unsettling bloom of unwelcome color. Finally, when I were near to collapsing, I squeezed Cody's arm. He started, missing a step. I mimed drinking. I could feel the relief wash out from him. With heavy legs, we both lurched to the ground.

Cody and I slumped back to back, sitting on our packs on the hard ice below us. My whole body ached with the cold. Cody handed me back the flask of water. I slugged back a long pull, the liquid running down my throat like fire. I stumbled to my feet.

Cody groaned. "Jorie, I don't think I can get up."

I stretched out my hand toward him. "You can. We can rest at first light, I promise." We were still too close to Bass to stop now.

Gritting his teeth, Cody grasped my arm and I yanked him up. We hefted our kits up onto our shoulders and with groans got to walking. One foot in front of the other through the uneasy night.

Dawn hit like a sudden shock. A burst of golden light, it cut across the path, cascading across the skin of the world, mixing the reds and greens and whites, torching them away.

We ate a little of what dried meat Dev had given us. It were salty and sweet. I really hoped it were deer. As I pulled at the last stringy rips, some of which found their way to catching in my teeth, I'd an idea.

"Cody, move your pack over here, will ya."

"Why?"

"Just do it, alright." With stiff arms and a hiss against the pain, Cody complied, mouth still working slowly against his portion of our beggar's feast.

When I'd finished we'd a shallow curved hole in the snow three feet wide. I maneuvered his pack and mine around the outside, balanced like a set of timber beams. A frame.

"What are you . . . ?" But then Cody got it, grabbing his own handful of snow. Insulation.

Within no time, we had a rounded, hollowed-out dome of snow. It weren't a tent, and it weren't really out of sight. But it were a shelter.

Dropping to my belly, I slithered through the narrow entrance and drug myself inside. Cody were in a moment later. He kicked up snow across the entrance, sealing us in. I pushed my finger through a couple of places in the roof, to let in air and breath out. Protected from the cold but suffocated under the snow were no better than being froze. Dead were dead.

Cody gave me a tired smile, which I returned, shifting around to sit back to back. My fur-covered head resting against Cody's, his shoulders curled close against mine, I finally let my eyes close.

No howls came as we rested. No one broke down the snow around us. I had more than half expected to be yanked from our sleep kicking and screaming. Instead, when I awoke, I had to kick my way out through an extra foot or so of freshly fallen snow.

It was midday, the weak sun at its zenith. Not a long sleep, but long enough.

All around our shelter, the Flats were blank. Not a scrape or footprint—animal or otherwise—marred the perfect snowy surface of the land. Like the porcelain skin of a doll, it were white against white, low clouds coating the horizon. Merciful, the wind had died in the night. Though along the horizon the gray-green promise of yet another ice storm were blowing in from the west. Usually we'd a day at least between them. Now we'd only hours. Faster, harder. The storms were getting worse.

Cody handed me the compass. "I think it'll work now."

I flicked open the cover. The three happy little metal hands pointed south. I turned round in the snow till those hands found home. Pressing a palm to the comforting warmth of the stone at my neck, I spun, coming to a dead stop facing our new path. Facing Nocna Mora. I marked the path and snapped the cover closed and held it out.

"Keep it," he said, eyes fixed as hard as mine.

"Ain't mine to keep." I shook my head and pressed it into his palm.

With a faint shadow of a smile, Cody slid it into his coat.

We ate our meal in silence. The unwarmed fat crunched between my teeth, surprisingly sticky.

"How much farther?" Cody asked, swallowing the last of his food.

"A day, day and a half at most." It's what Dev had said, hoping it were true. But the fact we hadn't yet been run down and weren't dangling at the end of Bass's bad mood were all the proof I needed. Dev hadn't lied. Least about helping us get away.

"Good. Cause I cannot feel any of my toes."

I winced. I had been wondering about that. He'd been limping something fierce. Like as not his toes were the size of plumped grapes, red and bloated. It were the first thing they did before they turned black. And rotted off.

I slipped off my gloves. My pinky fingers were none the better. Plump as fish left out in the sun. And they hurt. Still, red and painful weren't black and dead. Gloves on, I stood back up. Hand wrapping tight around my revolver's grip. Rest over.

The rolling hills soon turned into an unnerving sea of smooth sheets of ice. Freeze that should have been many feet thick. Only it weren't. And the farther out we got, the thinner and more uneven it became. Worse if we were to be unlucky enough to meet what I knew passed silent and hungry beneath the ice. White and eyeless, sleeper sharks lurked under the ice. To make matters worse, the fresh dusting of last night's snow added more slip than grip to our track.

Made for right treacherous walking. Cody had fallen twice. And even I had slipped. The heel of my hand still smarted wicked from my fall. Not that I were complaining. It were the least of my hurts. I rubbed the pendant between my cupped hands, letting the warmth seep slow into my palms. The white mist of my breath swirled delicate soft around the stone, leaking out and away from between my fingers.

We were only an hour out from dusk, passing in the shadow of a great glacier, when I caught it. A muted shifting. I'd heard it for about an hour, and dismissed it as just the wind. Only as I slipped off my hood, the world pressing cold and dangerous still against my skin, there weren't no wind. The hairs on the back of my neck stood up.

"Cody, hold up! Stop!" I said, pulling my stride up short, skidding a few inches. My right hand thrust straight out in front of me. My arm. It was shaking. Not with cold, but with the moving of the ice below my feet.

Yards in front, Cody came to a slithering stop, his rifle raised quick. He turned back to look at me. His face a mask of worry and confusion.

"What is it, Jorie, are they back? We are almost—"

A low cracking, like the rumble of a sea giant's bones, reverberated through my body. I stood motionless, my breathing taut, and looked down.

It came again. My eyes went wide and I looked up. Cody dropped his gun to his side. His gaze snapped onto mine.

The sound. It were coming from the ice.

CHAPTER 26

Under Thin Ice

R un!" But there were no need to have hollered it. Cody were already sprinting. In the wrong direction.

In front of him, big splinters of ice shot into the air, churning freezing water and slabs of crystal shot to the skies. They shuddered with a controlled violence.

"Cody! Turn back! Come on," I screamed it. And I don't know if he heard me over the din, but he did turn. I waved frantic. He began running toward me.

And then he reached me, slipping and grabbing my arm. I caught him.

"You alright?" I asked.

"I think so." He brushed hair from his face.

Heart racing, I helped Cody regain his balance.

"That was—" Wicked lines of black burst into the ice under our feet. Horror seized me. The whole thing was breaking.

And we were still on it.

"Go!" I shoved Cody out in front of me. "Run."

We ran. I darted to my left, away from the snaking black under my feet, and picked up my pace. I didn't right know where I got the speed, but I reckon if I hadn't found it, I'd be dead.

Panting, I collapsed, staring back the way we had come. There weren't nothing there except a great gaping hole. Lashing water. Churning house-size ice boulders were tossed into the air with no more effort than a drunk tossing his dice.

A moulin. A vertical well of fractured ice, it plummeted down into the blue abyss below. A crack split up from the beneath, its tendrils slinking and cracking the meters thick ice all around it. Tears in the frozen skin of the world.

As I stared, a wicked-sharp horn thrust through the surface of the sapphire-clear water. A massive gray narwhal, his back covered in scars and red slashes, crested bright and proud.

I gaped as the beast tossed his giant head, spraying water and ice into the air all around him. I'd never seen them that big. The whale could have fed an entire village on meat and oil and fat. For years.

Then as quick as he materialized, he were gone. Swallowed whole into the blue heart of the freezing waters below. Cody and I exchanged a long look. The serenity of the moment only ruined by our laughter. Hiccups and hollers dispelling the sharp cut of adrenaline snapping through our bones, making it easier to breathe.

"Did you see it?"

"A whale!"

I wiped the frost from my eyes and stood up, sobering quickly when my vision, blurry with the flush of flight, broke sudden into focus. My stomach dropped.

The ice were unstable for hundreds of yards around. Fractured. In every direction. Save one. The way we'd come.

"We're gonna have to go back." A deep groan escaped my lips. Wincing, I hefted my pack and got to walking. Cody following quick at my side. From the sky overhead, little flakes of snow began to fall. Cold and pure and picturesque. And very much unwanted.

We broke for lunch late.

"Who do you think we'll find in Nocna Mora?" Cody asked.

I glanced in that direction and away. "I—I don't right know. Bren, I hope."

A flicker of a smile played across his lips. "I know, me too. Hoping, I mean. But do you think we will find the Rover?"

"Yes." We had to. There weren't no other options to entertain.

"Do you think he'll be waiting for us? Him and that wolf?"

"Yes." It certain weren't a pleasant thought. True ones hardly ever were.

Cody looked thoughtful for a long time. "I just can't shake the feeling we are running into a trap. One we can't see."

"Worse comes to worst, we fight. You shot that ox well enough." I ran a hand over my bruised ribs.

Cody snorted. "I guess I did. But that was different. We didn't have any other choice. It came at us, not the other way around. If I hadn't shot it, the beast would have killed you." He pushed the snow in a circle at his feet. "I never have been very good at fighting. My uncle always said so. Told me I'd not the aptitude for it."

"And you think I do?"

Cody looked at me doubtful.

"Fair enough." My stomach gave a funny little lurch at that. But I'd no right to it. The notion that I were anything but that uncaring, that hard. I'd given him no reason to think anything else. "Whatever happens, you and me, we'll handle it, alright?"

Cody frowned.

"I'll just figure it out when it comes." Like I always did.

"When it comes is not a plan. You said you had a plan." Unappeased, Cody sunk his teeth into one of the last pale yellow fish Dev had given us.

"I said I would think of something and I will. We've been a bit too busy trying not to die, if you ain't noticed." Even to me my words came out defensive and harsh. I cringed. Cody were right and I knew it.

It were long odds, us makin it alive. Even longer were the chance of us making it there with all our wits intact. High risk, high reward. Sometimes one bad shot were all you got. Way I figured, if you had it you took it. From over his dinner, Cody looked up at me expectant like.

"Well, I ain't planning on taking 'em by force, if that makes you feel any better."

He raised an eyebrow and smartly held his tongue.

I tossed my hands into the air.

Only thing worse than a man who were right was a man smart enough not to tell you so.

CHAPTER 27

A Hollowing Light

I t were there. Right there.

I'd swear to it, though in the two days we'd been out here, I could bare tell what were real and what were delusion. I rubbed at the ice covering my eyes, at the pain of the crystals forming at the edges of my skin, the cracks in my lips. Though it did no good. My vision, it didn't right change. There weren't no mistaking it.

A light. Bright and burning.

From out in the misty darkness, a single lantern shone. So small and dim at first that I could bare understand what I saw. I stumbled in the snow. Cody, not three paces behind, staggered to catch me. We had walked near to all day and all night, though I could no longer be sure, as the heavens had become more and more alight until naught but red skies burned overhead. It had been alright, until a storm had blown in.

But even the thick blanketing of the snows and the raging of winter winds could not dampen the skies. And so, we had stumbled. And now I were seeing lights in the darkness.

Yellow. The color brushing bright against the dark. A light swaying with the lurching gait of the person holdin it. Their face half-hidden by a hood pulled high.

Great spikes of burned and broken buildings erupted from the crimson ash-flecked snow. The holder limping straight toward the center of the ruins, a spark dancing down the spine of the hollowed-out carcass of a town.

I knew it in my bones.

Nocna Mora.

We had made it.

CHAPTER 28

Out of the Mists

———◆———

Behind the figure struggling down the main street, an empty black mountain loomed ominous and alone. Heads and hoods lowered against the approaching storm, we pressed in after, following close as I dared.

Main street were littered with the shells of burnt-out buildings. Hollowed-out houses, inns, and stores, now little but wooden carcasses jutting from the snow. The sad remnants of a once-prosperous mining community lay silent and broken, bare before the coming storm. At the very end of the road, closest to the mines, only one building still stood tall.

I darted behind the nearest shelter. Heavy winds stirred, eddying the man's lonesome lantern light. I shifted my legs.

Taking Cody's hand, I ran forward, ducking in tight behind a rusted-out water tower. Cody pointed downward. Footprints—two sets of footprints—lay all round the water drum. One human. One very far from human. The Rover. It had to be. Cody took a step toward the street.

"Wait." I put out an arm. "Watch."

Cody stilled.

At the end of the lane, the trembling light paused on the threshold of the house. For a long moment, the man did naught but stand before the door. Finally he pulled something from his pocket. Only to drop it in the snow. He scrambled round for a long minute, before standing with a grunt. A moment later he lurched forward and rammed the door with his shoulder. Spikes of ice cascaded down over his head. Bashing the dirt and snow from his boots on the step, he shoved the door the rest of the way open.

A shimmer of hot air leaked out around the doorframe. He paused on the threshold. Lips moving, but this far away his voice were nothing but air. Another moment and the man staggered, falling back hard into the snow. The lantern fell to the ground; flame sputtering out against the white. With an obvious effort he righted himself and disappeared inside.

Disbelief washed through me. He were drunk.

In the highest of the house's first-floor windows a blue light snapped into existence. The light went out. Then back on. Then out. No, not out. Moving. As if it were being dragged, or—

A hand gripped my shoulder. I jerked back.

"Stars, you scared me," I said, moving a hand to my chest. A familiar warmth curled up my fingers.

"Sorry," Cody whispered, kneeling at my side.

"We have to get closer, figure out if it's him." It had to be, it just did. "And if he's really alone. We can start with—"

"Jorie," Cody said urgent.

"What?" My eyes on the house where the blue light had finally stopped.

"Just look!"

"Really, Cody." I tore my eyes from the house. "This had better be—"

There, stalking silent between the twisted-out ruins of the town, were a sliver of shadow, black mountain mines smooth behind its path. A wolf's shadow.

The Rover's Tracer.

The beast's eyes glowed unnatural gold. Snow began to fall faster. Not a flake landed on it. As if even the storm were afraid.

I bare breathed. My hand stiff on Cody's. Then the wolf gave a massive shake of its head and turned its path back down the lane. Away from us. A hand brushed down my neck. A whisper of laugher. I glanced over my shoulder. The red night howled, but there were no one there. I scrubbed a hand over my face. Hard enough my skin burned with the contact. Cody's hand squeezed my arm.

"Alright?" He narrowed his eyes at where I were looking.

"Fine. Never better."

He raised a brow.

I shrugged him off. Cody frowned, but dropped his hand. Out in the lane the wolf was gone. This was it. We had to get to that house. Now. Before the wolf came back. Before the Rover weren't alone.

Quick as a snow fox on the hunt, I sprinted from our outpost and across the street. The bastard was not going to get away. Not this time.

CHAPTER 29

Hide Your Fires

———◦———

The building was snugged up tight to the side of the black mountain, a splinter lodged deep in the otherwise perfect smoothness of the stone.

The place were in better condition than I'd thought. It were also larger. But for all its windows, it mercifully had only the two external doors. Done circling, we slunk careful to the back. I ran my hand over the rusted door, catching on the lock. Icicles cracked under my touch. Broken, they scattered to the ground. I glanced over at Cody. He nodded. He'd wait a minute to make sure no one were coming after, then follow.

Bare breathing, I turned the knob real slow. But the door was not locked and gave easy at my pressure.

Quiet as I could, I pushed it open. And entered into a disaster. Painted cabinet doors hung at all angles off rusted hinges and thick strips of paint curled from the wall like peeling skin.

Dirty pots and pans were stacked high in a cracked stone sink. And what surface weren't covered with broken things were covered in rubbish.

I stepped into the room. A moment later and Cody were there. Grimy ash-covered floorboards moaned with the pressure of my boots. I cringed. A path wound across the room and through a high molded archway leading into a dim hallway beyond. From which the smell of smoke wafted in eddying bursts of cool air. Someone had smothered a fire. I exchanged a long look with Cody. Recently smothered.

A slow grinding, dull and muted, came from the second floor. Right above where we stood. Cody and I froze, listening hard. But the noise died and didn't come back. I gestured toward the hallway. Cody nodded.

Pressing tight to the shadows on the walls, we slunk forward. I struggled to keep my breathing smooth. To stay quiet. The hall were warmer than I'd expected. Broken and dusty paintings hung at odd angles, some fallen to the floor so we had to take care to step over the fractured frames.

Three rooms led off the hall. What had once clear been a dining room and two small bedrooms were now all of them empty, save the moldy overturned furniture. That left only one place to go.

Ahead of us at the far end of a hall, a single set of high-railed wooden stairs loomed up and into the darkness of the second floor. Slipping out of the last of the bedrooms, I raised my gun.

"I'm going up," I whispered. "You can stay down here if you want." There were no way the Rover had just left. We would've seen him.

"No. If you are going, then I am going with you." His eyes searched the dark ahead.

I nodded grim and took a deep breath. No noise came down from the floor above.

At the top of the stairs, I slunk over the decaying threads of a once-blue-and-green rug. Heels catching in the rotting fabric.

There were four doorways here. A tall window stood dim at the end of the hall. The floor behind me gave a squeal of protest and I whirled, gun raised. But it were only Cody. He came to a stop beside me, his body warm next to mine. We searched the rooms. Like downstairs, there weren't anyone here.

But unlike downstairs, it were clear there had been. We stood in the last of the rooms, a sitting room. The reek of tobacco and wet dog filled the air. Ash and dirt and long black fur covered the wood floor. Outside, flurries of snow beat against the windows.

"He couldn't have left," Cody whispered, peering out at the now near whiteout of the storm outside. "Where could he have even gone? He cannot just have vanished."

"Not far, that's for certain." That wasn't a real answer. Outside the wind howled. I tried not think on the Tracer. I ran an uncertain eye over the room.

It didn't instill much confidence. I moved to the far side from the door. A broken mahogany table sat under the window. The red flame of the candle at the center of the table sputtered and went out. On its once-ornate surface the remains of a card game—embossed but dog-eared playing cards—littered the wood.

I ran a finger across the silver-and-blue face of the queen of spades, imagining that the heavy paper was still warm. So close. I ground my teeth. The house were impossibly empty.

"We must've overlooked something." *I* had overlooked something. "Maybe look for a door, a window, something we missed. If this place is like any of the thieves' dens I've heard of, like as not there's a smugglers tunnel hidden . . . somewhere."

There was only one other piece of furniture. A large wardrobe pressed tight against the fireplace. While it rocked heavy full when I kicked it, were itself no hidden door.

Around the fireplace a thick ring of tarnished silver seeped out of the large black river rocks, curving into the stone.

Circle upon circlethe metal inlay spiraled in upon itself. And at the heart of which was a raised wooden carving. Amateur, clear done without an artist's tools, it was plain enough. A wolf's head. I pressed a palm to it. The necklace at my throat went cold. And for a moment there were two distinct heartbeats.

Like a flare in the darkness, that second beat roared inside me, thumping steady behind the warm curl of my ribs. The world blurred. Not again. I jerked away from the stones. No, not the stones. From the silver. I took out the chain. *What have you left us, Ma?*

"The house really is empty," Cody said.

I snapped the necklace back under my clothes. "Is it?" My voice strange calm. "We need to keep looking." I glanced at the wardrobe, resisting the urge to press a hand over my chest. The second heartbeat had disappeared.

"Jorie?" Cody looked at me with concern.

"What?" I turned away.

Cody frowned. "I said, have you noticed it?" Cody had picked up the red candle and were pushing the fresh wax about with his fingers, brows furrowed tight.

"Noticed what?" I pushed aside a thick row of moth-eaten furs. A stack of rotting books filled the back of the wardrobe.

"How wrong all of this is, how out of place." He gestured over the room. "These types of wood—even in the South they are not cheap. And these pieces, they are old. Really old. Like this chair—by the quality of it, it should be in an academy hall, a museum. Not"—he gestured around the room—"wherever this is."

The room spun.

"You alright?" he asked.

I nodded, pressing a hand to my temple. *Focus, Jorie. Don't get distracted.* Must be the cold. Though even as I thought it, I knew I were lying. There was something deeper here, something in Nocna Mora that were more than the lingering strangeness that lived out in the Flats. Unease rolled inside me.

"I'm fine. You're right." I scanned the place with a more critical eye. The pieces here *did* feel misplaced. Heavier. Older. Darker. I stumbled a little, managing to catch myself against the edge of the wardrobe. Which under my weight gave a threatening lurch. Books came crashing out. I froze, my head snapped clear. Cody froze. The air went dead still.

"Merciful stars, I—" A sudden whip of wind snapped my loose hair about my face. I spun round. The distinct reek of whiskey filled the air. All the hairs on the back of my neck stood up. Leaning in, I studied the wardrobe and then pulled back. Looking at the fireplace.

"There's a hole."

"It's a fireplace, Jorie, they tend to have holes," Cody said, coming over to my side.

I gave him the scowl that comment deserved. "That ain't what I mean."

A little smile caught at the corner of his lips.

"Look," I said.

Cody peered into the wardrobe. The breeze stirred again and his eyes went wide. Because at the back of the wardrobe where the books had been, he saw it.

A piece of rusted metal were wedged in tight against the grain, curls of air leaking past its uneven edge. Moving Cody aside, I yanked at it hard. And hissed back a breath. A gaping hole, big enough for a man to crawl through. That were what was behind it.

With the metal sheeting removed, the low whistle of wind filled the room. Bringing with it long trails of hearth ash. Like streaks of sand dragged out by the tide, the swirling ash rushed into the air from the passage beyond. Taking a step back, Cody went and knocked on the stone above the fireplace. We exchanged a look.

Standing up, I pushed my shoulder hard against the heavy wardrobe. I moved it maybe an inch. "Cody, give me a hand." A narrow way in meant a narrow way out. And without knowing what were on the other side, I wanted the widest way out I could get.

Together we pushed the wardrobe away. And there, rimmed in the same tarnished metal as the fireplace, like a gaping black mouth, were a doorway.

CHAPTER 30

What Lays Buried

———◆———

W e need light." I whispered, hunched and awkward near the tunnel's opening.

"Agreed," Cody said.

We were maybe fifty yards in, and the passage had become unbearable close.

"We could burn this," Cody suggested. He pulled out the red candle from the Rover's room.

From my pack, I pulled out the fresh bag of powdered sulfur Dev had given us and rubbed a pinch onto the warm wick. The candle took quick to flame. Which I regretted.

Five feet tall and only two wide, the hand-hewn tunnel walls were propped up with all manner of rough wooden pillars. Insect holes and frost damage plain enough to see.

Cody knocked a hand against the nearest one. Ash and debris filled the air. "These don't seem too stable."

"That's cause they ain't." I kicked the base of the one next to me. Dust went everywhere. "See."

Cody watched wide-eyed as the whole cage of pillars shook. "If you find that reassuring, remind me never to tell you I'm afraid of heights," he said, finally letting out long breath and pushing his hair back. "Especially if we climb anything taller than a horse."

"See, who said you weren't getting cannier?" I said, smiling wide.

"You." He dusted his shirt off. "I believe it was this morning."

"Was it now?" In truth I *were* worried. Mines collapsing weren't uncommon. But I didn't want to worry Cody any more than he already were.

Besides, the Rover *had* gone this way. And so would I. A league or so in I came upon two sets of familiar footprints. Squeezing sideways, I inched us down deeper into the dark.

We must have gone on for a good third of a league before the air changed. The close musty smell of the passage became wetter, thinner. Colder. And in moments it became clear why. This were only a connecting tunnel. Light held out high, I walked down a set of stone stairs out of the Rover's tunnel and into a much larger one.

Hissing a curse as wax dripped hot down my hand, I missed the last step and landed hard on the rough rocky floor below. A sharp breeze greeted me from the left. Outside. I could even smell the bite of fresh fallen snow. The smugglers' tunnel weren't too far from the mine's working mouth then. Not that it mattered now.

Cody landed lightly at my side. "You alright?"

"Fine," I grunted.

"What is this place?" Cody asked, awe plain in his voice.

"Abandoned mine," I said, pointing at the long sets of parallel metal tracks feeding into the distance. Some of which had carts piled high with what suspicious looked like old sticks of dynamite. "We are in the mines of Nocna Mora." I kicked at a pile of old soot-covered stones.

"I thought you said these mines were dry?" Cody asked, running a hand down the cold rock of the wall behind us.

"They are," I said, furrowing my brow. The glitter of quartz blooms sparkled in the candlelight. Veins of what looked like metal coursed through the crystal.

The way the crystals clung looked more like buds on a vine than layers of lifeless stone.

Cody raised an eyebrow. "They don't appear to be that way now."

"They certainly don't," I said, turning away. "Least it answers why Rovers would still be here. Leave it to rats to be scavenging at bones."

Cody thought for a long moment. "The only trouble with that theory, Jorie, is that if these mines aren't dry now, they were never dry. So if that's true, if there was still gold to be had, what made the people here abandon it in the first place? What could do that?"

He weren't wrong. We stared at the dark silence surrounding us.

Cody shook. "It's not right. I don't know much about Northerners, but I know no man walks away from treasure like this." He picked up a piece of quartz that had fallen on the ground.

I blinked. A small line of the precious metal ran through the rock. "Trouble. That's why. Which I don't need to be reminding you, we already got." I snatched the rock from Cody's hand and replaced it. Only reason a man walked away from a little money were because there were much more money. Somewhere else.

Like say, an entire city of gold, locked away deep in the ice. Cody had named the sagas *Aurum et Glacies*. Gold and *Ice*. The clatter of falling rocks echoed from ahead.

"Let's go," I said, and pointed ahead where the tracks split. Sets of footprints ran toward them and then stopped. "He must be walking the lines."

"Seems like it."

The farther we wound, the higher the tunnels grew, and they just kept going deeper and deeper into the mountainside.

As we moved, strange green lights appeared on the ceiling. Little enough at first that I thought it were my imagination. But soon a bed of neon stars covered the cave.

"Never thought I'd see these this far north." Cody's voice a soft whisper at my side. "They usually die in the cold."

"The lights?" I asked confused.

"Amazing, aren't they?" Cody put a hand to his throat. "Up there all alone."

I gave him an odd look.

"They are worms, you know. They've never been reported up here, least that I know of. They tend to like more temperate climates. Coastal tropics and the like." He stumbled a little as we walked, his gaze on the lights.

"Worms? You're telling me all those little lights are *worms*?" I pulled a face.

"They're called night crawlers. The University has an extensive collection in the entomology department. I'd go there when my uncle was too busy, and the other kids were . . ." He shook his head. "They're related to fireflies, though these prefer to hunt in the dark of caves. That green is their bioluminescent light. The worms make it. Acts like a lure, snaring insects as they pass. Beautiful, but deadly. Toxic."

Cody gave me a small smile and we walked on, deadly worms hunting high above, undisturbed by our passage.

The farther in we went, the more different the world around us became. The rough hand-hewn walls of the early mines gave way to rock smooth as melting ice. Walls that radiated a strange heat. I began to sweat, thin streams running down between my shoulder blades and into the top of my pants.

My hands, my feet, my face, they all ached something painful fierce. As did the metal of the pendant around my neck. I tugged it away from my skin.

Too soon, however, we came to an impasse. A tumble of rocks and shale had fallen across the tunnel, blocking it.

Just at the edge of the fall, a slender line of darkness cut through the rocks. A narrow slip of space, just wide enough for one person to squeeze through.

"Someone's made this intentionally," Cody said, pulling on the sides of the passage. "Not even loose."

"Only one way to find out," I said, and pressed myself into the opening. No more than a few yards in, a sudden breeze spat through the space. The candle snuffed out.

I gave a little curse. The rock walls were ragged; edges of stones snagged at my skin, my clothes, my hair. And like tiny teeth, some of them drew blood.

Working hard to control the rising panic, I shoved my body through the high narrow space. Behind me, Cody were doing the same. Only by the rate he were breathing, his fear less contained than my own. Then sudden, without warning, the slither of tunnel exploded upward into the darkness above.

A vast cathedral opened out before us. I relit the wick and scanned the chasm. Directly ahead, like the sun off a fish's scales, a blue flicker of light reflected back at us. So too did the steady clink of metal on rock. Of ax on stone.

In unspoken unison, Cody's hand went to his rifle, mine to my revolver. We were no longer alone. Hasty I pocketed the candle, extinguishing any remaining smoke.

We moved across the space, sticking to the sides of the cave, guns ready. The heavy smell of burned wood, sulfur, and something I couldn't put a name to filled the air.

At the far end, round a series of massive sparkling stalagmites, a slender slice of deep blue light illuminated the air. Bathing us in an uneasy shimmer. As if we was walking below the ice.

Cold air slammed into my front. Like a wall. Goose bumps raised over the front of my arms. After a moment, I gleaned why. Ahead, a wide circular opening gaped in the ceiling of the cave, edges sparkling with piercing spines of melting ice.

The far side of the chamber were dotted with openings to other tunnels. Like numbers on a half-broke clock face, they sat dark and unlit. Eight of 'em in all. Any one of 'em could be the one we wanted. All had footprints going in and out. But there was one tunnel bigger than all the others. Only one with a wolf's prints. A spike of adrenaline shot through me, making my already warm body flush.

It were the one over which a thin stripe of silver had reflected back fish-scale blue. We peered down it. It went—somewhere. Just to see, I looked down the ones on either side. Both of those dead-ended not three hundred yards in. Cody said the same about two of the others.

"Where do you think it goes?" Cody asked.

"No idea. But we gotta pick." I ran a finger cross the swirl of silver. "And this ain't done us wrong yet."

"I don't like it. The air in here *feels* wrong. Like we're pushing through it."

A low, long rumble, like the breathing of the mountain, swelled from the tunnel ahead.

Coming to a bend, the path split three ways. One straight ahead billowed with cold gusts of air. The right one ran warm and smelled of iron and blood. And the left one? It were as cold as the first. Only it weren't black; it glowed with a deep sea of light.

Cody placed a hand on my arm. "It could be a trap." His voice anxious.

"I know." *We are too far in.* So with little other choice, my gun ready and like a moth to the moon, I moved us into the light.

A small half-opened doorway appeared in the stone wall ahead, like a scar of light.

Heart rate spiking, I pushed an eye to the narrow opening. In the dim, a lone male figure crouched over a smoldering fire. A figure I knew well now. I scanned the tiny room, no sign of no one else. No Bren. Desperation bloomed. I made to open the door. A hand caught me. I spun, temper rising.

"Let go," I snarled.

Cody's expression flashed hurt as he took a half step back, but he didn't let go. Scowling, I shook him off. Or tried to.

"Cody, this ain't the time. The Rover is right there, let me go." I hissed it, my hand hovering just over the door. We were so close.

"Jorie, wait. Look," Cody whispered, urgent. He pulled something out of his pocket. "It's not perfect, but it's better than nothing."

I stopped. There were something in his voice. "How did you . . . ?"

Cody shot an uneasy glance over my shoulder to the room behind. "I stole the paper when you were talking with Dev, been working on it when I could. I didn't want to tell you in case I couldn't make it." He shuffled his feet. "I did my best. It won't fool him for long, but it might just be enough to get your sister back."

"I . . ." Words stuck in my throat. "You made a copy of the map. Of Vydra." It felt like someone had shot fire straight into my veins. Everything went hot and numb and burning inside me all at once.

"You said we needed a plan," he said. "And now we have one."

No one had ever in my life given me something near as perfect as this. He were giving me—giving us—a chance.

I didn't know what to say. But meeting Cody's eyes, I knew I didn't need to. He gave my arm a squeeze. And so, straightening my spine, I turned and thrust open the door.

The Rover were crouched over a smoking fire, his hands busy tearing at whatever he were holding in front of him. The air stank of filth and burning fur. He were jabbering on to himself, his entire body moving, jerking odd in the firelight.

Then he half turned, half fell to his side. The entire world slowed.

I took another step into the room. I had the Rover. I had the map. And he would give me my sister.

"Stand up, you coward," I said. "Now." My hand steady, my gun raised high.

Slow as molasses, he stood.

CHAPTER 31

Vengeance Burning

———◆———

J orie, is it?" the Rover asked, chuckling strange. Voice off in a
way that were like he had just stepped to the side of normal. "I
never did ask you your name right and proper like. Too busy,
weren't we?"

My skin crawled. It weren't right. He weren't right. He shifted his
feet, scattering a pile of coals. Little embers, fresh sparks of red over
stone, rolled across the floor. Coming to rest against piles of boxes
and the broken support beam stacked against the wall. Heat snapping at the wood. Hungry. I glanced at them.

I pointed to what he held in his hand. Bren's sweater. "Where is
my sister?"

Smiling slick, he raised what he held in the other hand. A long,
bloodied knife. He met my stare, eyes wild. The look of a man burning desperate. I went cold all over.

"And who else have you brought me to play with? A brother, is
it?" His words slurred together. He swayed ever so slight on his feet.
He spread his oily glare over me and Cody, raising his knife.

There we were, all of us, in the middle of a dead mine.

"Jorie, what's wrong with him?" Cody whispered.

Stars above, those eyes. They were near to completely bloodshot.
Runny red lines webbed over ivory globes. The man was clear gone

off. He were wicked thin now, as if something had melted the fat from his bones, sucked the muscle from out under his skin. Like he'd been hollowed.

"I brought what you wanted." My voice burned colder than ice. "Where is my sister?" I brandished the fake map Cody had made.

The Rover laughed and laughed. His voice a deep hungry echo. It were the kind of laughter that saw unlucky men into their dark and lonesome graves. "You're too late, little girl. Your sister's long gone. I don't need what you have, not no more."

"Liar!" I took a step toward the Rover. "You are gonna tell me even if I have to drag it out of you, intestine by intestine, inch by bloody inch."

"Like to see a wisp like you try," Rover growled.

I shot. Bullet hitting the wall not a half foot from the Rover's skull.

The man's eyes flashed with surprise, and then rage. I smiled. Smiled real wide. Cause I knew then that *buried* was gonna be too good for him.

"I told ya she's gone, traded her on for something better," he leered. "Looks like I didn't need you after all."

I had just three bullets—two now—but the Rover, he didn't know that. I narrowed my eyes, steadying the weight of the gun. "I'll have the truth of it right now—all of it, mind—or so help me I'll shoot. And I promise you I don't need one than one shot."

Ahead of me the Rover didn't move, just widened his drunkard's smile.

An itching sensation, one that I were somehow the one at the wrong end of this exchange, began building in me.

I clenched my jaw. And like all women worth their grit, I doubled down.

"If you don't think I'll do it, you're dead wrong. You don't start talking sense, I start shooting." I near shook with them words, but my hand stayed steady.

"Oh, I'd wager, girl like you, you'd do it alright. Given half the chance." He sloshed a little to the left. His blink slow. "Too bad you got even less than that."

"Not by my count," I said.

The Rover waved his knife in front of him, arm swaying. "Maybe I'll tell ya, maybe I won't. But you tell me something first. Who sent you? Was it that fanatic and her worshipers? Couldn't stand it, could she? Me being right after all this time. Bet it got her down in the banks when they figured out ol' Reeves ain't that easy to kill. Well, it's not me that's the traitor, not anymore." He laughed. "But I ain't too worried." A fervent glint flashed in his eyes. "It's them that'll get what's coming to 'em. I've seen to it right and proper this time, I have."

My finger eased over onto the smooth metal of the trigger.

"Jorie." Cody's eyes reflected glassy and wide in the firelight. "We need to go."

The Rover looked at him up and down, as if seeing him for the first time. He wobbled ever so slightly on his feet. "Look just like your uncle, you do." He were swaying bad now.

"Pathetic," I hissed. "That's what you are." No one said nothing to Cody but me.

"You killed him." Cody didn't scream it, but his voice were deadly still.

A flash of something akin to focus crossed the Rover's expression, and then it were gone. "So what? I did what I did. It's them that's gonna regret it, not me." He tapped his temple with the blunt end of his knife; it came away wet with perspiration.

"You murdered an innocent man and all you have to say for yourself is *so what?*" Cody said incredulous.

"Deserved it. Underhanded, gutless man. I were owed. He tried to cheat me. Took my words, tricked me into telling him things he'd no right to know. Steal a man's coin is one thing, steal his memories—that's another. So I showed him too." Reeves swayed on his feet.

I shot Cody a worried look.

"You deserve worse." His voice brittle, gaze unflinching fixed on the man. The man who'd killed his family. All for the price of a single sheet of paper. For the scratches of a Scholar's pen.

Running the back of his hand over his dripping nose, the Rover laughed ugly. "Oh, I got a lot to say, boy. But here, I got something you can tell 'em." Feral smile spreading like oil across his face. "You tell 'em I ain't sharing nothing with her and her filthy lying pack of Warders, not a single forsaken thing. I *earned* this." He stumbled backward, heels crunching into the coals. He made no move to step out of the flames. "Said it can't be done, but here I am." The Rover coughed, pink-tinged saliva sputtering onto his chin. "And I ain't dead yet, am I?"

Only he was. A thick stain leeched across his shirt, black and red. I knew a mortal wound when I saw it. Little sparks of red and gold licked at his pants. But he only had to live long enough to tell me one thing.

"What have you done with my sister?"

He laughed. "You couldn't save her even if you wanted to. Creature like that woman, a spider in her web, she is. Stories ain't lied about her, no they did not. She were so pleased when she saw what I'd brought with me. . . . Said your sister smelled just right, she did. That she's been waiting for her."

I blinked. "Who, who did you give her to?"

Rover shifted his weight, not hearin me. Little red droplets cascaded from his right side to the ground.

I demanded it again. Rover leered deep. "The woman in the ice, that's who."

"Ice?" The Rover had lost it. "What are you talking about?"

"And all I had to do were hand her over. Some sniffling girl in exchange for everything I'd ever wanted. Everything."

"So where is it then? Everything you ever wanted?" I gestured round the cave.

"Don't have even have the first clue about any of it, do you? About what's here. What's buried in these walls." Eyes flashing, he ran a slow palm down the bare stone, the sickening shadow of a smile leeching over his face. His fingers tracing nothing. There were nothing on the walls. Just exposed rock and frost. "About what I am *owed*."

There it were again. *Owed*. He kept saying it like I should know what the stars he were raving about. I glanced over at Cody, his body rigid, eyes hard, angry. Leaning over, I put my hand on Cody's arm. Mistake.

Seeing my attention swing, the Rover lunged. I turned my head and raised my arm. Bracing for the impact. A shot rang out first.

The Rover screamed, staggering back and against the wall. I weren't sure whose gun had gone off first, mine or Cody's.

Eyes fixed on mine, the Rover wiped at his mouth. A wicked smear of blood scraped along the yellow enamel of his teeth. He licked it away. The bullet had grazed the edge of his cheek. My stomach tightened. Close weren't close enough.

"Foolish brats, you won't win." He spat the words. "I'll walk out of here one way or another. And if you get out of my way and I might just let you live." Laughter high and sharp bubbled from his throat. Blood dripped steady from the wound, pooling in the soft curve of his collar. He raised not a finger to staunch it.

Redoubling my grip on my revolver, I squared my shoulders. "We may be fools, but there is only one loser here. And just to give you a clue, case your little brain needs the help, it ain't the ones pointing the guns."

The Rover smiled feral.

Cody let out a blood-curdling cry. I spun, just as the Tracer sprang from the darkness.

With a scream, the Rover surged right at me. Before I could dodge, he was there. Body looming over mine. His rancid smell thick.

I couldn't move. I were back in the hall with Bren. But then Cody slammed into me, sending both of us tumbling to the right as the wolf passed bare inches over us.

Hitting the ground, I rolled and raised my gun. A dark figure loomed above us. I shot. A man cried out. The Rover stumbled and fell. The cave churned with smoke and confusion. Chaos.

I could hear Cody. But I couldn't see him. The world tilted, as if the very ground were moving. Above me it were all shouting and gunfire.

I pushed up to my side, my hand coming to a stop atop Bren's sweater by the fire. I grabbed it and sprang to my feet. I'd no bullets left. Yanking on what I hoped were his arm, I tore Cody and me out of the room. As we did, Cody turned and fired the last of his shots. An unnatural piercing shook the cave. Filling the air. I didn't look back.

We made it all the way back to the large cathedral when I pulled us up short, panting. I could barely breathe. Cody slumped next to me, hand pressed to the cavern wall. I looked at him. He were covered in blood.

"Jorie. I—I shot him. I've never shot someone before, I didn't mean . . . all that blood." Cody panted.

Neither had I. If the Rover were dead, it were as like my own bullet as Cody's. Unease, guilt, shame swirled in my gut. "First time for everything," I said.

Cody gave a little scuff of a laugh. Weren't no humor in it.

I glanced back over my shoulder. A thick heady smell drifted up from the tunnel behind us. Something hot and rabid. Like the ox.

There weren't time to dwell on it. From behind us a bone-rattling howl seared through the darkness.

We ran.

As we did, the smell of sulfur grew stronger. Sharp. Small stones rained down from the rock overhead. A low rumbling began to fill the air.

"Uh, Jorie." Cody stopped. "What's that smell?"

Fire. Another boom came from the tunnels. Dust billowed out from behind us. The entire world began to shake. Blasts came as fire found the old deposits of explosives. Rotting wood finally gave way.

"Run." My entire body thrumming with fear.

"What?"

I grabbed his arm. "I said run!"

The entire world began to shake.

We ran for our lives.

Smoke pooled in the air above our heads. It were getting harder and harder to breathe. Sprinting, we turned the last corner, squeezing past a large fallen boulder and collapsed beam support. And there— the smugglers' tunnel.

I put a hand over my mouth, coughing from the smoke. But in a boom of rock and earth, our exit fell out of existence. I blinked frantic. There had to be another way out. There had to.

There.

All those metal tracks converged on one tunnel. We ran for it; a whip of fresh air swirled the smoke around me like ghosts.

"Go!" I pushed Cody ahead of me.

From behind us a gunshot rang out. It hit the tunnel over my right shoulder. A howl soon followed.

I bit back a string of curses. The exit was ahead of us now. My heart sunk. Not cause the way were blocked. But because outside the exit, the world were a wall of gray. A storm.

I glanced back over my shoulder. Another shot rang out, as did the rumble of breaking rocks. On the threshold, Cody and I exchanged a long look. Neither of us had any bullets left. Between the fire, the rocks, and the Rover, there were only one option left.

"We may have shot him," I called out, wind whipping at my face, "but we ain't killed him." Yet.

Hand in hand, before I could think better of it, I threw us out and into the waiting mouth of the raging storm.

Stars save us.

CHAPTER 32

The Taste of Hunger

———◆———

We made it maybe twenty paces.

A whitewall of storm battered us. We must have emerged somewhere just outside of Nocna Mora. I could tell no more than that. A crack of wind tore at my back, driving me to my knees. I bare felt the impact as Cody's hand was ripped from mine. His body tumbled away. Flotsam against the freezing ridge around us. Panic gripped me. I could not see him.

My ears rang with wind and cold. I scrambled to stand, to rise against the onslaught of the storm. My feet slipping again and again against the ice. Finally, I got to my hands and knees.

"Cody!" I screamed it. The only reply were the unrelenting tear of the wind. I fell to my side. Desperate, I gasped for air. The hammering of my heart a dull pain against my bruised ribs. I tried to stand. To do anything. I fell.

"Cody!"

No reply. I had to get up. Gathering what little I had left, I forced myself to my feet, muscles straining into the wind. I tried to raise my scarf to protect my face. Some measure of warmth. It weren't there. I gasped out into the white. There weren't nothing but storm. I stumbled.

I clasped a hand over my eyes as the snow moved faster. As it twisted around me. Pressure, like unseen hands, snagged at my limbs, pushing at my back. Forcing me down. Panic rose, slick and red in my belly. This were it. Stars, this was how I died.

In the haze, a body, heavy, stumbled into me. I cried out. The weight a spike against my side. I reached out. This time my fingers closed round something real. Solid. An arm out of the storm.

And then the body covering me, blocking out the worst of the wind. Cody's face met mine. Relief washed over me. All of it gone a moment later as a massive gust of wind tore us apart. I lurched, finding his shoulder. And I held. I held on to him tighter than I ever held anything before. Bracing against the blizzard, Cody mouthed something. I couldn't hear. Eyes on mine, he gave a pained twist to his lips.

Stars, we needed to get out of this storm. But the entrance, even if it weren't collapsed with fire and rock, had long since disappeared.

Again Cody tried to speak. But the wind were still too loud. He pointed to his left. With great effort Cody tugged at my arm and stumbled us a half step forward.

"Don't let me go." I screamed it. It were naught but a whimper past the blaze of my teeth, but he must have heard. His grip doubled on mine.

We staggered to the left. The wind shifted, tossed us yards to the side. My back slammed into rock. My eyes watered at the impact. Snow slashed into my skin. I spread a hand over the stone. The mountain. Merciful stars.

I hugged my body tight against the crag. Pressing into the solidness of it. Next to me Cody, struggling, did the same, his hand still wonderful tight in mine. Now we just had to find a way to get back inside.

Again and again we pushed ourselves away from the rock, only to be slammed back. No cave or crack or refuge in sight. A cry pierced the air. I stilled. It came again. The whole world stilled, as if the storm itself had simply paused. And in that uncanny breath of calm I heard it clear.

Singing.

A woman's voice. The song rose and fell in crashing melody. Whipping through me. Notes like a caress ran through my hair. Sounds trailing smooth along the curve of my throat, over my skin. Gentle. I shook my head. The song snapped. The world crushed back into me. Cody were there. Mouthing words I couldn't hear. Staring at me, hair beating in the storm. I must be losing it. I wondered brief if this were what you heard at the end. When the ice-fever took hold. When your mind could no longer separate dream from life. The story from the real. When it were time to stop.

Not yet.

The words screamed up from somewhere deep inside me. Somewhere raw and primal and alive. A pulsing living heat at my core. And like the snap of a whip biting at your skin, determination tore through me.

I gripped Cody's hand. *Not yet.*

The fight weren't over till it were over. And I for one weren't anywhere near done. I scanned the mountain. There had to be something here, some opening, some crevasse, some—anything.

And there.

A miracle of a small fissure in the face of the cold rock. It might just be enough. It had to be enough. It would be enough.

My back braced against the beating wind, head down, legs burning and lungs pumping, I pulled us both toward the shelter. Inch by freezing inch. I pulled us both.

Not yet.

CHAPTER 33

Tombs Made of Stone

———— ◆ ————

The weight of the storm fell from my shoulders. Sudden as the dropping of a stone.

I collapsed to my knees. It took hysterical long to settle my gasps into something more like breathing. Inside the fissure of mountain, it were a different world. Silent.

Panting, I pressed my arms to the hard earth below. My ears rang with loss of the wind. My face and limbs burned with it.

I shoved Cody up to sitting. Before I fell against his side. The wind scratched at the entrance. Hungry. Angry. Waiting. Around us long veins of silver ore spiraled into darkness above. A chimney of perfect stone.

We had been so close.

I am so sorry, Brenna. I am so sorry. I tried.

I took a long shaking breath, ribs rattling against my burning lungs. Cody's head resting against my shoulder. His breathing shallow and painful.

I pressed a hand to Cody's head, leaning my cheek to his.

Breathing with him. Out in. Out in. Just breathing.

"I'm sorry, Cody," I whispered. His hand tightened in mine. And I knew in that moment, in a spike of painful clarity, what all those people out there on the Flats had learned long ago. What they knew as they felt the blood freeze in their veins, their breath pool in their lungs. No one was coming.

Because out here there were no one left to save you.

My head went light as a growing warmth built on my chest, as the storm, cold and hungry, blotted out the rest of the world.

CHAPTER 34

A City of Ice and Bones

⸺ ◆ ⸺

I did not expect to wake. Honest I didn't.

I blinked into the unwelcome glow of an unfamiliar space and sat up. My head swirled. All around me sheets of solid ice, perfect as crystal, formed the stories-high walls encasing me. Not a window or door to be seen. And above it all a massive dome glittered like the facet of an insect's eye.

Through it light dripped, syruped and slow. Beams of a glowing gold that fractured inside the walls, threading color through everything in the room.

Every once in a while, the path of light would catch and then disappear into the ice. Gone as surely as it had been swallowed whole, only to reappear impossibly, colors that were there and then gone again in the blink of an eye. Like the flash of a fish under a darkening tide. I began shaking. I must be dreaming.

On aching feet, I stood and pressed my palms into the wall. Cold burned through me and I drew them to my chest. Cause despite the fact that I weren't no colder than if I were standing by a fire, the walls were made of real ice. I stared at them for a long, slow minute.

An ice-fever dream, that's what this were. What it had to be. But try as I might, I did not wake. Everything around me were undoubted real. And it were all made from ice. The basins, the shelves, the chairs.

All ice. Flakes of gold and green sparkled within the clear freeze of the waters. Glimmering in the kaleidoscope of light.

Including Cody.

His body were laid out against the smooth floor, a soft pink filling his cheeks. I put a hand on his chest. Gentle rise and fall telling me he were still alive.

"Cody," I whispered, trembling his shoulders careful like. His eyes fluttered open. And flashed with a brief look of panic, whole body going rigid under my hands, before he saw who it were waking him.

With care I helped him sit. He tilted his face up to mine. "Where are we?" His voice a bare whisper scattering out in the vast ice world around us.

"I—I don't know." I stared at my hands. At the little moons of gray under my nails, the dirt and grime. The memory of the Rover, bloody and crazed, flashed behind my eyes. "But it is certain real enough."

"Help me," Cody pleaded and, with a hand under his arm, I got him to his feet. We traced the perimeter of the high-ceilinged room.

I frowned. Cody's limp were gone. As were all the cuts and scratches on his skin. None of our clothes were torn. Panic struck and my hand flew to my neck. Bren's necklace were still there. But our guns were certain gone.

"Is there no way out then?" he asked.

"No." But even as I said it, it was wrong. Across from us were a slim door cut out of the ice. Its entrance folded over on itself, so you could only find it if you looked at it just right. A foot left or right and it looked solid as the walls around us.

We walked over to it. Silver bars trimmed a doorway just wide enough for one person to slip through. Beyond it a great slither of stairs curling down and away.

"I don't like this," Cody said.

"Neither do I." And though it certain beat freezing to death in an abandoned mine shaft, I had a more worrying thought. We didn't walk here ourselves. Nor did we tend our wounds. I eyed the doorway.

Despite begin able to see all around, every angle, every direction, there were the unshakable feeling that—*we are being watched.*

Sudden as a storm, waves of ease ran through me, warm. It was safe here. And I was so tired. Yawning, I blinked slow down at the floor, eyes aching with sleep. I should lie down again. Rest. That would be best. Just sleep. And let everything go away. Dream.

I jerked my head back, eyes flying open.

"I . . . what?" I said confused, finding I had already lain on the ground. I gritted my teeth against that feeling of ease, comfort, of warmth. Because it weren't right. We weren't safe.

The moment I thought it, like the sheen of oil over water, the false feeling of comfort slid smoothly away. I jerked to my feet. Next to me, Cody were curled up, a tight ball against the ice.

"Wake up," I said. This time when I woke him, I weren't too gentle. "Something's real wrong."

He blinked sleepily up at me. "But I am so tired, Jorie. Aren't you tired? We should rest." His voice were hollow. His eyes smooth as the light dripping down overhead. I shook his shoulders till his teeth right chattered.

"No, we should not."

The glazed expression on his face rippled away. He began to shiver. My gaze drawn, moth to a fire, to the door that stood in front of us, waiting.

"Maybe we're dead?" Cody asked optimistically.

I snorted before I could help myself. "I don't reckon I'd end up anywhere like this. Considering."

I ran my fingers over the oxidized silver edges of the door. A shiver passed through the cold white of my bones as a sense of déjà vu near to overwhelmed me.

As if we had been here before. Had this conversation before. I grunted.

That couldn't be right. Couldn't it? I took a step toward the open doorway, and as before, a sense of calm filled me. But that weren't right. I weren't *anything* like calm. And there were nothing right natural about that feeling. From down the hallway, a flicker of light caught my eye. But when it didn't come again, I pushed it aside. Trick of the light, was all. Must be. I shifted my feet over the slick floor.

"Jorie, are you alright? You look"—Cody raised a brow—"strange."

I frowned in reply.

In the silence, Cody ran a hand over the smooth ice of the wall at his side. Awe covered his features. "You know what this place looks like?" he said, voice low and breathy.

Yes. "No." *Don't say it, don't make it real.* But wishing weren't going to work.

"Vydra. My uncle was right. It's real and we've not just seen it, we are in it." He slid down the ice wall to sit, legs splayed out in front of him.

"Maybe." I fixed Cody with a long stare. But our location weren't what had pins racing down my spine. Alive or dead, there should have been someone here. "But if you're right and this *is* Vydra, what I want to know is where precisely is the Ice-Witch."

"The Witch." He whispered it, mouth opening a little in surprise before he closed it quick. "We need to go." He made to move for the door.

I grabbed his arm. A sudden thought struck me. "Is that what the Rover were rambling on about? Giving Bren to her, to the Witch?"

I needed to think.

I pressed the palms of my hands into my eyes.

Footsteps, fast and hard, fell from out in the hallway. Cody and I jolted to our feet. When had we fallen asleep? Why could I not stay awake?

The footsteps grew closer. And faster. We exchanged a look. I ran to the ice door, pressing my body flat as I could against the side. And careful peered out. From the far edge of the corridor, I caught a flash of figure. Slender and running. A wave of blond hair. And then it were gone. *She* were gone. My heart jumped into my throat.

"Bren!" I screamed it. It had to be her. But before I were across the threshold, Cody's arm flashed out in front. Nearly making me fall. I batted it away. "What's wrong with you? That's Bren. You saw her."

"Maybe." Cody's frown deepened, face skeptical, reserved.

Everything I should have been but couldn't make myself be.

Hope, as deadly as a dagger pressed to my ribs, were intoxicating. My body burned with the push of it. For Bren it didn't even matter if that feeling were real. Even if there were the brittlest of chances, I would gamble for it. Part of me heard Cody, heard the logic of what he were sayin. The impossibility of our situation. But the rest of me? The rest of me reared up raw and ragged and grabbed hold of that voice and drowned it. Drowned it down deep, till it were nothing but a whisper pressing against the soft underbelly of my heart. Cause I would find her.

"We are following. Now."

Cody shook his head. "It could have been anything. We can't trust what we see in here, Jorie. All those books I've read, they've all have one thing in common."

"And what is that?"

"The power here, it distorts you, twists you up until you cannot tell what is real and what's not. You can't fight what you can't see, Jorie, what's inside you already. We can't just—"

I didn't care. I shoved his arm out of my way. I had already lost her. I wouldn't do it again.

CHAPTER 35

The Ice Garden

———◆———

This hallway was made from the same shining slick ice as all the others.

Two stories high, the carved walls coiled around themselves, the frozen body of a hollow serpent. The floor was so polished it reflected our footsteps back up at us. Walls rippled with the passage of our shadows through the light. I ran until my lungs burned. Cody panting at my side, saying words I weren't listening to.

I lost count of the turns and slowed to a walk. Caution, which had begun a slow buzzing at the base of my spine, were now blaring bright. We were doing little but spiraling in upon ourselves. The air began to take on a colder, heavier edge. I slowed.

But I needn't have. There weren't no one here.

Finally the corridor came to an end. A tall arched doorway loomed before us. I exchanged a long look with Cody. Either we went on or we went back. And I for sure weren't going back. Together, we walked through it.

A massive chamber erupted grand and cold before us.

A deep river-blue bathed the mammoth space, swaths of light echoing off every bend, every dip and curve. And it weren't empty.

We slipped inside. The great forms of animals pressed in on us from all sides. Their bodies encased by ice, as if simply caught. A life suspended. I ran a hand over the thick curve of ice, fingers lingering in the smoothness of the cold, as I passed under the heavy jaws of what at first glance was a bear.

I took my hand back from the bear's mouth, shivering at the teeth. Where there should only have been one, a second and third row lingered behind the first.

The farther we went, the stranger and more obvious the distortions became. As if someone had played around, taking bits of one animal and linking them into another. It were a menagerie of impossible creatures. Each different. Each one more unsettling than the last. And it didn't seem to end. An eagle with the body of fox. A great ice bear with the tail of a serpent behind.

Row after row of incredible things. Only here and there, small gaps existed in the order. A place where a creature had once been. Only now it weren't.

I missed a step as I passed a particularly fierce-looking wolf. Its coat thick with not fur, but with vines and branches, bits twisted as an old oak. A painful burning built against the hollow heat of my chest. I pressed it down as I made my way into the center of the great cavern.

Cody were already there. He were stopped, looking up into the snarling face of a massive ice bear. This one were different than the others. Thorny cords of black and green wound tight around the bear's body, digging sharp into its chest and neck. Cords that looked the same as those I'd seen winding about the neck of that white ox out on the Flats.

And where the thorns broke the hide, tiny drops of frozen red— little blooms of ruby in the ice—hung suspended. A few, those closest to the animal's throat, swirled with something else. A black twisting just under the red's surface.

The echo of slow dripping water filled the room. My hand stilled as I suppressed a wave of unease. Next to me, the muscles in Cody's jaw cracked tight. But nothing moved.

The strangest one of all were yet to come. Set back, it were near as big as all the others combined. Massive scales the size of a prospector's sifter covered a thick, ropy body. Long limbs were tipped by thick claws, talons gouging into the floor below. A thin collar of red encircled the sinewy neck, above which swirled deep blue eyes near as big as my skull.

"What is it?" I whispered.

Something akin to awe spread over Cody's face. "I've read about these before." He ran a hand over the curve of a talon. "Never in anything but story books, but they—uh—seem rather large."

That were an understatement.

"One spoke about a great beast, stories long, that swam in the Northern Sea. With impenetrable scales of gold and ice, it roamed the ocean hunting prey. They say the last thing you would know were the crash of the harsh Northern Sea and a great pair of eyes that shone like slivers of ill-fated moons over the water. And when men tried to capture it, the beast would simply vanish in a burst of golden foam. Sailors said the breaking of a rose-red sky at night was omen for the beast's arrival."

"That don't sound a very pleasant thing."

"Oh, it really wouldn't be. These teeth"—he reached up—"are shaped for tearing. Can you imagine the damage they could do?"

Well, that didn't take much imagination. I opened my mouth to tell Cody so. A flicker of motion crossed the far wall. I jerked Cody away, darting us behind the sea beast's leg. Pressing a finger to my lips, I pointed to the far wall. "I thought I saw something. Moving."

"There," Cody hissed, pointing to the far end of the chamber. "It looks like a cage," Cody said, confused. "Why would they need a cage? Those creatures are all made of ice, aren't they?"

Fear, quick as a knife in the night, bit into me as I glanced over my shoulder to reassure myself that yes, they were. But nothing had moved. I didn't know what would be in a cage in this room, and I didn't right want to find out. Besides, that itch were getting worse. I shivered. "You hear that, Cody?" A sudden awful line of thinking hit me.

"Dripping water?" he asked, picking up on my worry.

"No," I said, gripping his shoulder. "Melting ice."

Cody went still, nostrils flaring, fear replacing the wonder on his face. We crouched there, terrified for a long minute, just silent, just listening, neither breathing.

"Jorie, is it just me or did the temperature in here just get a little . . . warmer?" Cody whispered.

It sure had. "Cody," I pointed. "That sure ain't a shadow." A slim strip of fabric protruded from just around the edge of the metal cage. "That weren't there a second ago. I'd swear to it."

A soft whimper broke the silence.

"It's hurt," Cody said.

We exchanged a long look.

Cody shifted to his feet. "I can see it."

I grabbed his arm. "Get back down, or you trying to get us killed?"

He shook me off.

"Cody, get back here. Cody." But he didn't listen.

He waved back at me. "Jorie, come on, come here."

I hesitated. Something in his voice were strange. Withdrawn. The pendant at my neck pulsed with a discomforting cold against my skin. The soft rumble of a mountain just before the fall. Before the avalanche broke free. That feeling of being watched were like a wildfire beating against my chest now.

"Cody, what's wrong? What's out there?"

He didn't reply, just walked on.

Cody rounded the corner of the silver cage. And then, just when there were nothing to see save the shadow of where he had been, he let out a high-pitched cry.

I sprinted after him, sliding to a dead stop right beside where Cody were crouching down. Cause there, hands and feet bound, mouth covered, were a girl.

The most impossible girl I'd ever seen.

CHAPTER 36

The Girl and Her Pieces

———— ∘ ⇒∘⇐ ∘ ————

The girl lay on the ice before us.

Her breath a canopy of mist above lips the palest pomegranate pink. Face illuminated by two golden-flecked eyes that hung over cheeks tinged by the softest of robin's blue. Hair so white it shone silver spilled over her shoulders, save one piece. A thin lock of black hair, like a drip of warm oil, fell from her left temple.

From her position against the ice, the girl's eyes met mine for the barest of moments. Before I could stop him, Cody moved away from me. Concern clear written across his face as he neared the girl. She couldn't have been any older than him.

I held out my arm. To reach for the girl or for Cody, I didn't right know. This girl. She weren't real. Couldn't be real. As if she had walked out of one of Cody's favorite stories.

"Wait, Cody." I'd taken too long. The girl took Cody's arm, fingers digging into the warm fibers of his sweater.

"We must help her. I—I think can help her." His voice held a note of awe.

"Maybe, but we don't know what's—" I lurched a step forward, words dying as I tripped over a tendril of ice snaking across the floor. I had not seen it there before.

"Cody, stop."

He looked up.

"We don't right know who she is," I said.

He tilted his head, gaze swinging between me and the girl on the ground. "Maybe not, but I know she needs help. One worthy heart, Jorie, that's all it takes. Remember?" he asked earnest. My heart gave a lurch at the almost-eager look he turned on me. "Come on, help me untie her."

The girl didn't seem to notice nor care that two strangers were having an argument at her side. I pressed my lips thin, hesitation. Sadness flashed across Cody's face. Disappointment.

What were wrong with me? He's only trying to help. Like I should've been doing, if I were a good person, like him. While I stood still, Cody were already struggling to get the ropes loose.

"Here, let me help with those." I near to whispered it as I reached down. I took her bound hands in mine. I frowned. "Your skin is freezing. Whoever bound you here ain't done you no favors."

My hand grazed the edge of her throat. Near to perfectly still under my ministrations, the girl's stare faltered for the barest of moments. My vision blurred. My whole body froze, as if I had just plunged into the sea. But then the girl was smiling at me, her face warm, eyes full and honeyed. And I forced myself to relax, to be less worried. To be less . . . me. Next to me, Cody smiled and finished removing the cloth cover from the girl's lips.

"Better?" he asked.

The girl nodded, some of the stiffness in her arms and shoulders sliding off. I twisted at the long-ended knot binding her hands. Digging numb fingertips into the rough cords, I bit back a curse. I were only making the bindings tighter. The girl smiled at me calm.

But even if I undid the ropes, the nightmare around us weren't changed. We were still trapped. In Vydra. The Rover gone and with it my chance to find Bren. I'd failed her. The ice-stone grew near to painful warm against my throat.

I failed. I were a failure.

The girl shifted a little on the floor. Rougher than strictly necessary, I tugged at her hands, scrunching my focus, narrowing it to the bindings. Forcing the world to this one task. The knots were strange. They were like the ones you used on fishing lines, but not. I cursed, twisting the braided cord round and round. Until I finally found the right strand. With effort, I leeched just enough slack into the thread. The knots loosened. A moment later and the cords fell free.

Deep impressions, pressure marks, ringed the girl's skin. In the well of which gray bruises bloomed. Seeing my gaze, the girl jerked her hands quick back to her side, pushing them in the fabric of her dress. An expression I didn't understand flashed cross her face and was gone. She didn't need to be ashamed. Reflexive, I reached for the long scar on my face.

I blinked the memory away, a little dazed. I don't know how long I stood there, just staring at her, the bindings, the bleakness of this place around us. Then Cody were helping the girl to her feet.

Clear weak, she leaned heavy into his shoulder. Heat flashed inside my chest. I should have thought to help her up. Why had I just let her lie there on the ice when I knew she were cold? I found my hands straying to the pendant at my neck. To the pulsing of it. *The cold made you everything worse than you were.*

The girl balanced heavy on Cody's shoulder. Stars above help him, the boy blushed to his toes. Cody put one hand at her elbow, the other around her shoulders.

"I cannot thank you enough," she said soft. "I've been in this prison so very long."

"My name is Cody."

"Vela," the girl said, face turned to his intent like.

"Just like my favorite constellation." The green of his eyes caught the blue aurora of light around us.

Vela blushed. An embarrassment of emotion. If anything, the creamy red of her cheeks made her more ethereal. A rose in the ice. Enchanting.

Neither Cody or the girl paid me no heed.

"Great." I cut into their murmur of conversation, the pull in my gut tellin me we should be gone by now. "Seeing as how we three are all familiar, I think that it's past time we got ourselves out of here. Cody, don't you agree?"

"Ah, yes. Right, leaving. Are you well enough to walk, Vela?" Cody asked.

Vela blushed again, giving a little stumble as she took a step. Cody reached out a steadying hand. She took it. "I'm sorry, I must be more tired than I thought. Thank you." Slow, she reached up and brushed that strand of black hair from her face.

Cody looked to me. "We can't just abandon her, Jorie. She needs our help." Admonishment crimped the edges of his tone.

I took a step back, surprised. "I ain't never said to leave her here." The image of a boy, too cold and too foolish, slumped against a pine tree, flashed remorseful inside me. I'd not left him, but I *could* have. I could've done it and not hurt about it. Not for long. But now? I glanced at Cody. Is that really what he thought of me?

"I can help you," the girl said, brushing a long strand of silver-white hair from her face. I blinked at her. But she were looking at Cody, not me.

"She can help us," he said.

"Yes, she just said that." I frowned at Cody. I had ears. "How?" I said to the girl.

"There is—"

"Maybe she knows a way out of here." Cody cut Vela off. Something sharp flashed in the girl's eyes, there and gone again. Oblivious, Cody ran a hand through his hair, scrubbing his face, eyes brightening as if a thought had occurred to him. "What if she's seen your sister? The Rover said he sold her on. . . ." He let the implication hang. Vela were a prisoner. She had to have come from somewhere. And someone here kept girls. A bubble of memory burst to the surface. Of a Witch made of winter.

I dropped my fingers from Bren's chain and went dead still.

"A sister?" The girl's gaze widened on me for the first time in what I reckoned to be a genuine interest.

Way she said it, my heart sank. "She don't know nothing, Cody. How could she, locked up in here like that?" I took a step toward Cody, only to have him step back. "What's gotten into you?"

Cody gave his head a little shake.

"A girl?" Vela said. "Maybe fifteen? Blond. With one blue eye, one brown." Vela's mouth a perfect little circle of concern. "I have seen her."

"What? When?" My turn to be surprised.

"Time is so hard to tell in here." Vela gestured to the impossible starless world of ice above us. "But I do remember she was not alone. She was with that man and his wolf. He did go on yelling so much." Vela's voice were bare a whisper, her lips twitching ever so slightly upward at the corner.

"Where was this? Was Bren hurt?" I asked. A dangerous hope flickered beneath my heart.

"I cannot remember."

"Please try." Cody's expression turned practical heroic. This were the story he'd have written for himself. Well, it certain weren't mine.

"Try harder. This is not some game." The words cut out of me. That dangerous bead of hope hardened into something else. If the cold made you everything worse than you were? Well, I were already freezing.

Disbelief flashed in Vela's face. "Please, I only want to help." Vela spun to Cody. "Tell her. I will help. I can lead you out of here, but she does not know what she is asking."

"Jorie, be reasonable," he said, looking at me if I'd sudden grown unfamiliar. A flash of hurt drowned in my cold.

"Reasonable?" I said, snapping my arm back. "I am the only one being reasonable. Or have you forgotten why we ran into the Flats in the first place? Bren, Cody. This girl's seen Bren. And she will remember where. She will show us."

Cody frowned. On his other side Vela had gone still as stone, her eyes fixed on mine. She did not look away, did not blink. "I will take you. If that is what you want."

I crossed my arms. "Look at that, she does remember." That cold knot inside me tightened, making it hard to swallow.

"Jorie . . ."

I waved Cody off. "Good. She helps us and we help her, but she's your responsibility. I don't need another one."

Cody nodded grave serious.

"And Vela? You can start by showing us exactly how to get out of this room. Then we find my sister."

CHAPTER 37

A Single Hound

⸻◆⸻

We walked, the three of us, for what felt eternity.

Curve after curve, archway after veiled archway, all marked by a slow downward slope through the never-ending string of tunnels pearling out before us. From high above, little glimmers of light hummed down through the darkness. Pools of cream and gold. They seeped along the cold walls, doing little to dispel the gloom around us. And even less to scatter the sensation rising in my gut that we were very much not alone.

"This way," Vela called, turning down another corridor. I don't know how she saw the entrance. But she did. And we followed.

More and more I stepped away from the high walls and into the center of the hallways, avoiding a darkness that had begun creeping 'long about the edges.

Vela appeared at my side. I started. I were certain she'd been ahead of Cody. Not behind me. I gave her a sideways glance.

"I should thank you," she said, her step falling in perfect time with mine. So that only two sets of footfalls and not three filled the dark. "I have been in here so long, I forget what it is to be free." Her gaze trailed over my face, the words unsaid. *Do you?*

"Don't trouble yourself about it." I rubbed at a spot just under my heart. The cold there gone painful.

"I won't." Vela gave me a flick of a smile. Her fingers tracing slow circles over the back of her hand. The ticking sensation in my chest grew faster. "You worry about your sister. Tell me about her."

I near to missed a step. As if for just that moment there had been no floor beneath me. When I looked back up, Vela were very close. A flutter of regret at my earlier anger rose inside me. She *were* helping. And the tunnels were long enough that the righteous flare of anger had settled into something else. A rawness I didn't want to right look at. The glances Cody kept shooting at me didn't help either.

"Tell me about this place," I asked, avoiding her question.

Vela's smile faltered. She ran a hand over the curve of her neck. Fingers tapping at the sharp edge of her collarbone. "Are you concerned I will get you lost? You do not need to worry."

"I won't." I echoed Vela's words back at her. She gave me a thin smile. "I should thank you for helping us."

"Hardly all I could do," Vela said, her fingers stopping their tapping. She looked away. "Do not thank me yet."

Before I'd replied, Vela darted ahead. Her arm finding Cody's, who had appeared right in the center of the tunnel no more than a few yards away. A light laughter trickling sweet from her throat. I frowned at her ease. Cause nothing with other people were ever easy for me. I wrapped my arms round my chest, trailing behind.

Vela didn't try to speak with me direct again, instead choosing to walk at Cody's side. I didn't blame her. I weren't good company at the best of times. Still, every once in a while I would catch Vela staring at me. But never for long, and never long enough for me to say nothing back.

Finally, we came to the end of the tangled passageways. A low metal door rested on rusted hinges. Lonesome and very much closed.

Whispering something I could not hear, Vela leaned into the metal. A moment later, she pulled back and waved a hand to indicate Cody should open the door. Under his hand the hinges opened with not even a squeal of cold protest.

Past the door were a poorly lit chamber, and it took me a long moment to focus in the low light. Expecting more of the same, more cold and ice. Only here the floor, walls, ceiling, everything were made entirely of uneven black rock.

It may have just been my imagination, but I could swear the air here smelled of trees. Of fresh-drained sap and slashed heartwood. Without hesitation Vela drifted off into the dim, her feet bare gliding light over the floor.

I turned to exchange a glance with Cody, only to find that he weren't looking at me. The urge to talk to Cody grew, but he were already trailing after Vela. So I too had no choice but to follow.

That first dim room soon turned into a series of interconnected chambers, not unlike catacombs. Each lit by a different colored light. Some of the honeycombed spaces were empty, others were not. And all of them were vast different. As we entered a dim room whose ice walls were the color of smoked glass, a flash of white caught my eye. High up in the turreted corner. All the corners. Emerald-eyed storm petrels. Hundreds of them. Only they weren't moving. They were frozen into the ice.

"Do not touch anything," Vela warned.

"I hadn't planned on it," I said.

Vela's shoulders stiffened slightly, but she didn't turn around, just kept striding onward. Over his shoulder, Cody shot me a strange look.

We passed into the next connected space. This one was covered with green, with deep veins of silver snaking through bright emerald walls.

"It is unusual, isn't it? It was her sister's, I think." Cody's voice echoed from where he and Vela walked through the middle of the vast space. "No, I do not think she would. I have never seen her without it."

Vela's reply were lost to the dark between us.

"What's that? What about my sister?" I called, bristling.

Cody slowed. "Vela was just asking about you two and where your—"

Before he could reply, Vela came to an abrupt stop. Twisting, she turned to face me. Her expression careful neutral. Completely gone was the simpering little flake of girl.

"What about my sister?" I repeated my question.

"Did I say something wrong?" Vela asked, fingers tracing a slow circle where they'd held to Cody's arm. It sudden hit me. What had been bothering me.

"No." I tugged a confused-looking Cody over to me.

Vela gave him what I could only assume were a tolerating smile before walking on. "We must keep moving." She didn't wait for us to follow. She didn't need to.

"Why's she asking *you* about Bren? If Vela wants to know about me or my sister, I'm the one she should be talking to."

"She's been here a long time, Jorie. She isn't good with people. And you scare her." Cody gave me a troubled look that were a long time in leaving his face.

I crossed my arms. "That's a load of bull crap and you know it."

"Do I?"

I scowled at him. "Yes, you do. If anyone should be scared here, it is us, not her. She's been living here and she's still alive, ain't she?" I let the implications hang.

"That doesn't mean anything." Cody swept a long look over the girl walking ahead of us. "People live in all sorts of horrible places. Not usually because they want to. I've studied plenty of—"

I yanked Cody a few paces farther away. One eye on Vela, who were humming to herself, ahead. "Well, this ain't one of your books. She isn't some damsel in distress. This is the real world."

"I know that."

"Do you?" I arched a brow.

Cody crossed his arms.

"Fine. Just don't you go telling her stuff about me and Bren. It's not her business to know." I knew it were right the moment it were out of my lips. "What do we even know about this girl? Just cause she looks it, don't make her a damsel needing rescuing."

"I haven't said anything that really matters, not about—"

"Look around you, Cody; this ain't your pleasant University world. I thought you'd have learned that by now, we can't trust no one but each other."

Cody tilted his head, sad. "Oh, Jorie."

Pity. He were looking at me with pity. As if I were the broken one.

"Don't *oh, Jorie* me. I ain't the one begging to be friendly with strange girls I find in the ice. Besides, aren't you the one who's been going on about myths of Vydra? Trying to convince me they're real? Well, you win, Cody. I finally believe. I believe *all* of it." I fixed him with a meaningful stare.

A troubled expression passed over his face. Then just as quick he were shaking his head. "You heard Vela; she's a prisoner here just like

243

us. For stars sake, Jorie, she was bound and gagged in a cage. I hardly call that magical."

"Depends on who did that binding. And why."

"Tell me what choices we have." Abruptly he took my hand, his fingers warm in mine. When he looked up, his eyes were clear. "We cannot stay here, and we do not know the way home. If we do not at least try to trust her, we are leaving behind our only hope of finding your sister. Of making any of this worth our lives. And if I've learned anything from you, Jorie, it is that we don't give up. Not when there is a chance. And right now, to find Brenna, Vela is that chance."

"You don't need to tell me that." It felt like I were scrambling in a game where I didn't know the rules, let alone where the players were. Didn't know what to believe.

"Why are you arguing with me on this?" he asked.

"Why are you?" I shot back. "With all we've seen—"

"*Exactly*, Jorie. With all we've seen, Vela has seen far worse. She's been telling me all about it. She's been living by herself here for years. Says she can't remember it all, only bits and pieces. Only the warmth of before and the ice of after. Run out of her home, she wandered the Flats alone. Until she found this cave in the side of a mountain. And then she was just here." Cody drew a clutching breath. "Sound familiar?"

"And you believe her?" It were like he were seeing something I weren't. Like I was missing something. Like there was something broken in me, like I couldn't feel right. But try as I might, there *was* something not right about all of this. The rot in a wintered fruit. If this were a story, if this were a myth, there should be some great creature. Some monster. Only I didn't see one. Which worried me all the more.

"Yes," he said.

I opened my mouth, but jolted to a stop when Vela clapped her hands, the motion as cutting as a blade in the dark.

"Be quiet," Vela said.

"Why? This ain't none of—" Footsteps fast and growing faster filled the room.

"We do not have much time. Come." Vela, smug, took up Cody's hand and turned. "If you want to see your sister ever again, I suggest you run."

I ran.

CHAPTER 38

Cold Harvest

———— ◆ ————

I ran and ran.

Sped through room after room. Catching glimpses of great golden archways, impossibly high keystones dripping thick with icicles the size of men. Rooms where gems bloomed like many-colored fruit from pale crystals of frost, caverns so thick with blackness they sucked the very color from your veins. And then, sudden as a squall, Cody and Vela stopped. I skidded to a halt behind them.

A door, white as fresh fallen snow and marred with five long lines of rose gold, stood shut before us. I shot a glance over my shoulder. The footfalls.

I ran to the door. But there were no handle. Nothing to grab, to swing, to—

"Move," Vela said. I stepped out of her way. She leaned a slender shoulder into the stone and pushed. Inch by inch the door began to open. Cody took my hand. His skin as light as the brush of sea silk across mine. Cold and warm all at once, I stepped into the warmth of the body beside me.

"Cody, I—" But whatever I thought about Cody, the door, any of it were muted by the next words out of Vela's lips.

"Your sister's in here."

I slid my hand from his and stepped away. Hurt flashed across his face. I shoved aside the answering flutter in my chest. Then I were not looking at Cody anymore, there was only the door and Vela.

At the center of the high-vaulted room, one block of ice waited all alone. Only it was not empty. Bren, hair cascading over a near-colorless face, lay upon it.

Her hands were clasped tight across her chest, resting over her heart. Like she were sleep. I darted over the slick floor. Behind me the door shuddered closed.

"That should keep us for a while," Vela murmured to Cody.

"What *was* that?" Cody glanced over his shoulder. "Those foot-falls?"

"I said I was not alone." Vela smiled at him. Picking at the edge of her gown. "And trust me when I tell you, Cody, there are things far worse than me in here." Behind her the shadows shivered.

"What does that mean?" Cody said, surprise mixing for the first time with doubt in his voice.

I slid to a rest on my knees next to my sister. "Brenna, wake up, it's me. It's Jorie." I smoothed the long strands of hair from her face, my fingers dislodging a flurry of tiny crystals, a dusting of frozen stars. Bren didn't respond. Not a flutter or a twitch. My heart jumped painful in my chest.

"Bren," I said soft. As if, just by my whispering it, she would wake up. As if I only had to ask right. But my sister didn't move. Closing my eyes, I picked up one of her hands, clasping it in mine. She were so very cold. But in the crook of her neck there were a slow, steady pulse. A flutter of life beating under her skin. She were alive, if only just. I lowered my cheek to hers. Soft wisps of air swept out of lips that did not move.

Wary, I pushed open the veined blue of her eyelids. There they were, one blue eye, one brown. Only there were something else too. Right in the corner of her right eye. A red-gold speck. As if a tiny pin had gone in and lodged itself in the warmth of her eye. I made to wipe it away.

In a heartbeat Vela were at my side. "Do not touch that," she said, placing a hand on my shoulder. I shrugged it off. Vela frowned, but she weren't looking at me.

"Why?" It did not look very much of anything.

"It is a Witch's mark. You must leave it."

"Well, if it went in, then I will take it out."

"No!" This time her fingers curled around my wrist. I went dead still. Her skin burned with cold. It were the first time she had touched me. She snapped her arm back. "It is all that holds her here to this place. If you take it out now, she will in truth be dead."

"What do you know?" I asked, rubbing at the pain in my wrist.

Vela's mouth twisted. "Enough."

"And how do you know it?" Shaking, I pushed back from my knees.

Vela did not speak. Instead, she turned to Cody. Who a moment later were at my side. His hand squeezing my shoulder. "I do not think she is lying, Jorie." Like his grip, I bare registered his words. "What would she gain for it?"

"I don't know." I wanted to shake him, to make him see that we were in more danger now than we'd ever been out in those storms. Cause in all those stories Cody told, not a one of them said nothing about this. What good were they, what good was their very realness, if they didn't help? Cody had said they were supposed to help. I pushed tears from my eyes.

Shaking, I turned to the only thing that mattered in this room. I placed my hand right over her heart. "Brenna, you have to wake up. I'm here. I've got you now." I were crying in earnest now. When I looked up Vela were kneeling, silent as flotsam against the shore.

She too was holding Bren's hand, her skin near so pale it were glowing, her lips hiding a thin smile. Slow, she turned her gaze to mine and moved her hand over the soft curve of her neck, fingers lingering over her too smooth skin. Eyes wild. Starved. The expression were gone, replaced in the flick of a heartstring by softer. Lighter. Something tamer. She pulled away, eyes downcast.

Vela flicked a corner of her hair away from the muted pink of her cheek. Eyes flashing to me and away again.

"If we cannot take it out, what can we do?" Cody asked her.

"I do not know what you would be able to do," Vela said.

I lifted my face, my fingers curled into a tight fist. A first fissure in the ice.

Vela looked down at me.

I set my spine. "There may be a lot of this I don't right understand— near all of it, to be honest. But there is one thing I do know. And that is I ain't come all this way to fail her. If it were done, it can be undone."

Vela pursed her lips, her expression pinched.

I turned to face Cody. "Help me lift her. We are leaving." I slipped a hand under Bren's cold shoulders. Her muscles flexed beneath me. Nausea welled in my throat. A doll. She were like a frozen doll.

"You won't make it, you know," Vela stressed, her tongue darting out to lick at her lips. "Even if you get her out, she will not wake. She will only get worse. She will slow you down. Leave her and there may still be time for you two to get out."

I ignored her.

"What is her life even worth to you to now, what little there is left of it?" Vela demanded.

"What is her life worth?" I spat back, incredulous. "You may as well ask what is the sun to the moon? Or the shore to the tide." All the memories that made us who we were, that made a family what it was, every one of them had Bren in it. My hand clasped over the ice-stone of my necklace. My mother's, and then Bren's. Strength, warm and welcome, flooded me.

The good, the bad, it was all there and would always be. But it was *ours*. Mine and hers and Ma's and Pa's. In a world of ice and hunger that ate away everything good in people, slow year by year, till there were nothing left but the bitter whites of their bones, Bren's unwavering kindness were as near to true magic as I'd ever known.

It takes courage to live your life with gentleness, when all around you is nothing but easy anger. Nothing but the worst of who you thought you were.

An odd sort of pity floated up inside me for this strange girl. What kind of life is left to live when there ain't the memory of anyone you care enough about to live it for? When you can't even remember your dreams? Cause what are dreams, after all, but stories we can't bring ourselves to tell?

"Life ain't something you can simply trade, Vela, one for the other. This for that. We ain't just things." I were near to shaking. "You ask what is one life worth? I say that ain't no right kind of question." I took Bren's hand in mine, interlacing our fingers. "Because life is everything good and right in this forsaken world. And no matter how small or insignificant it may seem to you, that will always be worth fighting for."

Cody's grip on Bren slacked the smallest of fractions as he shook his head. "Vela, please, if you know something, anything, help us."

Vela narrowed her eyes. "It is too late. She may be breathing, but she is as good as dead. There is no fight left for you to win." Silence filled the room, heavy and alone.

"The stars there ain't." I stared at the soft rise and fall of my sister's pulse, the subtle twitching of her muscles, the movement of little veins of red pulsing under her skin.

"If I know one thing, it is that *as good as* ain't final. And Bren ain't dead yet. And if she ain't dead, there is still a chance." I fixed Cody with a piercing stare. "And we, Cody Colburn, we ain't gonna let my sister die. Not today, and certain not here."

His mouth went a little slack just for a moment, but his eyes, his eyes turned hard. "Of course we won't, Jorie." A dazed expression on his face. "We are leaving. And either you help us, Vela, or you get out of our way."

"'Bout time you found those brains of yours," I said.

Cody gave me a half smile, hefting Brenna's arm up onto his shoulder.

At her sides, Vela's fingers twitched. A flash of disbelief flaring behind gold eyes. "I did not mean for you to die here with her, surely you see that." She reached a hand out to Cody, but he pulled away, disoriented.

"Then show us where it is we want to go."

Vela looked at me, mutinous. "It is not safe."

For you, maybe. But I only pulled Bren's other arm up high and over my shoulder. "I know what I'm askin. Now, are you gonna help us get out of here like you promised, or are we all gonna have to die trying?" Cody took up Bren's other side, her head tilting between us.

Bren weighed less than I were expecting. It took a good few paces for Cody and me to sync up our steps instead of fighting each other, each trying to lead. We finally found some semblance of an awkward rhythm.

But as I glanced at Vela, who had opened the door and were darting restless around the tunnel ahead of us, I think I finally had a plan.

Vela, whoever she were, prisoner or Witch's creature, I didn't right know. But what I did know was that one way or another she were going to betray us.

In fact, I were counting on it.

CHAPTER 39

Dwindling Dawns

———◆———

W hat is that noise?" I spun my head right round. Instead of cold tunnel air, warm air swirled about me. The floor beneath us grew . . . wet? I looked down. Ice. *Melting* ice. And then just like that we emerged into a vast rumbling chasm of a cave.

At the center of which a massive waterfall crashed down into a waiting pool. The great watery mouth hiding away unseen in the dark high above. At the pool's edge, thorny horned orange sculpins, graylings, and long-whiskered chars darted below the surface. Multi-colored mollusks, gray and blue, silver and red, clung to the rocks. I blinked, unable to account for the world we had passed into.

Here, in the middle of a world of ice, the perfection of the palace were eaten slowly away. Its stillness melted by promise of movement. Like grains of sand, small beads of water showered down from the breath of the falls, landing soft as velvet across my face. My hair, my eyes.

My dry body drank in the liquid. Welcoming it. I brushed the water from Brenna's face. Her breathing were still steady, but her eyes were still closed. She looked a little less blue. A little flush to her cheeks.

"We can rest here," Vela called, darting out of sight behind a massive chunk of polished ice on the far side of the pool.

My neck and shoulder ached. When were the last time I had

slept or ate in this place? Though I didn't feel tired or hungry. Cody gave a groan and together we careful set Bren down. I made sure she were propped up against a smooth stone. She stayed sitting. I brushed the hair from her face.

Cody plopped down next to her. "Merciful stars, even my bones hurt."

I let out a low rumble. "Careful now, Southerner. Keep on rambling out things like that and someone might mistake you for a boy from Shadow Springs."

Cody raised a brow. "From you, Jorie, I'll consider that a compliment."

"Always did say you'd more brains than wits." But I were smiling.

Cody's answering laugh turned quick to a racking cough. I pressed my lips in concern. I rubbed a hand over my eyes and let out a long sigh. Cody were staring at me. A blush crept over his face, and he lowered his eyes. I had the strangest urge to reach over and brush the dew from his long lashes.

"What is this place?" Cody asked, rubbing hard at the muscles of his shoulders.

"We are near the old drift mines, as your friend requested," Vela said.

I hadn't seen her come back. As if my surprise pleased her, she smiled and took up her own perch, cross-legged in front a low rock shelf. Her palms resting on exposed knees, eyes closed. In the watery light, her skin glowed. A small ruby beetle scrambled across a patch of moss.

Vela, eyes sudden wide, cocked her head. The insect were trying, but the combination of its short little legs and the slickness of the moss meant it fell as much as it made it forward. Vela's hand snaked out and plucked it from the green. The beetle scuttled across her palm as she rolled her hand over and over. It were near to helpful as I'd come to expect from her. Right. I cleared my dry throat. If there were one thing this place didn't lack, it were water.

"Where do you think you are going?" Vela asked, the little beetle cradled in her palm, red in a sea of white.

"Water."

Vela's lip ticked into a frown, but she didn't divert her attention from lurching insect. "Well, do not go too far. It's dangerous out there alone." Her eyes snapped sudden to my chest. She stared at me, unblinking. It weren't an enjoyable look.

I picked my way over to the pool's edge and kneeled down. The water's crystal surface shook from the waterfall, blurring my reflection. I dipped my hands in; it were unexpected warm. I took a long drink of the water. In the pool below me, a brave sculpin darted to the surface, biting at the drops of water as they fell from my cupped hands.

Unfed, the fish darted away, disappointed. I took another drink before ripping a strip from the edge of my wool undershirt. Wadding it up, I submerged it in the pool. Like a breath, little bubbles of pressed air escaped from the fibers, bursting where they hit the water's surface. I let out a long sigh, twisting the fabric till it could hold no more. Soaked the cloth until there was nothing but the smell of stone and water to fill me.

When I returned, Cody were already sleep. I let him rest. Moving slow, I cupped one hand under Bren's chin. Bren's eyes fluttered but did not open. Her skin was still too cold. But it weren't as bad as it had been, back in that catacomb of a room. The farther we got from the heart of the ice, the warmer she became. But it weren't enough.

"I told you she will not wake," Vela said. "Water will not change that. No matter the source it comes from." Her attention flickered to and away from the waterfall.

"Yeah, thanks for that." I ran my hand over Bren's forehead, wiping away a stray hair.

Vela let out an uncertain huff, picking up a small red pebble from the floor as she stood. Rollin it smooth through her willowy fingers. Over and over. Falling water swirled in the silence between us, pulsing in the cold. A scattered echo of a slowly beating heart.

"Your necklace, I saw it as you were arguing with your friend." She gestured toward Cody.

"What of it?" I reached up involuntary.

"An unusual stone." She tilted her head to side.

"An heirloom. Our Ma's."

"Indeed." Vela gave a wry twist of her lips at that. "I am uncertain how much your friend has told you. Or what it is that you already know." The pebble rolled across the back of her right hand. Weighing. "I do not like not knowing."

"And why is that?" My arms ached something fierce. I rubbed at the sore muscles, not meeting her eye.

"Surely that is evident by now." She tossed an uncaring hand at where Bren lay.

"Try me."

Vela circled closer. Eyes intent, roaming from Bren to myself, searching. For something I weren't sure that even she knew. "I loved my family once. As you love your sister. I gave of my heart freely." Her body had gone perfect still, knuckles white where she gripped the red stone. I hadn't seen when she had palmed it. "She is your light. You carry that love within you, tucked in tight against the world. I only ask that what-

256

ever it is you think of me, that I too have carried that light. And I know what it is to live on when the world around you turns dark."

Reflexive, I placed a hand on Bren's shoulder. Vela's lips twitched.

"In the end, we are all proved too weak. And I too young, too fallible. The light is not what makes you strong. It is what will break you."

"But they were your family, you loved them." It were all I could think to say. Her words felt hazardous close to something inside me I didn't want to see.

Vela gave an unexpected laugh. It was light and sweet. "A mistake I hardly plan to make again." She looked down at me, her eyes bright. "Once, I think, we may not have been so different, you and I. But that was a long time ago. Another life." Her chin tilted ever so slight, throwing her already sharp features into piercing relief, a finger tracing a circle across the smooth curve of her throat. Without thinking I raised my hand to the silver chain around my neck. Flushing, I dropped it back to my side. I'd give her nothing to see worth stealing.

A flick of a shrewd smile. "Just remember, Jorie, what is shattered once can hardly be broken again."

I wanted to object, to say something. Instead I worked hard to keep my face calm. This felt dangerous close to that first crunch under your boots. Right before the ice gave way and the cold swallowed you whole.

Then, smooth as a bird in flight, she turned and strode off into the waiting darkness of the cave. Not a footfall or crunch of heel on stone came back. I shuddered in a breath, and glanced to the rock where she had been standing. To the pebble she'd been playing with.

There weren't nothing left of it but a scattering of shattered red dust.

CHAPTER 40

A Trick of the Light

———✦———

Careful, I wiped Brenna's chin dry, coiling the cloth up in my hand. And slipped the ice-stone pendant from around my neck. I stared down into the jewel. An heirloom, I had told Vela. But it were more that than. It were like a piece of my Ma and of Bren, lying there in my hand. Like dripping silver, I let the chain hang between my fingers. The shine of the metal catching and tossing the crisp blue light of the cavern in long cold slivers over my legs. In the silence the faint glow of the stone swirled in the heat of my palm.

Weighing the stone my hand, I stared at my sister's face. At the face that looked so much like our Ma's. Her breathing was shallow but steady. Her heart still beat. Her lungs still worked. There was so much I didn't know. About all of it. I ran my fingers over the smooth face of the stone. I leaned in close. Close enough that my breath stirred the stray blond hairs on Bren's cheek.

What if?

Ma had always told us it were special. What if that weren't just a story? What if? A strange bloom of hope shivered through me, aching desperate in my heart. If all those other stories were real, if Warders and Tracers and even Vydra—for stars sake—were real, why not this? And before I could think better of it, think it false, I slipped the chain over Brenna's neck.

The stone flashed sudden bright against her skin. I held my breath.

"Come on, work. Fix her." I cupped my hands over the stone. "Just wake up, Bren. All you have to do is open your eyes. I'm right here." My words, like my hope, just loud enough to be real.

Bren took a sudden inhale of breath, a shudder running through her. I leaned harder on the stone above her heart, faith flaring my own. But then . . . nothing. The light faded. And did not come again. Bren didn't wake. And as quick as it had blazed, belief died away.

"You are a fool, Marjorie Harlow," I said harsh. "What did you think were gonna happen? That you'd slip some stone over her head and she would, what, just be alright again?" I scoffed at myself. Even if the world were full of fairy tales, living and breathing and desperate trying to kill us, I certain weren't one of them. I had no more power in me than did a starless sky. Tucking her coat tightly about her shoulders, I pressed my forehead to my sister's.

My lashes growing thick with the salt of my tears. But just cause we weren't stories lost in the night, that didn't mean I couldn't use the ones we'd already met to get us out of this. I just had to find them.

When our rest were finally over, we got ready without speaking. Not that there were much to do. Cody took one side of Bren and I took the other. Vela strode away. Mutely, we followed.

Soon the ice of the tunnels took on a more familiar cast. Rock. And ash. Lots and lots of it. We were entering the Nocna Mora mines.

The next time Vela disappeared round a corner ahead of us, I jerked my head toward the side of the path.

"What?" Cody asked.

I nodded again, this time slowing my step as I did. We set Bren down. She had been odd recent. Not awake, not really, but I could feel her growing restless. Little tremors under her skin. It were right worrisome. Because they wasn't smooth, gentle movements, like someone waking. But sudden and sharp. Like someone struggling.

"You okay?" Cody asked, rubbing his shoulder.

"Yeah," I said. "But are you?"

Cody winced as he rotated his shoulder. "I think so."

I eyed the darkness ahead of us. "Cody, there is something I've been meaning to tell you."

From under his lashes, Cody shot a tired look to me. "What is it?" He leaned heavy against the wall, slumping. As if his muscles had simply given out.

"What's wrong—?"

"We must keep moving."

I started at the sudden cut of her voice. "Stars, Vela, you startled me." *Again.*

Ignoring me as she had done since last night by the reflecting pool, Vela glided to Cody's side, her face tense. It were like there were two of her. This girl clinging to Cody's side. And the other. The one I had seen circling ever so slowly below the surface. And why wouldn't Cody see it too?

"You must get up. No resting. Not when I am this close." Vela's cheeks flushed red, her fingers dancing along the neckline of her dress. She shifted her weight back and forth on bare feet.

She were a well of unspent energy. It were troublesome, but that weren't what was bothering me. Not really. I needed to get us out of here. And do it before Vela decided we weren't worth her troubles any longer. I were mildly surprised she hadn't already. I didn't know what she were, but I'd an idea, a wild one. But what about my life weren't lost in the wild now? The memory of dripping ice—melting ice—in that chamber had been my first clue.

If something had melted, something had been let free of the ice. And with all those lions and bears and all manner of near to right beasts standing round that ice garden, why could there not have been a girl too? I eyed Vela as she darted out in front of us. It would also explain her story. Prisoner might not have been totally right, but it also might not have been wrong.

"We must keep moving. This is the only true passageway to the outside I am able to follow. If we slow now—"

"Just give us a second," I said.

"A minute only, then follow." Vela spun, her shoulders stiff, and strode back out of sight down the tunnel.

I cocked an eyebrow in Cody's direction, and held out my hand.

"I suppose we should keep going," he sighed.

Taking his hand, I stood. He pulled away. I held firm, tightening my grip. "Cody, she ain't right. And you know it."

Cody's frown deepened. This time when he yanked his hand, I let it go. He turned to check on Bren. "Jorie?" Cody's voice hitched on my name.

"What? Is something wrong with Bren?" A tint of panic filled me. I rushed to his side.

"I . . . no. Well, not anything new."

"Don't scare me like that."

"I—sorry. I wanted to ask you something. Let's just say that for argument's sake we make it out of here."

"And?"

"Jorie, we can't carry her. You and I, we barely made it ourselves. How can we carry her home like this?"

A spark of fear. I swallowed it. Cause he weren't wrong. Good thing I'd already thought of that. "I have a plan."

"Like the last time you had one?" he asked. "When we ran in blind and were almost killed and then burned by the Rover? Or the time before when Bass and her people took us prisoner? For once, Jorie, maybe you let someone else help you."

"Cody, that ain't fair." Hurt roared up in me. I wanted to tell him he were wrong. That he should trust me. But like a sudden weight, leaded and hard, the truth in what he were saying settled heavy on my chest. But it weren't the only truth.

It were Cody that had shot the ox, Cody that had pulled us from the Rover. I lowered my eyes. But this time I weren't lying. I had a plan. "Vela may say she knows a lot of things, but she don't know everything. She don't know me, and she sure as stars don't know us. You have to trust me."

"But we barely made it out there, just us. How are we gonna make it home, carrying a girl who can't walk on her own?" he repeated.

I bristled. "We will find a way. We always do." Cause even when the hare had no chance of avoiding the fox's jaws, she didn't stop running. Didn't stop fighting. My skin went sudden hot.

"Will we, Jorie? How can you be so sure? We have nothing left. Even if we get out of these caves, then what? We were barely able to drag ourselves through the Flats, and then with your sister . . ."

"What are you saying?" Anger, all of it I had held back, that I had forced aside, came flooding back. And that little fissure of doubt, like a wound that ain't ever healed right, tore. I didn't need no one. How stupid I had been to think there were some kind of we. There was just Bren and me. "If you want to go with Vela, just say so and be done with it. I won't stop you. Stars, Cody, I can't stop you even if I wanted to."

"That is not what I mean." But Cody wouldn't meet my eye.

"Leave then, go on. I thank you for your help, but I don't need nothing from you anymore. I ain't never asked you to come in the first place." My voice burned in the darkness of the tunnel. I were surprised I didn't glow with it.

A slow creep of a blush brushed across Cody's cheeks. "That isn't what I am saying, Jorie, please."

I kept my lips firm closed.

"I'm sorry. Please, I didn't mean it like that." He reached out into the space between us. "I am just so tired and worried."

"I am too, but you don't see me giving up, do you?"

His hand fell to his side, untaken. He took a long time to compose himself, fidgeting with his fingers. When he looked back up his eyes were an odd sort of glossy. "I've never been brave, not like you. And this has all been, so, well"—he gestured to the space—"awful. And my head, it's felt so muddled, like I can't think straight for days. But, Jorie, please. I want to help you and Bren."

I scoffed, but my anger slipped ever so slight away.

"It is all I want." His voice trailed off small, quiet. "You are all I have." He looked up at me then slow, careful. Sincere. My stomach gave a turn, and the tension drained out of me. A tear fell onto his upturned palm.

I knelt down at Cody's side. I put a hand on his shoulder. And that wound, that space that had opened between us, got a little smaller. Because trust, it were a choice. And I chose it. For once in my life, I would choose. And I chose this boy. For good or bad.

"Then we stick together, Cody," I said. "We take care of family. Forever. Even when they are pigheaded, spoiled, untested. . . ."

A small smile flicked at the edge of his lips.

"I know it seems impossible. Stars, I am pretty sure it is impossible. But we will get home."

He smiled at that, and my treacherous, stupid heart give a flutter.

"And I can tell you what that don't mean. It don't mean that we give up. We ain't never gonna give up. So we will get us all home. One way or the other, I swear it. I really have a plan this time."

His eyes found mine. "Then what are we waiting for? Let's get this team home."

My heart gave another treasonous beat.

"I'm just tired is all. My head has been so muddled lately. Did I mention that? But I'm better now," Cody said. "Come on. Let's get her up."

We stood and balanced Bren between us. A feeling not unlike comfort welled inside me. And as I glanced at Cody's profile, I knew it were the scariest thing I'd ever known. And for the first time in my life, I didn't know how to get rid of it.

Soon, lines of untapped metals began appearing in the rock and ice. Like great beams in the thick white streaks of quartz. All of 'em one contiguous metal. Silver ore.

How would the men who lived here have left them? These were mines, a prospector's paradise. Solid earth turned to rubble and grime for a man's profit. So why would these, clear and bright in sweeping lines across the tunnels, still be *here*? The farther we went, the more frequent and organized they became. Embedded in the stone, they looked near to almost . . . purposeful. Like bars. They were just like a cage's bars. So where were the guards? An idea, as unlikely as it could be, struck me.

Ahead of us, Vela had been getting slower and slower, her movements stilted as little pools of wet began to fill her footprints. Now her body sagged, her breath came in deep shaking rattles. Cody and I exchanged a long look.

Vela stood, blocking the way forward. Her silver hair just gently swaying in the breeze of the tunnel before her. And she were shaking.

"Vela?" Cody's voice was achingly hesitant as he stopped a yard behind her.

She half turned toward us, little ripples of motion rendered up and down her thin frame. She was really shaking. And deep rings of blue, heavy bruises loomed under her eyes. Her hollow cheeks so pale they were nearly clear.

Her eyes burned. She weren't shakin cause she were cold.

Slow, we came up next to her. I near stumbled as we stopped. Vela turned her glare on me, her mouth a thin line of pressed rose. Cody cleared his throat.

"I—shouldn't we keep going?" Cody asked, shifting Bren's weight a little more onto his shoulders from mine. Gritting my teeth, I shifted it back.

"Yes." Vela snapped her teeth loud enough that the crunching bone echoed through the chamber. She made no move to go on.

Cody and I exchanged a look. *What were she waiting for?*

"And?" I promoted.

"And nothing," Vela shot back. "This is the way you want to go."

My eyebrows shot up in surprise. Vela didn't want to go down that tunnel. Something were making her uneasy. And she were angling away, holding her arm strange like. But whatever it were, even I could feel the difference in the air. There were a new sharpness to the cold. Like a closing of teeth through snow. There were a storm outside. Near enough to taste it. We were so close.

Vela stood silent in the dark crescent of the tunnel, cold wind snagging at her clothes, her face, her hair. A silver tempest in the growing dark, as all around her the barest of hints of a setting sun pooled liquid and gold around her silhouetted body. Something were dripping from where her hand clamped her upper arm. *Water?* No, it weren't water. It were thicker than that. More like liquid mercury . . .

"Vela?" Cody hesitated at my side, giving me a look. I took Bren into my arms. He approached her, strides even. Slow. "What's wrong?"

He were close enough to reach her, but he didn't. "Is this the way out?"

I didn't like this. I didn't like the stillness. Made my skin crawl. I made to step toward them. At my side Bren began a low, breathy moan.

"Bren?" I turned to my sister. Her eyes were rolling something fierce under the lids. "What's wrong?" The farther we left that passage, the more animated Bren had become. I checked her pulse. Racing faster than it had any right to. As if she were afraid.

I spun. A clatter came from the tunnel behind me. Followed short by Cody's cry. Pain. Warning. Only it came too late.

One moment I were standing at Bren's side, the beat of her heart under my hand, and the next I were falling.

Vela, eyes vicious wild, had grabbed hold of my coat and were dragging me down.

Nails scraped at my skin. Cold and unrelenting. Tearing the fur from my neck. It were all I could do to focus. To put up hands, useless against the wild of the girl above me.

"I saw it," she screamed. Scraping at my chest, my coat, my neck. "Where is it? Where is it?" She kept repeating the words. Over and over. Desperate. "What have you done with it. It is mine!"

Where her hands set upon me, great threads of ice began to grow across my skin. Burning with cold. I gasped. Vela's eyes were . . . untethered. Glowing. There weren't nothing left in them to recognize as the girl we had found. Nothing.

"I don't—understand." I tried to roll. To be anywhere but here. Tight as chains her fingers clamped down around my wrists. Pain tore through me. "What do you want?" I panted. Under her stare I struggled, hair whipping at my face, the uneven tunnel jutting into my spine, cold burning at my bones.

Then quick as a snake her weight were gone. Gulping down air, I scrambled to my knees. And saw her, sprinting down the tunnel. Running right at Cody and Bren.

"No!" I screamed. Then I were running.

But it all began to slow. The shock in Cody's eyes, the sway of Bren's body at his side, but there weren't nothing I could do. As Vela ran into them, and a hand on each, pulled them into the darkness of the tunnel and the waiting black beyond. A silver chain sparking bright in her hands. The ice-stone pulsing silver-red in her grip.

In that single moment, the rock unhinged massive jaws and swallowed them whole. I called and called. Yet nothing came back at me. No Cody, no Bren. No Vela. Just the cold echo of the rocks around me. A burst of wind scuttled through the space, bringing with it heavy flakes of snow.

I ran. Stumbled. Forced my way forward.

A scream erupted in the stillness. Vela.

The cries grew louder. So too did a scent of snow. A deep rumble filled the space, joining a crunching of ice and rock under my thundering feet. Vela, Bren, Cody. None of them were there. This was the only way they could have gone. I ran faster. My heart thundering, my body screaming.

The Flats—cold and white and hungry—burst out before me. Heedless of the pain, the cold, of anything else, I threw myself out into their waiting embrace.

CHAPTER 41

This Echoing Dark

———◆———

A face in the cold stared down at me.

"Bass." I pushed to my feet.

"Pigeon!" The blond woman smiled for all the world as if we was long-lost friends. "How nice to see you again. Our last meeting cut so unfortunately short. Sneaky, sneaky. I'm certain Dev told you there ain't nothing out here I can't find. Even when it tries so desperate to hide from me." She shot a look over her shoulder. "Let's just call it my secret gift, that." She tapped the side of her nose.

Frantic, I searched the snow around her. On either side, Bass were flanked by what must have been twenty men. And their wolves. Their Tracers. And the reason I reckoned Bass would find us. Sooner or later.

"Jorie," a small voice croaked out behind me. "We're here." I spun. Cody were there, propped up against the rock wall of the mine's opening. At his side, his arm clasped protective like round her shoulder, were Bren. Somewhere behind me Bass barked out a crude laugh.

I lurched, hitting my knees on the hard black rock as I came to their side. I grabbed a hold of Bren. She didn't look no worse. I ran a hand over her forehead. But also no better. "You alright?" I asked Cody.

Eyes focused over my shoulder, he tilted his head. But whatever small moment of comfort I had, it were cut short. A woman were approaching.

"And who is this? A third one now, is it?" Bass asked. "You sure are picking up a lot of strays, pigeon."

"My sister is none of your business," I snapped.

"A sister? Of course there is." Bass let out a rolling belly of laughter, hand on her stomach. After a long while, she wiped at her eyes. "Tsk, tsk. So rude. You haven't even thanked me yet."

I glared. "For what? Asking stupid questions in the snow?"

"For saving your ungrateful life." Bass looked me up and down, smile sweet and slow, her finger trailing a long line down the side of her neck. She reached out to the space between us. I recoiled.

"Rill!" Bass snapped. Behind her, the largest man struggled with something in the snow. After a moment, what were giving him no end of grief came into view.

Vela.

Vela with a wide silver collar choking tight around her neck. From which linked heavy chains. Clunky shackles bound her arms and legs. Vela's body twisted. Patches of red flaring hot and angry everywhere the metal seared her skin.

Rill yanked Vela to her knees, thick fingers gripping the chains. Vela were hissing, face a mask of rage. Under her in the snow, the darkness of her shadow flickered.

"Cost us a pretty number of men and women, she has. Never have been able to lure her out into the snows whole enough so to catch her." Bass leaned in close and tapped the side of Bren's face, a lingering smirk in her eyes. "At least this one looks like your mother."

I blinked between the three of them.

"Seems I only needed to set the right bait to catch a me Witch."

Bass gave me a flick of knowing look before turning away. Gesturing over her shoulder for Rill to bring Vela. He obliged. Hefting her weightless as a sheet of silk onto his shoulders.

I could feel Cody behind me, his breath warm on the back of my neck. Ignoring Bass and her gunslingers, I lay a gentle hand on Bren's face. And took a deep breath.

"Cody, are you sure you're alright?"

"I've had better moments, I must admit."

I gave him the wry twist of lips the comment deserved. He coughed.

"What's that?" Cody asked.

I followed his gesture. "The ice-stone," I said surprised. And quiet as I could, I stole over. My fingers closing round the gem in the snow, its surface cracked open. Broken. As if something had fallen out. Deep fissures ran into the metal settings. I closed my hand around it. A jolt shot up my arm.

"It was what she wanted."

From behind me Cody spoke, eyes tired. "When we were in the tunnel, Vela went wild. Screaming about pieces. Where were her pieces, she could feel them. The scent all over us. And then she found that." He indicated the necklace. I placed a hand on my chest where it had been. *Where Vela had been searching.*

With careful fingers I opened Bren's eye. I don't know what I were expecting, but I was sore disappointed. That mote were still there. Red-gold and perfect. I wanted to claw it out, right here. Right now. Instead, I raised my hands, spun, and spit right into the face of the man sneaking up behind me. Eyes furious, he wiped it away as the others closed in on us, a tight circle. Guns raised.

"Into the sled with 'em. It'll do 'em good to see what they've been missing. And there's some mighty big questions I'd like the answers to." Bass barked order after order to her men, bare a glance in our direction, as five sets of hands descended upon us.

This time they didn't bother with the hoods. And though our hands were bound, they were loose enough that they didn't cut into my skin. Though they mightn't have troubled themselves. It were as if all the wounds I'd sustained before the ice palace slammed back into my bones. Even my marrow hurt. Whatever power had kept us unaware of our hurting clear weren't working now.

I couldn't have run if I'd wanted to. And I didn't. We needed to get to Bass's camp. In fact, as I pressed a tired shoulder against Cody's at my side, I were counting on it.

We passed through Nocna Mora first, Bass's men driving the wolves fast, until the town's fallen buildings were naught but crumbling black specks behind us. After an hour, my teeth felt near to rattling out of my skull. My lids became heavy with a thick clotting of frost. Gusts of wind swirled around us, methodically picking their way under cuffs, collars, and wool alike. I fixed down the thin bearskin they'd given me to cover Bren. Another hour passed. Then two, three. Finally, an outcropping of white unlike the snow around it came into focus along the horizon. The musher snapped the reins, sending the wolves snarling as they kicked up speed.

As we got closer, the wind shifted and the smell of burning wood and tanning hides drifted out from Bass's camp. I swallowed hard. This was sure about to get interesting.

CHAPTER 42

What Lingers on the Soul

———— ·◆· ————

I were tossed to the ground rough, knees skidding on the familiar floor of Bass's tent. Cody slung out right after me.

The tent flap opened again as two men between them brought Bren inside. With care they set her down on a pallet of blankets in the corner. Legs like rubber beneath me and brain spinning light, I crawled to Brenna's side. Cody joined me. Vela and her silver chains weren't nowhere to be seen.

"If you done hurt her . . ." I ran a hand over Brenna's face, searching. But there weren't a scratch or bruise on her that weren't there before.

One of the men gave a short snort before letting the tent flap fall back into place. My threat were idle and they knew it. I tucked a blanket up under Bren's head for a pillow. What troubled me was the change. A deep blue tinged her mouth, and little lines of frost had begun growing along the creases of her cracked lips.

A moment later a woman appeared. Dressed in the same gray clothes as the rest of 'em, she didn't make eye contract as she came into the room and set down a pitcher on a small wooden tray. She left it on the floor just inside the tent flap.

Slow, Cody lurched and retrieved the tray. On it sat a flask of melted ice as well as three cold, smoked sweet vetch roots and some salt-cured herring. Vetch never had been a favorite, though bears and caribou did have a mighty fond taste for the mealy tuber. Cody gave them all a long sniff. My stomach growled. So too did his.

Cody handed me some of the herring. Even if it were drugged, that at this point drugs would be better than starvation. I took a long swig of water. And nothing happened. No smell or taste, no shaking of my blood. Carrying the flask over, I tilted up Bren's head and gave her the water.

Finished, I came over and sat cross-legged by Cody's side, offering him some. He took a long pull before setting it down again. Everything hurt.

"I'll eat it first, and if I don't keel over dead . . . ," I said, tearing off a slim strip of fish meat and mashing it with some of the smoked white root.

Cody let out a little scoff. "We'll eat it together then." He took up a piece of the sweet vetch and popped it in his mouth. "Really could use some salt."

I gave him a small smile.

Together, we ate the sparse meal in silence. When we were done, we each fell into sleep. Alone.

A heavy shouting mixed with canine howling racked me from my uneven sleep. I jolted straight up. And immediate regretted it. I raised a hand to my pounding skull. Felt right like a narwhal were trying to spear its way out from behind my eyes.

Careful like, I pushed myself up to a sitting position against Brenna's pallet. Across from me Cody were already on his feet. The tent flap snapped open.

Three heavily armed men strode in, Bass right behind. A sliver of moonlit sky flashed in and out of brilliance before the tent flap once again closed.

They arranged themselves across the entrance. Bass gave us a critical eye, roving between the three of us. After a moment she gave a brusque nod, as if something had been decided.

"Get 'em up," she said. "They're coming with me."

The men jumped to Bass's order. They were certain prompt, I'd give the bastards that. One took my shoulders, draggin me to my feet, the others picked up Cody and Bren. I scuffled with the one holdin me, but he only laughed. I fought his grip as he tried to pick me up.

"I can right well walk myself!" I said, baring my teeth. The man looked at me the way an amused cat might look at a drowning rat.

"Suit yourself," he snorted.

Growling, I pulled up every ounce of what I had left and on shaky but working legs walked. Outside the moon were still clinging to the new ripening morning sky.

The tent we were taken to was four times the size of all the others I'd seen. Two heavy men, their faces covered with thick wool scarves, waited sentry outside. As our party approached, they exchanged a few words before pulling back the tent's entrance.

The heat inside was an unwelcome warmth. One that stank of beer and unwashed bodies. It made my skin feel like it were on fire. Arrayed all around the inner rim of the tent like some human rind, people and wolves stood silent. Following us with eager eyes.

Three empty chairs—two together, one just a little apart from the others—rested in the cloying heart of the tent. Torches and lanterns hung about the room, giving off smoke and casting trembling shadows about the air. The man holding me marched us to the center of the circle, onto a floor thick with rugs.

They stepped back, leaving Cody and me alone. I rubbed the pinched, bruising skin of my neck. Bren they deposited into the arms of the single largest man I had ever seen. He took her weight as if it were nothing but a bolt of starlight.

A low anxious murmur began. A few people shuffled their feet, rocking back and forth, exchanging half-hidden mutters. Eyes fixed not on Cody or me—or even Brenna—but on the empty chair in the heart of the tent.

Unlike ours, this chair were fixed and crisscrossed with tarnished metal chains.

Howling split the night. Tent went dead silent. I spun in my chair, metal slick below my legs. Bass strode into the room. Her back stiff and head high. Right next to the chain-covered chair.

"Warders!" Bass turned about the room, meeting eye after eye. "We are people who have known little of this life save blood and ice and toil. Who have starved, who have lived and died for this land. Who have suffered. And for what? So that we may watch our world—our friends and families—be swallowed, year after year, by an ever-hungrier winter tide. To have lungs and breath and life only to stand by silent as our very bodies grow cold and our lives stolen away in the night for a bargain we did not strike. I say no. I say enough." Bass shook her head. Her whole body boomed with her words, the power of her will. The room buzzed with it. "We do not have to be beholden to some arcane promise our ancestors made out of fear and desperation. I say that there is another way. And that now, here today, I will rip us free. I will see us thrive."

Fevered on her own words, Bass's smile grew and grew. She held up hands for silence. The room stilled.

"Our lives, our children's lives, our very liberty cannot be the cost of victory. We are not prisoners to the past. We are not the promises of our forbearers. And to those of you here that ramble on about old sins and long shadows, I say you are wrong. I say that we, every woman and man and child, every Warder, deserve a life of their own choosing, of their own wanting. To those amongst us who flex and bow to convention, to promises long past keeping, I say this most of all. There can be no true victory without survival. And this." Bass gestured round the room. "This is not surviving."

Heads nodded. The room thrummed with her every word. And she knew it. Bass raised her hands. "Bring me the Witch and I will break her heart. I will kill her and set us free."

The room erupted. A raucous roar, one that shook the very earth under my feet, vibrated down the white length of my bones. Warders beating on their chests, Tracers howling at their sides. All of them hungry.

Cody and me spun in our seats as three women, heavily armed and dressed in thick coats woven tight with silver threads, dragged in a lone supine figure between them.

A figure with hair as silver as the freshly falling starlight.

CHAPTER 43

On All Sides

———◆———

Vela." I didn't scream it, didn't say it any higher than a whisper, really. But nonetheless Bass flashed me a triumphant smile.

Everything, every look and gesture Vela had ever given, every word she'd said or lie she'd told, they all slammed into existence inside me. Next to me, Cody's mouth were near to on the floor. Whatever he had been thinking, it certain clear weren't this.

The women placed Vela, her head lolling limp between them, into the chair, securing her chains. None too gentle. And like the circling of desperate seals under the ice, the crowd were closing in. Fast.

My heartbeat thundered in my chest. The room suddenly too hot, too small, too—too everything all at once. I tried to stand. Only to find a hand slapped down hard on my shoulder. And myself back down on the chair.

Bass were standing right over me. Smile wide. I craned my neck, seeing little other than the worn gray furs of her coat.

"You gave us quite the chase out there, pigeon. Though to be honest, I didn't think we'd find you again after that last storm. Nasty one, that. Miracle, really. Though Rill and Vig near lost your trail a few times, we found you in the end. Just like I said we would."

Like Dev said she would. *Please do not let Bass have killed him.* I scanned desperate the faces around the room. He was not here.

Bass's hand squeezed tighter and I cringed. "Nothing to say about it? Well, that's alright, isn't it, men?" She spun round to room. "We all have to thank you, it seems. What a treasure our little bird has brought us tonight. I'd ask you how you managed it all, though I think it would spoil the effect."

The room laughed. Bass's eyes sparkled. I ground my teeth. Cause nothing good out here ever sparkled. She leaned in close, her next words for me only.

"Some of the men said you were *her*. The Ice-Witch." Bass shot a glance over her shoulder to Vela, who were now moaning low. "But not me, pigeon. Not me." Bass gave me a gentle pat on my cheek. "You're far too smart for that."

I spat.

Bass, sidestepping it, ignored the gesture. "All this is just as my gran foretold. She said, 'Sebastia, watch for the signs. For when our winters have grown too long, for when the ice refuses to let in even a single flicker of green, that'll be the time. The Witch, with her gathered pieces, is testing her cage. And when her heart has come back to her, when she thinks she is the strongest, she will be at her weakest. With that mortal heart comes a mortal life. When that happens, you strike. And strike hard. It is what Warders were born for. Not to guard her, but to finish her. To shatter the Witch once and for all.'" Her voice had dropped, a shiver of something real. And gave my cheek a hard enough pat to leave my skin stinging. "I've no intention of lettin her down."

She spun from me, arms raised high. Buoyed by the chants and calls of her people. Of people born into the ice, lives forged by myth and shadow. Born destined to break the heart of a waking Witch, or die in trying. To do it before she killed them.

Unease flared raw and red in my marrow. Vela had certain fallen into the Warders' hands mighty easy.

A hungry sparrow with a meal in its beak didn't always feel the hawk watching.

Behind Bass, Vela stirred.

"Ah," Bass said, clearing her throat and coming round to crouch in front of Vela's chair. "Seems our guest has finally awoken."

Vela snapped up her head quick as lightning and lunged forward. Wild.

"Oh, I wouldn't try that if I were you. Chains, you see. Silver. Haven't had a proper chance to use them yet, but we made them new, just for you. But of course, you don't mind, do you? Stories say you do like silver real well."

Vela glared at Bass. I were surprised the other woman's skin didn't catch on fire, right there in the middle of the tent. Enough hate spilled out of those rose-gold eyes to burn a town to the ground. To burn it to ash. Hair obscuring her face, Vela's lips began to move in a near-silent whisper, like gathering winds before the squall.

"Nothing to say for yourself? No desperate pleas of mercy? No apologies for the suffering you've caused my people?" Bass's eyes blazed. "Any last curses, Witch? Before I shatter your heart?"

Vela hissed then, throwing her body against the restraints. She only managed to rattle them before the force of her body against the metal made the red welts on her wrists and neck begin to bleed.

Only her blood, it weren't red. Thin lines of silver spilled out of her wounds. The smell of it odd familiar, sweet almost. Like a piece of meat left too long in the sun. A low rumble of laughter filled the room.

Something Vela had said, it clawed at me. Digging to get out. *What is shattered can hardly be broken again.*

Oblivious, Bass strutted about the now-bleeding Vela. "If there is no survival without victory, we, my Warders, we will not only survive, we will thrive!" Bass called. "We shall shatter this curse, break this Witch now and for forever. We will not be held to the mistakes of our ancestors. I will finally free us of this charge. And our children and their children, they will be free!"

Shouts of "Bass, Bass" and "victory" went up in a hearty chorus. Bass, circling back, leaned down in front of Cody and whispered. I couldn't hear. Cody gave a start. Bass said something else, trying to press an object into his hand. Cody jerked his arm back.

Bass spun abruptly away. And stalked to her prisoner. She leaned in, all bravado and sway. I caught a sliver of Vela's contorted face, a tick at the corner of her lips. Bass reached out a hand to Vela's chin. Their eyes met. A pale glowing light began to pulse under the surface of Vela's skin. Bass didn't seem to notice. Vela's eyes snapped to Bass's. Ever so slow, Vela licked the blood from her cracked lips. Bass's shoulders went taut as she growled something I couldn't hear. My mind raced. Stars, something were wrong. Very, very wrong.

I stood. We had to get out of here. On her pallet, Brenna began to shake. Seizing. Spit leaked out of the corner of her mouth, tinged red where she were biting her tongue. Then behind me Bass were screaming. Everyone were screaming.

And into that rising red chaos, Vela began to laugh.

CHAPTER 44

Whatever the Cost

———————

The chains around Vela's neck and wrists were glowing red. Dark lines curled up her arms, her neck. Great sheets of frost formed and melted and reformed all across her skin. Until, from in between the cracks in the icy covering, a thick black-green water began to leak. Running down her legs and arms. And with every wild laugh that burst from Vela's blistering mouth, Bren's body grew colder, twisting under my hands.

And then, the chains simply broke. "Time, I think, you learn that silver, like Witches, are not all made the same." With her words the hiss of smoke rose, the smell of melting metal and a rotting sea, sweet and bitter and cloying, filled the air.

Dark drips of molten metal cascaded to the floor. Her chains gone, her body once again growing over with ice, like a second skin. With eyes glowing bright as newly forged steel, Vela got to her feet. All her welts were gone. With a little flick of smile, she flung the scorching metal out into the crowd behind her.

Vela stood and surveyed the thunderstruck tent around her. A woman screamed as the metal seared into her skin, pulling useless at her furs as the blistering chains heated through them, catching fire. A few of her fellow Warders turned to help her. Finally, her cries died away, leaving an open, uneasy hush.

"Such little creatures, so frail, so weak." Vela sneered, eyes blazing bright as stars. "So very mortal. How naive. How limited. How very small. Always so confident in what you do not understand. You say there will be no victory here without your survival." She raised her arms. A small ball of pale white light, a cold and burning sun, swirled into life in her palms. Hair eddying around her with an unseen wind. "Well, I am happy to show you otherwise."

Outside the tent, the world trembled, and the very air began to scream. For a long moment time was suspended, held still by unseen hands. Every nerve in my body ringing. And then, into that perfect storm, Vela let the orb of light go.

Confusion erupted throughout the tent. I pushed hands to my ears, trying and failing to block it out. My pulse ripped through my veins, adrenaline spiking and painful. Making it hard to breathe.

I scrambled to my sister's side. I put my hand on her brow, her head tossing under my fingers. Stars. Instead of cold, she were scorching. So cold she *burned*.

What is happening? I dug my fingers hard into the furs over her, tying to keep her down. But the violence of her convulsions tore her from me. Her back arching impossibly off the pallet. And then Cody's hands were on mine, his weight helping to hold Bren. The world behind us erupting into chaos.

"Brenna, hold on!" For a brief shining moment, I thought she heard me. Her eyes opened and focused on mine. But then it was my turn to start screaming.

The mote, the one in her eye. It weren't small any longer. In its place a red-rimmed blackness spidered, spreading outward. All from that one little red-gold spot. The Witch's mark.

A knife flew over my head, the edge of its blade just brushing the edge of my ear. I ducked reflexively, barely feeling the cut. The blade snagged into the fabric of the tent in front of me, falling to the ground. At the same time the roar of bullets began to fill the tent.

"Jorie! We have to go!"

I shot a look over my shoulder. People were churning all over the tent. Shots and knives flying. The tent opening was flapping in the wind, the just-lightening sky swirling with what could have been snow, but the soft red glow said otherwise. It were smoke. The camp was burning.

Vela was nowhere to be found, but I had no doubt she was at the center of it all. I gripped Brenna by the shoulders and looked up at Cody. Cody frowned, but agreed. "Hold on."

Under my hands, Bren's skin continued to burn hot. Cody darted out into the fight. The tent overhead began an ominous creaking. In a second, though it felt a hundred, Cody fell back.

"Here."

He handed me a short-handled revolver.

"It has only two bullets, but it's something."

I didn't want to know whose it had been. Bloody fingerprints littered the grip. I wiped them off onto my pants.

"If we—"

Someone slammed into my shoulder, rolling off. I shoved at them, not seeing their face as they spiraled into the crowd. A second later, another face, this one familiar, came tearing in our direction.

Her shirt was torn, exposing long welts and a massive gash that ran deep from ear to hip. A red scar trailed from the eye of the great serpent inked on her side. As if the snake itself were weeping. Bass stumbled toward us, eyes raw. "This is all my fault. I should have listened to Dev. But I wanted to help my people, my family. It is all I have ever wanted my whole life. And I have failed."

I shook my head.

"I have. I misjudged her strength. I'm too impatient, always have been. I thought it was me, that I could kill her. I were wrong. But if we hurry, you might still have that chance. You can still free our people from this curse. To let us all just—live." We both glanced down at Bren.

"Me? How?" Everything were happening so quick. Like I'd not the air to make it from one breath to the next. "I don't know anything."

"You don't need to. It's in your blood."

"What are you talking about?"

Bass shook her head. "Look, the Witch's magic, we ain't ever found a way to kill it. Only hold it, hide it. But that kind of power, it don't take to settling real nice. It finds ways out. Maybe it's only a little at first that you don't notice, but it leaks out all the same. Why do you think our winters get worse year after year? We can't stop it, we can only slow it. Didn't you ever wonder about that necklace your sister wore, about why it were only passed from mother to daughter for generations? Well, it ain't cause we needed to keep it warm. No one can be that close to that much power for as long as your family and not be changed by it."

Realization dripped cold at the edge of my thoughts. The Warders. The prison. The stone. Bren. This woman had known Bren, and then me, had carried the last piece of the Witch's heart. That it were leeching into us slow and corrupting and had done nothing about it. Stars, she had not even told us.

"Jorie, look at me. I were wrong. But this ain't over yet. The Witch, she still needs your sister." She were begging me to understand. "She needs her body. She needs an unbroken shell to hold together the gathered pieces of her broken heart. Your sister is that shell. And if we let that happen, the Witch won't just kill you, she will cover the whole world in her winter. She will drown us all." Bass fixed on me then, eyes watery and more than a little wild. "Do not let her."

Bass took my hand and placed it over Bren's eye. "That spot, I've seen it before. It is a spike. Are you watching? A thin sliver of enchanted ice. It's how the Witch controls them, the people she chooses. Once she places it, the mark anchors them to her. She feeds from it, stealing their life one breath at a time. You need to get it out."

My head spun with the noise and the heat of the tent. With the words being said.

I opened my mouth, but then Cody were there, hand on his side, mouth pressed in a painful line. "She's coming!"

Vela was coming. Inside, my heart could not beat any faster. I could feel every spring of its pale muscles beating in my chest. Aching. Forcing blood through my veins, oxygen to my brain. *If you are still alive, Jorie, you had better pull yourself together.*

"Take this. It is the last true piece my grandmother ever made. Before our supplies ran out. I'm sorry there ain't more. I'm sorry for everything." Bass pressed a small silver coin into my hand. It was warm in my palm. A little buzz flitted up my arm from where the coin brushed my skin. "Your sister will need to swallow it. Like all creatures of her making, the Witch can't survive the touch of silver." Bass's eyes went wide then. "The touch of this silver." She pressed the coin harder into my palm. "Do you understand? Have your sister swallow this coin. It will loosen the spike. Only a little, but enough. You can pull it then, and once it is out, she will lose control and—" Bass gave a startled cry, her back arching to the point of obscenity.

A deep coppery-red blossom spread across her chest. A look of shock passed over her features. She placed a hand over the stain, her eyes gone wide, her fingers coming away wet. This was it. A hunter always knew a fatal shot when she saw one. A small smile flickered across her lips as she fixed her eyes on mine. Urgent.

"Go, pigeon," she whispered. "Go." With those final words, Bass slumped to her side. Sprawled body twitching, chest bleeding out across the rug underneath.

"Jorie!" Next to me, Cody was shooting hard. "Jorie, we have to move."

Raising Bren's head into my lap, I said a little prayer, for all the good it had ever done me, and shoved the silver coin through her clenched lips.

The moment the coin reached the redness of her throat, Bren let out a bone-splitting scream, her lips pulled back in a rigor of a snarl, her body tensing.

It was the most inhuman sound I'd ever heard.

CHAPTER 45

Of Snow and Ash

W hen we finally managed to stumble out of the tent, the night outside was freezing.

The stars above were fast fading into the dawning sky. A last hint of the aurora borealis haunted the horizon, a pale green specter clinging to vanishing glory, hounded by the fire raging behind. By Vela's white fire.

"This way," I called, striding in the direction of the supply tents. Least where I remembered them to be. We had just made it out in time. Whatever Vela had unleashed in there, it hadn't only flattened the tent we'd been in, but near to everything nearby. I stumbled as my boot caught a splinter of broken wood. I glanced down. No, not wood. Bone.

From overhead, thick flakes of snow began to fall, heavy and uncaring around us. A few settled on my eyelashes. I wiped them away. But they didn't go clean; instead they smeared. I looked down at my hands. It weren't falling snow. It were ash.

It were raining ash. Screams filled the air. My stomach turned.

Between us, we lugged Bren. Running farther and farther into the camp. At least she had stopped shaking. I frowned. I weren't sure if that was a good thing or a bad thing.

We rounded a corner.

"You. Stop." The woman's voice cut the air. Her black hair were disheveled, a thick river of red ran from her temple. Raising a hand to her temple, she swayed on her feet, eyes blinking far too quick to be right. But whatever swirled in her head, it didn't stop her from aiming her gun.

"Stop," her words slurred. "You."

I gripped Cody's arm. Her concussion must have been worse than she knew.

"We mean no harm. We were just leaving," Cody said, voice soft. Kinder than any words I could've mustered.

The woman ran a hand over her face, arm erratic. Jerky. "I think you'd better come with me."

I stepped toward her. But just then a massive boom erupted into the night. The woman staggered, stunned. Her gun fell. She soon after it. White light flashed across the sky. Followed quick by billows and billows of smoke. Vela were not leaving nothing standing in her wake. Which, I knew very keen, would include us. But first she needed to find me. I didn't need to be told twice. As the disoriented Warder lurched in the dirty snow, scampering for her gun, we ran.

Tent after tent, none of them were right. The first held nothing but straw and ice. The second and third were filled with people. All of them huddled against the white backdrop of the canvas. All of them, though scared, were nonetheless all too bravely ready to fight. The sky around us burned and burned. And so too did the Warders.

I had near to given up when, lurching into the fourth tent, I miraculous saw what we needed. There, stacked perfect against the pale canvas, were what I wanted. Supplies.

Packs of crates, stacked goods, it were all arranged about the space. Just as I'd remembered.

I took a deep swallow of the hot bile rising in my throat. I let out a little cough, my grip on Bren's waist loosening.

"Look for anything we can use. Food, tents, furs, flasks. Anything you think we need to get back home. If you can carry it, you grab it."

"Got it."

We set her down, leaning her back against the least splintery of a set of tall pine crates. She gave a little puff of an exhale. She was starting to show some signs of coming around, bearing some weight on her legs and fluttering her eyes. When we sat her up, she stayed that way without our help. It should have made me happy.

I pulled my hair back out of my eyes and started looking. We weren't out of trouble yet, not by a long shot.

We still needed a way out of here, but if we didn't grab supplies, we might as well just give up and starve now. A massive bang rocked the air, sending ripples over the goods around us. The screams weren't far behind. Neither was the increasing chemical smell of smoke.

I picked up a sturdy-looking canvas bag and hurried over to a promising pile of boxes. The first were empty. And the second. I moved to the next set of supplies. A sense of dread rising. Maybe this were where they kept all the things they rejected. The spoiled bits.

"Jorie!" Cody called. "Look here." In his hands he held something eerie familiar. My ma's sealskin pack. He tossed to it me.

I opened the ties. Inside were my possessions. Some of what we'd scavenged after the ox attack. I pushed aside a black sulfur orb—which were mercifully still warm—and my chest gave a little flutter. Cause there, sitting right there in the bottom of the pack, were two of my pouches. The black one and the white one. The one with the iron ore and the one with quicklime. I smiled.

Beyond the orbs and the powders, some bullets, furs, and a water flask were inside. It were a start. I rifled through the supply tent, filling the sealskin pack with everything useful I could find. A particularly fine-looking saw-toothed blade caught my eye. I picked up the knife. A sharp serrated edge sat perfectly balanced on a walrus tusk handle. It felt smooth and right in my hand. I tucked it away at the small of my back.

Pack full, I walked over and helped Cody load up his. When they were both filled—with a jumble of supplies I hoped would be enough—I slung my pack up onto my back. The muscles of my shoulders sank a little under the weight of it.

With an effort, we strung Bren up between us. A little wind-up marionette. My heart lurched as a groan, quiet but sure, escaped her lips. Time, I think, to find us some dogs. Covering my head, I pulled up the thick cocoon of my hood.

"I hear barking!" And I did. I turned us in the direction, hoping it weren't just dogs on the loose, but those still in their dens.

"Me too."

"This way." We turned the corner and ran straight into a set of working animals. One lonely pack. My smile spread from ear to ear.

"Fen!" It were too good to be true, but the second I called her name the dog bolted to her feet. She ran right at me. "You're okay!" The dog began nuzzling at my sides, hitting my hand, impatient like. I gave a little chuckle. She licked and nipped at my arm. Gods, small mercies. I were thankful for small mercies.

They were all there. So too was a sled. We stumbled over and set Bren in the litter, both Cody and I going about getting the dogs harnessed.

"Shh! Fen, settle down, girl. I know, I know, I missed you too." Fen was nudging along in my footprints, half inspectin my work, half bossin me around. I reached over and tussled her ears. Her tongue lolled. *Good girl.* She were a welcome relief I didn't even know I needed. Somehow everything just felt less . . . heavy.

When we finally had all the dogs harnessed, we was ready to move. We maybe might just make it out onto the Flats and then maybe, if we were lucky, home. So if we could just get out of camp before—

"Don't move."

I froze, the click of a barrel snapping against the back of my head.

CHAPTER 46

Dead Men's Burdens

———◆———

E ven through the thick fur of my hood the muzzle was cold.

"Lower your hood. And turn around. Slow like. Hands where I can see 'em."

I complied, anger deep and raw rushing in. I didn't have time for this. We didn't have time for this. A heavy wind whipped at my face as I turned around, gray ash-covered snow crunching cold under my heels. A man stood there, his blood-covered arm leaking slow waxy red drops into the snow, gun raised.

"Stars above, Jorie." The gun fell from me. "You're alive."

"Dev." I breathed it out.

We blinked at each other for a long time. He were shaking. A slow drip of red pooling into the snow at his feet. I didn't right know to be worried or mad.

"And you're hurt."

Dev gripped his arm. "This? Nothing to worry about. Just grazed. Here, let me help you." His voice unsteady, his movements stiff. That little pool of red growing bigger at his feet.

I frowned, worried. "You sure don't *look* fine. Let me look at that." I took a step toward him, but Dev took a step back shaking his head.

"Forget about it. I deserve it." Dev shook his head real slow, his face a grim mask. It weren't a look I right liked. "You need to get as far away from here as you can."

"Trying, Dev." I tried to say it light, only it came out flat.

Dev glanced over his shoulder. At where Bren lay. Frown deepening. "Jorie, I didn't know before how to tell you. About your Ma, about everything."

"Then tell me now." The answer urgent in a way it never had been before, that knowing.

"Don't matter anymore." Dev doubled over, pain on his face. Hand on his side. Blood leaked between his fingers. "Centuries of waiting and now it's too late." Dev laughed bitter. "This world of ice and pain and death, what is it all even for?"

"Uh, guys, I am pretty sure we need to move. Right now," Cody said.

Morning light sputtered over the horizon. So too did the big black billows of smoke. "The Witch is changing more than just the snows to suit her needs. I see that now. And I've failed you. Jorie, I've failed all of us."

"Dev, you haven't. I don't know what—"

"You saw the way she broke those chains?"

I had. That I understood well enough.

"We though we were ready. But she's too strong. I don't know how to stop her. Not anymore. Not when Bass's silver don't even pierce her. So just get out of here, Jorie, and live. All of you. Just live. It's all I can do for you now." Dev were rambling. The red pool growing slick at his feet. Muttering incomprehensible, he stumbled and, grimace on his face, started helping us load up the sled.

When we were done, Dev paused at the front of the dogs.

Bending down on one knee, he tucked his gun into the holster at his side and pressed his face into Fen. A little tear at the corner of his eye. He wiped it away with shaky fingers. Fen wagged her tail real slow, sending a dusting of snow swirling into the cold breeze.

"You take good care of them, Fen, you hear. Get them home. . . . I am so sorry. . . ."

Fen gave a little rumble and licked at Dev's tears.

I turned away. This were clear not meant for me. I busied myself helping Cody settle Bren into the litter as explosions rattled the air around us.

I glanced down at her eye. The mote, no longer flush, looked like a blister. She said I could take it out. Bass said I could take it out.

I took off my glove, fingers hovering just above it. With slow care, I began to pull. Slow at first, and then quick, the little red dot began to slip out. I suppressed a wave of nausea and kept pulling. Clean-sided and clear, it were just like Bass said. A sliver of ice.

It was first cold, then hot in my hand. I tossed it away. Wiping my fingers, which felt sudden as if I had plunged them into a fire.

When I looked back at my sister, she began to move her lips. My heart jumped. I lowered my ear to her mouth. Nothing but the warm motion of her breathing met me. I cupped a hand around her cheek and she let out a little sigh. I bent and kissed her forehead, her face for the first time restful.

Clearing my throat, I stood up. I slipped a long leather strap over Brenna's waist to secure her down to the sled. It weren't a lot, but it should keep her tight. I nestled a few of the black sulfur orbs in at her sides, covering her with a thick blanket.

When I looked up, Dev was looking down at Bren, her calm face the only visible bit above the furs, and smiled.

"You found her right enough, Jorie, just like you said."

"I did."

We stood there, looking at Bren and not each other.

"Jorie . . . she won't give up, you know. Not till she gets her back."

My hand tightened on the blade at my side. There was no need to tell me who that *she* was. Vela. Good thing I weren't gonna let her touch my sister. Not ever again. The smell of burning ripped by on the wind. The fire growing closer. I twisted my head around. A deep white light, the lick of an impossible flame, poured into the sky. It were coming straight toward us. Vela was coming. Dev saw it too.

"You aren't coming home with us." It wasn't a question. He had clear made up his mind. And no matter what I argued, I weren't gonna be able to change it.

Dev gave a sad little smile. The answer plain in his eyes. "I will slow her down." He patted the gun at his side. After a second, he reached into his pocket and held his hand out.

Slow, I reached out and took it.

"Thought you might want it back."

Ma's necklace. I closed the space between us. And hugged him. Hard. We parted, Dev clearing his throat. "Now you promise me that you won't stop for nothing, you hear me? Nothing."

I nodded, fighting back the well of hot tears. And without another word, Dev turned to face the camp. Gun drawn. His silhouette a flickering shadow against the flames.

The expanse of ice and frost gaped wide and fearsome before us. Unwelcoming as it were deadly. But somehow, after the chaos of the camp, the shimmering silence of the Flats were a familiar relief. That weren't something I'd ever thought I'd feel a fondness for.

We made it maybe half a day out of the camp before she caught us.

CHAPTER 47

Of Hail and Fire

The sudden stillness was our only warning. Bitter wind rushing into my face, I glanced behind. What had been the open ice were now nothing so much as an all-smothering wave of white. And it were getting closer. This squall was built of snow and ice and wind. Six stories high, it darkened the light of the sky.

I pushed the dogs harder. They picked up their speed, feet and fur churning ahead. They too could feel it. In the distance, a long line of black stilts came into existence.

The Petrified Forests.

Ice crystals like shards of glass, sharp needles hangin from their naked branches, freezing in the darkness. Storms died in there. And maybe, just maybe, if we made it there, we might have some semblance of cover. Small and desperate as that hope were. I harried the reins. Lightning and thunder rutted the darkening sky as heavy clouds, bellies thick with snow, swelled everywhere around us. My teeth rattled wicked in my skull.

The dogs pulled harder, their hackles raised, teeth bared. We raced so fast it were near enough to flying. I forgot for a moment it weren't.

The wind whipped at my face, blurring my vision at the edges where tears were torn from my eyes, cold air forced pore by pore into my body. Behind us, the press of the storm circled closer. A blizzard's eye.

We ran and we ran, the lines of individual tress becoming clearer and clearer at our approach. Only a few hundred yards away, I could just make each one out. But it weren't gonna be enough. We just weren't gonna be fast enough.

Sure enough, another three breaths and the forest paled from view. Ice and hail overtook our sled, sending everything around us into a swirling, roaring obscurity. The storm's embrace throwing us like rag dolls up and out from the safety of the sled. For a long moment I were weightless, floating in the frosted air, and then I weren't.

My already-aching body hit the ground hard, limbs and bones bouncing off then grinding against the ice pack below me. My body skidding to a stop. Dazed, I scrambled to my knees, feet slipping. Beads of hail the size of bullets scattered across the ice, making footing slick at best and painful bruises across our skin at worst. Sleet, sharp and sticky, beat against my brow. I pulled up the hood of my coat. And then, as violent as it had arrived, there were a sudden hush. Like the breathing of the ocean, it engulfed me.

I unbowed my head. All around me the storm raged. Just not where I was standing. The heart of the storm were as still as water trapped in ice. Outside of it, the world spun with the viciousness of the clashing snowstorm. But not here. Not in the center of it all. Here it was silent.

Maybe a hundred yards away, direct in front of me, the slim figures of the rock trees pierced the silent air. To my left lay the eviscerated remains of the sled. I drug my body over to it, forcing heaving muscles to move, burning lungs to move air.

Our possessions were scattered against the earth, cracked and broken. The harnesses at the front flapped empty in the fading remains of the wind. And the litter. It was empty. Brenna was gone. The world spun, and this time it had nothing to do with the wind.

"Jorie! Over here!" Cody's voice cut across the thunder.

I didn't move toward the call, but stood concussed, staring at the shattered sled. From somewhere outside the eye of the storm, the braying of dogs echoed about on the wind. And then from that nothing there were something.

A thick-gloved hand. It grabbed my shoulder, dragging me backward.

I went stumbling, the world falling. With both speed and care, Cody shunted me behind the skeleton of one of the petrified trees.

"There!" Cody pointed, shoulders hunched, muscles coiled tight.

I squinted into the haze. It took me a second of searching, but I soon enough saw it. And it weren't nothing to put my mind at ease. Cause out in the breath of the blizzard, she stood untouched by the winds and snow. Unmoving.

Vela.

And she wasn't alone.

Bren was next to her, my sister's body swaying on her feet. A fish on a line, her movements were unnerving smooth. And just like Vela, Bren was indifferent to the winds whipping around her. A shiver ran down my spine, sharp as glass. Vela's mouth moved, words I could not hear. Bren slid to her knees. Her head bowed.

Vela placed her hand on Bren's cheek. Slick as a flame, something passed between them. Dark and jagged, like the lines that had crawled up Vela's skin in the tent. When she were executing everyone. I jumped to my feet. Cody jerked me back down again. "You can't go running out there, she'll kill you," he hissed. "You can't help Brenna if you are dead." Cody's eyes latched on to mine, searching. His fingers intertwined with mine. He were beggin. For me. I took a deep breath. Cause he was right. I couldn't do nothing to save her if I were dead. There had to be another way. Another way I ain't thought of. Yet.

"Silver!" The answer hit me sudden. "It's what Bass used to control her. We saw it work back in that tent."

"Jorie, we saw it work—a little. Maybe. But even all those chains that Bass had, they did not hold her all that well." Cody shivered. "Besides, we don't have anything of the like. Let alone more."

Across the way, Bren's body started to go dark. Her hair curled about her face, like tentacles of some giant squid. A darkness scuttled under her skin, everywhere except one little place. A deep red pulse at her center. The place where that coin had settled in her guts.

But it weren't enough. Whatever had left Vela were leeching rotten inside Bren, dimming that light. As Bren grew darker, bright as the sun Vela began to glow. Dev's words floated to me. *They don't even pierce her.* But Vela could bleed. I'd seen it. She could be hurt. I had to find a way.

"But it worked. That's the part I care 'bout. It did. You saw them cut her, saw her bleed and break. What if the silver weren't on her"—I glanced uncomfortable at Bren—"but inside her? You saw how that it expelled the Witch mark. What would it do to the Witch?"

Cody blinked at me, running a hand through the wind wild of his hair. "Except we don't have any silver." His face fell for a second. "Maybe, just give me one shot . . . it might be enough to distract her. You grab Bren. And then you run, Jorie. You run. And you don't turn back. I don't know how long I can keep you covered, but I can sure as stars try." His face a mess of emotions. I reached out careful like. His cheek smooth under my fingertips.

Slow, Cody lowered my hand, bringing his face close, his breath floating near mine. With care, he pressed his lips light and warm against my skin, kissing my palm. A thrum of sensation rippled through me. Cody smiled sad.

Dropping my hand, he gripped his gun. His eyes resigned and angry all at the same time. He was going to let Vela kill him. For me. For Bren. I weren't gonna let that *monster* take one more person I loved. Not one more.

I shook my head. "No deal. I won't be leaving you to die. So you can just put that stupid heroic idea right of your foolish stubborn Southerner's head, Cody Colburn, cause I ain't got plans to let any of us die. Not today."

A small smile shifted at the edge of his lips before I reached up and brushed it away.

"So where do we get this silver then?" He began searching his pockets.

Out across the ice, Brenna began to moan, her body pulling back, away from Vela. She were fighting just the same as us. That soft glow, the coin in her belly, began beating against the shadow around her. I stared. The silver was—pulsing. Like a tiny heartbeat.

I ripped the broken necklace out from my pocket. And looked at it. At the broken setting. At the silver that had held the stone. A piece of a heart. Vela's heart. Held it and kept it. Silver-blue, the setting buzzed weakly in my palm. Just like the coin had. And the coin had worked. *This silver*, the look of realization on Bass's face as she had said it. Understanding slammed into me. This wasn't any silver. The silver of this necklace weren't just silver. It was pieces of the Witch's prison. It had contained a piece of her heart. And it would sure as stars stop it now.

The necklace, broken stone and all, burned hot in my palm.

CHAPTER 48

Breaking Darkness

T hank you, Ma. Thank you.

I shucked my gloves and began to tear desperate at the silver chain.

"Come on, come on," I muttered. "There." I pried the fractured stone away. Leaving the setting and its links. Together they were only half the size of my fist. My heart lurched. Would it be enough? I didn't know.

"We need more."

Without a word, Cody reached into his pocket and pulled out the silver compass. The words engraved in the surface flashed in the starlight. Could it be? I nearly laughed. Opening the top, he let the little coils of silver, parts of the broken compass, parts that had held something precious once, slide into his hand. Something from the North. We had enough.

I gave Cody's other hand a hard squeeze.

Wrapping all of the necklace pieces around the jagged edge of my blade, I spiraled it around. The rest of the silver I handed to Cody. I pulled out the two leather pouches I had recovered from our things at Bass's camp. The black and the white. The quicklime and the iron. Quick, I broke off a large chuck of stone bark from the tree.

I also broke off a long slender icicle from the lowest branch. With care, I upturned the pouch. A bright blaze of fire erupted, hot enough to force my hand away. Hot enough, I smiled, to heat the stone.

Snow melted into boiling water around where the bark sat, sprinkled in the iron ore. And then, the silver. Soft metal already, the shards of silver didn't take much heat to become malleable enough. To liquefy.

When they were a twisted mixture of black and silver, smooth as oil on water, I plunged the knife into the liquid. The metals bubbled. The handle grew hot, but I didn't drop it. Silver fused into the blade.

After a minute I pulled it from the mix. The thick blade of tempered steel dripped with the black of the iron and the molten shine of the melted silver. I plunged the blade into the snow at my side. It hissed something fierce.

I turned to Cody. He took out one of the shells from his gun, dumping all but the casing into the melt water at our feet. Deep breath—which I immediate regretted—I took the shell casing from his hand. And poured the remaining molten metal inside.

There were three bullets, one silver knife. It was gonna have to be enough. He had his, I had mine. Four chances. All we got. Except way I figured, it was better than most people ever got.

"Ready?" I asked.

"Ready," he replied, raising his gun and taking aim. Ready to cover me.

Outside the storm, Brenna screamed.

In among the bodies of the trees, Cody settled in, limbs digging into the snow and frost, body heavy. Bullets loaded, rifle raised, his sights fixed on the pair of women just outside the yellowed center of the storm. If I failed, he would take the shot.

This was it then. I pulled off my coat, set it on the ground. I did not feel the cold. Silver-coated knife in one hand, I made a rush for the waiting whiteness of the storm just beyond.

CHAPTER 49

Under Another Sky

———◆———

I hit the storm wall at a dead sprint. It hit me back just as hard.

Air slammed out of my lungs, I stumbled over the threshold. One hand pressed to my chest, mouth gaping. I gulped bigger than a two-horned sculpin on land. But hitting that wall, it were like running straight into water, the thickness of the storm unforgiving heavy about my bones.

The cold tore at my skin, the wind licking at my lungs. Finally I took a jagged breath. Gripping the blade at my side, I ran on, legs pumping against the exhaustion, adrenaline plunging through my veins.

They were in front of me. Bren and Vela. They were both of them on their knees. Vela's reed-like fingers gripping Bren's bowed head. Black lines twisted over Bren's skin. A kiss of darkness swilling in her veins, a contrast to the silver lines pulsing through Vela's. Not unlike iron and ice they were.

Snow pooled around them, a twisted globe of white. I ran for it.

Ten steps away. Five steps. Three steps away. My heart beat an uneven rhythm against the slick lining of my chest. Vela chanting high and urgent. Screaming words into the wind. Words I didn't know, but which Bren were repeatin, her voice breaking with disuse.

I flexed my fingers on the hilt of my blade. The metal colder than the plunging temperature around me. I dug my skin into the pommel, till I had no idea where my flesh ended and the handle began. Two steps away. One step away . . .

Vela's eyes shot to mine. I froze. Not cause I didn't want to move, but cause I couldn't. A low laugh played across her distorted features. Her fingers never left Brenna's head. If anything, Vela were even more beautiful than before. A burning star. She was radiant. And I wanted nothing so much as to stab my blade straight into her gorgeous beating heart. My muscles were aching with the strain of trying to just move.

A shot rang in across the ice. Right next to her, it grazed the shoulder of her silver gown. Vela's lips pulled back in a snarl. The snow began to whip harder. Faster. One step away . . . my arm shook with the effort, but I wasn't moving. Another shot. This one took her in the ear and she were forced to clasp a hand to it. Her blood didn't freeze. Just sat there, slick and glistening.

"I will break this world, rip it fissure by fissure, before you will take this from me. I will not go back to that prison, not now, not ever again. I will have this body." Vela whipped her head around as a bullet tore the air, the crack of ice singing in its path. I smiled. Keep it up, Cody. My heart cried, even if I couldn't speak. One step away . . . one more.

Vela looked down at Bren then, my sister's breathing ragged. A deep, visceral cry ripped through the air, tearing at the cold and haze and storm.

With a massive leap, Fen and Boz exploded out of the wall of snow and ice. Teeth and fur and feral eyes blazing. Great padded paws landed home and Vela crumpled under their combined weight, dispersing the snowpack under their fall. Snarls ripped through the air. They spun away into the wall of the storm. So too did Vela's screams. Sudden as silt after a storm, I could move again.

I ran to Brenna's side. I took her shoulders in my hands. Her head snapped up. Her eyes, near black in the pale sockets.

"Jorie?"

My heart stopped. I choked back all the anger and frustration and pain and tears. I spoke near as calm as I ever had.

"I'm going to get you out of this, I swear it. Just hold on, Bren. Hold on."

The blue and brown of her eyes blazed, the black retreating to the edges. A shadow ran across her features. Scowling, I spun, heels digging into the snow, blade tight in my hand. And stalked to the roiling pile that was Boz and Fen and Vela. My soul harder than ice.

Boz sunk his thick yellow fangs deep into the meat of Vela's arm. She let out a scream, tearing the dog from her skin. With impossible strength, she flung him from her. His body swallowed whole by the storm around us. His cries lost to the squall.

Panting, Vela got to her hands and knees. Around her, Fen prowled, darting in and out, snapping her jaws. Long lines of silver dripped from the pack leader's gums, from where she had already taken pieces of Vela. Vela snarled.

"I will have the freedom owed me, my bargain is paid! Have I not suffered enough, is this not enough?" Tears ripped frozen down her porcelain skin, her hair wild as a squall raging about her, her face turned skyward. And yet for all of it, for all her heartrending screams hurtling into the darkness around her, the call went unanswered.

Vela's face were contorted by rage. By pain. By loss. It were the nearest to human I'd ever seen her. And for the barest of moments, I believed her will were stronger than mine. That I would lose.

But it were only a moment. As with the next heartbeat a searing blast of pure resolve flooded through me, adding strength to my pulse and drive to my bones. No. She would not win. A flash of fur off to my left caught my eye. I ground my teeth against the cold and smiled. Cause, Bren and me, we mattered just as much. Not to mention Bass, all those people back in the tent, their families, their lives.

Just cause Vela had been torn from her world, it didn't mean she had the right to tear us from ours.

I looked at her this time and saw her. Not the fury and the anger, but the once-living girl, a girl who had to stand by helpless as everything she'd ever loved had been torn from her. As her sister and father and mother had been killed. Murdered by the very people she had called friends. And in that instant I understood why Vela had made that bargain. Why she had sold her life for the vengeance to which she had been owed. And honest, I did not know if I could say I'd have chosen different. And I knew then that it weren't hate inside me for what Vela had become, but pity for what she had been. For the life she had lost. Sadness for what she had become. Dark, twisted. Lost.

Even Bass had it wrong. No survival without victory? That weren't right.

Victory meant nothing without the people you loved. Because without love, without even the memory of it, there were nothing left to be victorious about. Even if Vela killed us all, if she found that vengeance, her own victory over the descendants of the people who had long ago killed her family, she would never be free. Not really. Not like this.

"Well, you are right about one thing, Vela." I inched ever closer. "I *don't* know that I can stop you. But I know I can try."

Vela snapped her eyes to mine, her face a snarl of rage. And in that moment lines of black flashed under her silver skin, a mirror of Bren. Vela did not seem to notice the change. "You think I care what—"

But whatever I thought, she didn't get time to tell me, cause Fen and I lunged at the same time, the dog from the right and me from the left. Vela had no direction to turn. I raised my blade.

Vela twisted away, as if she were the storm itself, ashen and mutable. Panic shot though me. I weren't gonna land the blow. I was gonna miss. After everything, I was going to fail.

Sudden as thunder, Fen slammed into Vela's blind side.

My arm fell.

The blade sank. Deep. Biting flesh and sinew and light.

The silver of my smelted blade kissing the very form of her muscles, snapping the fascia and tearing into the bone. Pressing it right up and between her ribs. Straight to her shattered heart.

A look of hatred turned sudden to shock. And confusion. Vela scampered back. Hands clutching to the handle of the silver-coated knife. Face scared. With a silent cry, silver cracks fissured through her skin. Breaking. Then, mouth open, silver blood spooling from her body like lines of starlight into a midnight sea, Vela simply ceased. Stopped.

Her shell just hanging in the cold, her parts sealed together by nothing so much as the memory of their closeness.

Her body just—dissolved. Skin and muscles, blood and bone, all scattered into a million flakes of ice. Perfect crystalline snowflakes.

Fragments of what they once were. Each one, one by one, were whipped up and away by the wind, scattering the pieces. Dispersing into the sky.

I stood motionless for a long time, staring at the hole where she had been. And seeing nothing. It were simply—empty. Vela gone.

A low whimper brought me back. I spun and sprinted to Brenna's side. A moment later, Fen was at my side, nuzzling into Brenna's outstretched hand. Bren's eyes were clear. Her skin clean. She was shaking with the cold.

Cody skidded to our side. "Did you see . . . I don't . . . is she?"

I nodded. "Gone. I sure hope so." I placed my coat careful on Brenna's shoulders.

"That was—"

Cody cut me off. "Brenna. I . . . I thought you were . . . that we all were . . ." He blinked down at my sister. "Dead."

She smiled shy like up at him, her face, even in its ragged exhaustion, more alive than I'd ever seen it. She turned her smiling face to mine and squeezed my hand.

"No offense, Jor, but exactly who the stars was she? And *who* is he?"

Cody flushed a very, very deep crimson. It looked good. Matched his hair.

The three of us alone on the open Flats of the ice, I let out a long, long laugh.

CHAPTER 50

The Pulse of Morning

The world didn't settle all at once. But settle it did. We gathered ourselves as the dogs limped back in, Boz included. The dark clouds slunk away, letting go of their grip over the sky, a last blush of night caught on the horizon. We had spent near an entire day in the heart of the storm. Under my feet, dense snowpack leaked into slush. Around us in the woods, icicles began to drip from the trees.

Deliberate, I lowered myself to Cody's side. His eyes stayed unwaverin on the slow pull of the horizon. Breathing out and in. Somber. I knew that look. I knew it cause it were my look.

It were a reckoning. Untangling the grief and guilt wound tight about your roots. Smothering, even as the sun rose, as the world pressed on. As uncaring as it always were. I laid my head on Cody's shoulder. He smiled and scrubbed a hand over his face.

Brenna were resting against the remains of the sled. The dogs tucked in tight about her, heads pushing under her arms, smiles big.

In the rising golden dawn, I counted my heartbeats. Counted the strong living beat that thumped inside. That resilient, wondrous beating. A tiny red miracle within all of us.

"Hurt ain't all there is in this life, Cody. I may not know much, but I know that whatever lies ahead, I promise you"—I raised my eyes to his—"you ain't gotta face it alone. Not if you don't want to. Not anymore."

I put a hand to my chest. As if I could feel it. The place where he had lodged when I weren't looking. That place inside me that knew that whatever came next, we were strong enough. All of us. Together. Me and Cody and Bren.

"I know." Cody gave me a shy smile as he stood at my side. The growing warmth of the sun flushing his face, catching on the curve of his cheeks and the familiar angle of his jaw. "And neither do you." He put out his hand. I took it.

I know. Heat swelled at the back of my throat. I brushed the snow from my coat. "That's right about enough sap for one day. Any more and we're as like to drown out here as freeze."

Cody beamed. Big and bright.

The certainty of its warmth—of *his* warmth—washed through me. I walked over to Bren.

She leaned on my shoulder, her breathing short and free.

Cody asked a question I didn't right hear. I pointed. There, on a low branch, in the very place I'd stolen that skin of bark, was a wedge of green. He followed my stare. Bren must have too, cause she gave a little intake of breath. They all saw it. The splash of color cutting across the bleak stone. A leaf.

A sharp, beautiful slice of the most perfect color I had ever seen.

I began to laugh. Cody cleared his throat, running a hand through his terrible, perfectly perfect red hair. Warm and comforting, a sensation I weren't right used to filled me. The swell of it slipped up and out my lips. And I smiled, a smile that burrowed into my bones. Cody gave a little shuffle of his feet in the slush.

Which made Bren, of all things, roll her eyes. I laughed again and enfolded Brenna in my arms. We stared all three of us out into the horizon.

"Where to now, Jorie?" Bren asked.

I smiled at her, wiping a soft layer of snow from her lashes. With my other hand, I reached out and grasped Cody's. He gave me a half-turned smile, and a blush that had nothing whatsoever to do with the cold.

In silence we stared into the fading light of the sky. A soft flutter of snow coiled around us before arching up and away, disappearing into the distance. Overhead the fading white lights of a thousand stars blinked down on us from their dark river of blue as the rising sun swallowed the horizon whole.

"Home, Bren. We're going home."

Acknowledgments

First and forever most to my parents, Marybeth and Randy, the best parents a girl could ever wish for. Who have shown me that hope is the fiercest kind of strength any girl could ever have, that no dream is too big if you believe in yourself. Thank you. To my wonderful husband, Quinn, who, no matter how cold and inhospitable the world around us becomes in real life, you somehow always make everything all right. I love you all. Thanks to my family, Donna, Maria, Marty, Bart, Patricia, Jessica, Bob, Ed and Verna, Rosie and Willard, Chris and Carollee, James and Ann, you are the best family anyone could ever wish for. To Jim, who reminded me that good people can persist in even the harshest of places. Thank you to my critique group, Amy B., Andrea, Amy S. and Cassie for being the first eyes, kind hearts, and wise sounding boards for my drafts.

To my editors at Simon & Schuster, Liz Kossnar, whose fierce championing of this world from the very start has made me more grateful than she'll ever know, and many tears of thanks to Alyza Liu, who honed and sharpened this fictional world till it shone brighter than the Flats, you have my eternal gratitude. Many thanks and praises also go to Dainese Santos, editorial assistant extraordinaire. Thank you to my agent Rachel Ekstrom Courage and the entire team at Folio Literary who saw the potential in Jorie and her story and who took a chance on me before anyone else. Thank you all.

To my publisher, Justin Chanda, and the entire dedicated editorial and publishing teams, including Katrina Groover and Chava Wolin at Simon & Schuster Books for Young Readers, I will be forever grateful that you gave me and this strange fantastical ice-covered world a chance. Many thanks to my copyeditor, Beth Adelman, for her hard work on this book. Thank you to my amazing cover designer Krista Vossen and the artist Lente Scura for bringing Jorie to life, as well as the entire design team at S&S BFYR for this stunningly beautiful cover. Thank you to Audrey Gibbons, Milena Giunco as well as the entire publicity and marketing teams who have worked for months to champion this novel, it means the world to me.

Many thanks to everyone else that I have inexcusably failed to name but have nonetheless lent their time, art, expertise or editorial eye to this book. And finally, thank you, dear reader, for reading.